'A heart-rate destabilizing novel . . . this is one fiendish, impressive book' **David Mitchell, author of** *Cloud Atlas*

'A startling vision of totalitarian Britain . . . Lelic creates a magnificent sense of place and deftly maintains the pace of his thriller plot . . . Lelic's crystalline prose is frequently utterly seductive and his compassion is deeply moving' *Metro*

'Nails the reader's attention from the off . . . there is simply no putting the book down at any point. Lelic's debut *Rupture* also had a striking central situation . . . The premise here is equally incendiary, with the bonus of a sure-fire setting: the secluded prison of the title, a hothouse of menace and corruption. Apart from his storytelling skills Lelic has two potent weapons in his armoury, his dialogue, which is scabrous and flint-edged, and his characters . . . As well as being an unputdownable thriller *The Facility* is a book with something to say about the price any country and its citizens must pay for security. However, Lelic never lectures us and when [they] reach the last chapter readers will be checking their increased pulse rate rather than their consciences' *Daily Express*

'A home-grown, high concept thriller . . . All in all, this is a deeply unsettling read' *Daily Mirror,* **Book of the Week**

'A classic story of a race against time' *Sunday Times*

'Lelic's follow-up proves he's no one-hit wonder. *The Facility* is well crafted . . . pacy and absorbing from the first page . . . Lelic has demonstrated once again his talent as a storyteller, keeping his prose fast-paced and always giving his characters distinct, believable voices. With *The Facility* he finds a niche as an author of solid, engrossing thrillers who could well turn out to be a serial bestseller' *Time Out*

'An elegant crime thriller about a falsely imprisoned man and his estranged wife, intent on finding the truth . . . Topical and fast-paced' *Red*

'Simon Lelic's second novel, *The Facility*, is timely indeed . . . Lelic has written a thriller for our times, whose plot is driven by a political machine that's oiled and ready in the real world . . . The plot grips not because of action scenes (although there are a few) but because we live in a world where feelings of mild guilt often slip into paranoia. This is Kafka meets Orwell in contemporary England' *Sunday Herald*

'Feverish imagination and expert plotting' *Observer*

'Lelic can plot like a demon and write wonderful dialogue . . . He has real talent' *Guardian*

Praise for Rupture

'Arresting debut . . . Lelic has an exceptional talent for voice. The pace is as ferocious as the subject, and some characters . . . are expertly grotesque. Lelic's novel may be his first; but you wouldn't know it, it is so controlled, yet confidently reckless' *Independent*

'Lelic's first novel is impressive in its scope and structural daring . . . [He] superbly captures the wildly different vocabularies and rhythms of speech of parents, teachers and pupils. This is a superior detective novel, proof that crime fiction can break free of the bounds of the genre into something much more complex' *Daily Telegraph*

'Absorbing, convincing and truly frightening . . . Lelic's novel fuses the police procedural and school genres, twisting many familiar situations and characters into the stuff of chillingly realistic nightmares' *The Times*

'*Rupture*, it turns out, is not necessarily a crime novel but one which trenchantly addresses a host of issues . . . It is a remarkable debut' *Daily Express*

'A brilliantly plotted detective story that kept me hooked. Lelic, once a journalist, writes crisp engaging prose in which every word counts . . . A remarkable achievement' *New Books*

'Confident and accomplished . . . Lelic's economical, oblique style successfully encourages the reader to work alongside Lucia to understand what has happened. He captures the different tones of characters' voices brilliantly and the novel is a cool, controlled view of various kinds of institutionalized cruelty and corruption . . . Definitely a writer to watch' *Spectator*

'*Rupture* examines one of the great horrors of our times – the school shooting. Slowly, painfully, by means of brilliantly presented monologues and spare narration, the causes are revealed, and they are even more shocking. It's impossible to believe this is a first novel' **Donna Leon**

'A powerful debut exploring the effects of institutionalized bullying . . . A gripping, disturbing read' **Marie Claire**

'Tight, impressive debut . . . Lelic's startlingly poetic ear for dialogue and knack for psychological ambiguity make for a superior piece of detective fiction' **Metro**

'There's a buzz in the publishing world about Simon Lelic's debut novel, *Rupture* . . . [Lelic] is set for literary stardom' **The Times**

THE CHILD WHO

Also by Simon Lelic

RUPTURE

THE FACILITY

SIMON LELIC

THE CHILD WHO

PICADOR

First published 2012 by Mantle

This paperback edition published 2012 by Picador
an imprint of Pan Macmillan, a division of Macmillan Publishers Limited
Pan Macmillan, 20 New Wharf Road, London N1 9RR
Basingstoke and Oxford
Associated companies throughout the world
www.panmacmillan.com

ISBN 978-0-330-52275-5

Copyright © Simon Lelic 2012

The
auth
with

All ri
repro
trans
phot
perm
act i
pros

The
any   es').
The
an e
prod

9 8 7

WEST DUNBARTONSHIRE	
D000016157	
Bertrams	12/10/2012
THR	£7.99
BK	

A CIP catalogue record for this book is available from the British Library.

Typeset by Ellipsis Digital Limited, Glasgow
Printed and bound by CPI Group (UK) Ltd, Croydon, CR0 4YY

This book is sold subject to the condition that it shall not,
by way of trade or otherwise, be lent, re-sold, hired out,
or otherwise circulated without the publisher's prior consent
in any form of binding or cover other than that in which
it is published and without a similar condition including this
condition being imposed on the subsequent purchaser.

Visit www.picador.com to read more about all our books
and to buy them. You will also find features, author interviews and
news of any author events, and you can sign up for e-newsletters
so that you're always first to hear about our new releases.

For Sue and Les

'The men . . . had come wanting to kill the kids who'd killed the kid, because there's nothing worse than killing a kid.'

Blake Morrison, *As If* **(1997)**

The world seethes. Headlights blaze and horns rage and the drivers behind her, as they broach the outer lane to push past, hurl gestures and obscenities through the rain.

It is calmer within but she does not feel calm. She feels battered, blown off course. The radio is on, though she is no longer tuned to what it is saying. She has her phone in one hand and her head in the other. She is staring at the mobile's screen: at her husband's name and a number she has dialled less and less these past ten years.

Did you hear? she could say but of course he will have heard. What happened? she could ask. Then, how did they ...? But he would not yet know any more than she does, nor tell her even if he did.

I'm sorry, she could say. She is not sorry, though; not remotely. And anyway it is not a bereavement, not in a sense that obliges contrition. It is a death but also a release. A culmination. A closing. Congratulations, then. Her sob is almost a laugh.

She lowers the phone and stares at brake lights through

melting glass. Then the wipers wipe and the world reforms and she shuts her eyes instead.

A hammering in her right ear startles her. She twitches and her phone drops and there is a face, when she looks, glowering through the window at hers. The face is framed in yellow; all about her is a flashing blue.

This is Brahms, she thinks. On the radio. Brahms or Berlioz. A lullaby, either way, and all of a sudden she has never felt so tired. It is over, then. They found him, they killed him. It is as definitive an end to things as there could ever be. So why, she asks herself, does it feel like another beginning?

The police car trails her all the way to her turn-off. When her exit approaches she indicates far too early. She eyes the unmarked BMW behind and contemplates switching the indicator off again. Instead she suffers its tut-tutting and wills the queue for the exit to pick up pace. Still the police car follows her. It joins the exit lane too and she grips the steering wheel tighter but at the roundabout the BMW dials past her and finally she allows herself a breath. She unsticks her hands from the wheel and shuffles in her seat. For the rest of the journey home, her attention is as much on the view behind as it is on the tarmac ahead.

The kitchen is dark and she leaves it dark until she gathers the will to boil an egg. The shell is fiddly, though, and scalds her fingers and in the end she cannot be bothered with it. She slides the plate away, toast and egg cup and all, and pulls her mug of tea and cigarettes nearer. Her phone, too. She checks the screen, just in case she has missed a call, even though the house is silent and the phone has barely left her grip. And, anyway, why on earth would *he* call *her*? She is the last person on earth he would think to call.

She would turn on the radio but she could not cope with it. There will be nothing new, she is sure. Just gossip and guesswork and a story re-told by those who have no business telling it. Also, she does not want to hear the name: *his* name, the child's.

'Sod it,' she says. She scrolls and finds her husband's number and hits call before she can change her mind.

It does not even ring. It goes to voicemail. She hangs up but then dials again because voicemail might actually be no bad thing.

'Leo? It's Megan. Meg. I hope . . . I mean, I realise it's been a while since we spoke but . . . I'm calling to . . . I'm calling because of the news. I heard, obviously. In the car, on the way home. I had to pull over. Silly really but for a moment I just couldn't see straight. Partly it was the rain, I expect, because it was raining, you see. But you know that, of course. I mean, you were probably driving in it too because it's hardly stopped, has it, these past few weeks? I suppose you might be driving now, in fact, because this is about the time you usually . . . you would usually . . . Look. Anyway. I was just calling because of the news, as I say, and also to—'

The tone cuts her off.

She walks the house. It starts as something to do that involves anything other than sitting and turns into a procession through what has passed. The living room, for instance: this is where Leo told her. She was seated here, at the bureau, and he was by the door and he was smiling, sort of, but also sweating and he said, Meg, listen, you'll never guess. But she did. Somehow, after hearing the evening bulletin that day, she just knew.

It is a coincidence, she is almost sure, that she so rarely comes in here any more. The kitchen is enough for her – the kitchen, a bathroom and half a bedroom. The other rooms, including the living room, she only ever enters to clean. Which is the pinnacle, now she thinks of it, of absurdity.

She should sell the house, really. She wanted it once – she fought for it, or was prepared to – but she does not need it. When they bought the place she adored that it was pristine but somehow it seems shabbier now than the Victorian terraces beyond the gates. Cracks border the ceiling, the skirting boards have wilted from the wall. The house settling, Leo called it. And if the house has settled, so has the estate, down into its shallow, overvalued foundations.

Look at the windows. They are uPVC, yellow where once they were white. There is condensation between the panes, as though an unseen face, shrouded by the cold night air, were pressed against the glass and peering in. She turns and closes the door a fraction too late to shut off the memory.

The staircase in the centre of the hallway entices her, its banisters like outstretched arms, but there is just the bathroom and her half a bedroom on the landing – nothing else up there that she is willing, in this mood, to contemplate.

The study: it was his war room. Empty now but for her laptop and some unfiled papers. He was in here late most nights, plotting the course of his defeat. For it was never the outcome that was in question, just the extent of it. Lose big or lose bigger or lose more than you could have imagined. She was engaged then, despite the stakes. She stood here, behind his chair, or perched here, on a cushion of papers.

Please, Meg, I have a system.

Dinner time, Leo, or the system gets it.

That was at the start, though. The joking soon stopped, her visits to his study too. They stopped when it became clear what her husband had got them into.

When Leo calls back she does not answer. She does not trust herself to. She is in the study and in front of her, on the screen of her laptop, is a photograph she has shied away from for years. Like the sound of the child's name, the image sickens her. I don't know how, she once told Leo, you can bear to breathe the same air as he does, inhale his . . . effluence. She struggled to find the right word but felt sure she had struck upon it.

Her revulsion recurs. The photograph, it is true, has been manipulated. The boy's eyes appear black, slit, pupil-less, his skin bleached of warmth, the shadows that frame him sharpened. It is quite ridiculous, really, how heavy-handedly the image has been altered. Unnecessary, more to the point, when the rot in the boy's soul was plain to see. Even in the other photographs Leo showed her, the boy, as a child, did not convince. Compared to the image of his victim, for instance, there seemed something within the boy that was contrived, artificial, insincere. Something dormant.

She scrolls and finds a picture of her husband. Not manipulated this one, though it would need to be if the man it showed were to resemble the man her husband has become. So much of that fudge-brown hair and he paid it such little heed. Even for a court appearance – for the most important court appearance of his career – he seems barely to have bothered with a comb. His suit is single breasted and looks, for one of Leo's suits and as far as she can tell, reasonably sharp – which probably means that at the time it was antipathetic to the prevailing style. Antipathetic to the prevailing style. It sums up Leo's younger self well.

And maybe not just his younger self. How much has he really changed, after all? Wasn't that the point: that he didn't change? That he would not.

In the photograph she can just make out the scar on her husband's cheek. Still pink. Still liable to weeping blood. It lingered, she recalls, but faded eventually. Some scars do, after all.

He has left a message. Her phone is buzzing, propelling itself towards the table's edge. She watches it until it almost falls, then rescues it and lifts it to her ear. The message plays but it is silence – for a second, two, then the message ends. He thought about it, then. He changed his mind.

She watches *Newsnight*. She decides she may as well. Her will to resist, after all, has already been breached.

The story features, of course, though it has been bumped from the headline slot to accommodate massive tragedy in the near abroad – the very minimum, perhaps, that could have provoked such a shift.

She switches off after the first segment: mentally, to what they are saying, not the television itself. She is not yet ready for a return to the quiet. She is not yet ready to go to bed. This is not over, it strikes her. This, the way things are: this is not an ending. This is not how she will let it end.

She stands. She picks up the remote control and hits standby just as the picture she should really have been expecting fills the screen. And that is what she is left with, as she hauls herself from stair to stair and slips her blouse from her back and her body between the sheets and lies restless in the shallows of sleep: the face of the child who killed. The child, as she will remember him, who cost them their own.

1

It had the babble of a celebration.

There were only twelve of them gathered in the office – twelve of a fifteen-strong practice – but he had lost track already of the number of times he had recounted his story. Just happened to pick up the telephone. That's right: the call centre, with a message to ring the station. No, this was at the office still but ten minutes later and I would have been heading off to court. So, yeah, I get the message and I call the custody sergeant. And the custody sergeant says she's looking for a duty solicitor and she asks me if I'm free. And by this time all I'm thinking about is a sandwich because I've been up since five and I've eaten what, a Mars Bar, since breakfast. Also, I've had just about enough after dealing with this Clemence character: you know, the drunk and disorderly? The football thing, right: three traffic cones and a whistle and he had the Plymouth fans driving round in circles. Not even a thank you, though. Not even a goodbye, come to that, or a glance as he walked out the door. So anyway, the custody sergeant, she hears me hesitate. She says, Leo, is that you? I say, it is, Gayle, but I was just about to head off to lunch. And Gayle, the custody sergeant . . . Do you know Gayle? She's the skinny one, the only Sri Lankan, she says, in the whole of Exeter. So Gayle says, Leo, I think you should take this. And it's the tone of her voice that does it. We get on well, Gayle and I, and I trust her. I sigh, I suppose, but I tell her fine. What have you got? Right, just like that. The biggest case in the county's history and it's mine, ours, this practice's, all because I happened to answer the telephone. Well, we'll see about that. Picking up that phone: it could just as easily turn out to be the worst mistake of my life!

He recounted it eagerly and did not wane in the re-telling. He took the call, he got the case. He should have told it with a shrug but like the others he was dizzy on caffeine and nerves. This was a beginning. For all of them but for Leonard Curtice in particular, this was where their careers would truly begin.

'So what's he like?'

It was Jenny, one of the admin girls, who had voiced the question but, from the hush that hurried in behind, she was clearly not the only one impatient to have it answered.

'What's who like?' Leo said, as though for a moment he had been genuinely confused. 'Oh, you mean the boy. You mean my client.' There was laughter and Leo savoured it because he knew he was about to disappoint. The truth was, he had spent an hour in the same room as Daniel Blake and not once had he heard the boy speak. Not once, that Leo saw, had the boy even looked at him, nor acknowledged his presence on the Blake family's side of the table. If Leo had not known better, he might have described his manner as shy. 'Quiet,' then, was all he could say. Also: 'Just a boy. Just, I don't know. Like a scared little boy.'

Collectively, his colleagues twitched.

'Scared? I bet he was scared.' Terry Saunders held his cup with his hand around the hot part. He jabbed the handle towards Leo. 'I should hope he was. Little fucker. I mean, sorry, Jenny, sorry, Stacie, but – ' Terry puffed his cheeks, as though his temper were straining just at the thought of it ' – but that's exactly what he is. A little. Fucker.'

The others, the blokes at least, nodded. Even the girls made fair-enough eyes into their coffee.

'I know what you're saying, Terry, but—'

'There's no but, Leo. I mean, sure, he's your client now and I understand, sort of, why you're acting like you've just won the pools . . .'

'Now hold on, Terry. That's hardly—'

'. . . but let's not lose sight of who this kid is, shall we? Of what he did.' Again Leo tried to interrupt but Terry angled himself to centre stage. 'If it'd been me,' he said. 'If it'd been me with that kid in a room . . .' Once again he inflated his cheeks. 'Well. Let's just say, when I came out, I wouldn't have expected to be allowed to practise again.'

Terry stood to the height of Leo's shirt collar and was an uncut toenail above ten stone. He might, Leo estimated, just about be able to handle a twelve-year-old child but his bluster was in reality nothing more than that. Still, it garnered appreciation. There was nodding and mumbling in general agreement. Jenny and Stacie both tutted but not, to Leo's ear, entirely wholeheartedly.

'Well,' Leo said. 'There's no denying it was a terrible crime. But the boy – Daniel – he hasn't been charged, not officially. He's barely spoken. And anyway it's hardly our place—'

'Did he do it, Leo?' This from Stacie. 'Surely they would-n't have made the fuss they did if they weren't sure he did it?'

'Now, Stacie, you know I can't . . . That is, I shouldn't . . .' But already her eyes were leaching disappointment and Leo was loath to let down the crowd twice. 'Yes,' he said. 'I would say he did it. There's not a doubt, if I'm honest, in my mind.'

Talk about bluster. He was worse, in a way, than Terry, with all his nonsense about beating up a twelve-year-old. *No, Jenny. Yes, Stacie. There's not a doubt in my mind.* For pity's sake.

'Leonard.' A hand on his shoulder. 'A word.'

'Howard. Listen. I'm sorry if I . . .' Leo gestured to the dispersing crowd, his colleagues drifting back now to flash-ing phones and rolls of faxes.

'No, no. Enjoy the moment. It's a coup, I grant you.' Howard revealed a troupe of too-white teeth. Falsies, was the rumour, and there were doubts as well about the authenticity of the pelt on his crown. It was too thick, surely, to be home-grown; too solidly the colour of honey when a man of Howard's age – sixty? sixty-five? – should have been struggling against a tide of baldness just like most of the younger men in the practice. 'A real coup,' Howard was saying. 'Well done, Leonard.' His boss's hand was on Leo's shoulder again. He found himself being led into a leafy corner of the open-plan office. 'How's your caseload? Got much on?'

'No, not really. A few odds and ends. Bread-and-butter stuff, mainly.' Drunk and disorderlies, exclusively, unleavened even by an ABH. There was such minimal variation in their work these days that Howard, really, should hardly have had to ask. Little wonder the office was so abuzz. Little wonder Leo was.

'Unload what you can, at least for the next week or so. Talk to Terence. Speak to me if he kicks up a fuss.'

'If you insist, Howard. I mean, I'm sure I can handle—'

'I'm sure you can, Leonard. But you'll have enough on your plate, I promise you.' Howard stopped and guided Leo round to face him.

'Howard, is something—'

'Are you ready, Leonard?' His boss gripped him on both shoulders now and sought out Leo's eyes with his.

'Ready? Well, I—'

'You understand what I'm asking you? You understand that this will be like nothing you have experienced before?'

'Well, yes, certainly. I mean—'

'He's a murderer, Leonard. He's twelve years old and he's a killer.'

Leo attempted a smile. 'An *alleged* killer, Howard. Don't forget—'

Howard squeezed. Leo could feel the man's fingernails through the polyester blend of his shirt. 'Don't piss about, Leonard. Enjoy the moment, certainly. Relish the attention if you must. But this little fucker killed an eleven-year-old girl.' Leo winced, as much at his boss's use of Terry's terminology as at mention of the crime itself. 'He goddamn nearly raped her. You are his representative. You, as far as the entire country will see it, are on his side. Think about that for a moment. Think about what that might mean.'

'I've got a thick skin, I promise you,' said Leo, even though it felt like the skin on his shoulders was about to break. 'Really, Howard.' He squirmed and his boss's hands fell away. 'I'll be fine. It will all be fine.'

'And Megan? Your little girl – Eleanor, isn't it? Have you told them?'

'What? No. Not yet. I will tonight. When I get home. I've hardly had a minute since I took the call. That was, what? Two-ish? And it's already . . .' Leo looked to his watch. 'Wow. It's getting late, Howard. I should get going. You should get going. Celia will be wondering where you are.'

Howard regarded Leo beneath eyebrows joined at the middle. 'Okay,' he said. Then, slowly, he unpeeled his alabaster grin.

2

He goddamn nearly raped her. It was true, he nearly had. And yet, in actuality, there had been no rape. Of that Leo was thankful because the rest was more than enough.

Felicity Forbes had been a few years younger than Leo's daughter. Ellie was fifteen and Felicity's twelfth birthday was approaching. It would fall, Leo calculated, on the two-month anniversary of her death. Not a vast gap in age, then, but Felicity seemed otherwise to have been a very different child. Superficially, for instance: Ellie was fair-haired, like her mother, and freckled and wiry; the Forbes girl had been auburn, sunned and stout. Podgy but not unhealthily so. In the only photograph Leo had seen of Felicity alive, she was grinning in a toothy, cheery way that seemed to vindicate entirely her parents' choice of name. This again was a contrast with Ellie. Ellie, when it came to having her picture taken, was bashful, even resentful. Stalking her through a lens was like stalking something wild, and the reaction, if she noticed, invariably equally so.

At their respective schools, both girls were considered

middling. In Ellie's case, however, Leo suspected – and not, he told himself, just because he was her father – a latency of potential. His daughter, clearly, was less than happy. She had changed schools when they had moved to Linden Park and possibly that was part of it. But even before the move she had lacked something that other children her age seemed to exude. Like in the photographs, for example. Ellie lacked . . . joy. It was a heart-wrenching thing to admit but Leo consoled himself, his wife too, that it was because Ellie thought too much. She was *too* bright, that was the problem. Her imagination could not easily accommodate glee because glee, in Ellie's case, would always be tempered by the worry about what might come next. That was why her eyes so rarely hoisted her smile. That was why her obviously fierce intelligence always seemed to be held in check. But her temperament would stand her in good stead, Leo insisted. It'll pay dividends, Meg, you'll see.

Felicity Forbes had hoarded no such angst. A steady Cs and Bs student, with the occasional A-minus in music and a blossoming predilection for the stage, she had spun between her schoolwork and her social life with dizzy delight. Certainly she had been outgoing, in the way the youngest in a large family is often compelled to be. Whereas Ellie was an only child, Felicity had left behind two brothers and a sister, all of whom had reportedly adored her. And it had not been just among her teachers and family members that Felicity had been popular. She had amassed a quantity of friends that Ellie, and indeed Leo himself, could never hope to. A people's princess, the *Exeter Post* – the self-anointed voice of the region – had dubbed Felicity. It was a shameless reference to events three years previous but not entirely unfitting given the quantity of foliage that had adorned her school's gates and the mass of mourners expected at her funeral. Indeed, that Felicity Forbes had so readily been beatified should hardly have come as a surprise. It was inevitable really, as much from the nature of how she had lived as the excruciating manner in which she had died.

He goddamn nearly raped her. Nearly, which meant not quite. And yet what Daniel Blake was alleged to have done was worse than rape. It was more brutal, more venomous. It was, in the coldest terms, more clinical.

Felicity, on her final morning, awoke to a January day that wore a frost like jewellery. Snow had been forecast but had failed to arrive and possibly it was a result of having already prepared herself for a day off school that Felicity dallied so on the walk in. It was not out of character – she was frequently late. She had, in fairness, further to go than most students; further, that is, to walk. Her family lived on the north-western boundary of the city, where the city itself was already lost to view behind wooded hills and the dilapidated halls of residence that disfigured them. Without the option of a lift most mornings, Felicity's choice was a walk along the riverbank or a lonely wait for a bus that was more reliably unpunctual than she was. It was, Felicity had long since decided, barely a choice at all.

She passed the Waterside Inn at twenty-five minutes past eight, according to the freeholder, already fifteen minutes later than usual. She had been a little behind on leaving the house, her parents had told the police, for no reason that they could recall. Gassing, her father had suggested, at which point the interview had been interrupted by her mother's tears. From the walkway adjoining the pub, Felicity crossed the pedestrian bridge and followed the river south. She had to climb a stile to access the footpath, the freeholder said; the sight of her in her crimson overcoat, straddling the fence and struggling to unhook her trailing rucksack, was the last he had of her. It was the last time she was seen alive by anyone other than her killer.

He goddamn nearly raped her. But he did not. He used a stick.

That, at least, was the pathologist's finding. The implement itself was never identified but the scratches – the wounds – were, apparently, unambiguous.

He used a stick. This boy, this child: he used a stick.

She was a flash of red clambering across a stile and next she was a corpse, trussed with a string of discarded fairy lights and bloated and blue after hours in the Exe. What happened in between could only be guessed at from the picture the investigators were left with. The pictures, in fact, because there were dozens of them. Only one in the file of the girl when she had been alive but six, for example, of her hands bound in wire. Seven, eight, nine of her ripped and muddied overcoat, which had washed up on a bank a mile downstream. Innumerable shots of Felicity herself: her face, streaked with silt; her injuries, puffed and bloodless; her fingernails, chipped and cracked – her only weapon against an attacker who had made use of anything and everything that had been to hand.

She drowned. She was drowned, rather. That, in the end, is how she died. Held under perhaps. Set adrift, more likely, still bound in wire and with gravel in her pockets and her book-laden bag on her back. The child, the boy: he had thought of everything.

He goddamn nearly raped her. This is what they all kept coming back to, as though rape were as bad as it could get. It had been enough, certainly, as far as the police had been concerned. Enough blood and guts with which to feed the press and more than enough to persuade the public to be forthcoming. The rest, the truth, would actually have been too much. For Leo, who had followed developments but not with the fervour – the fury – of others in the community, it was already more than he could contemplate. This boy, this child: your client. This is what he did. This is the case, then, fully disclosed. This is your cause for celebration.

He wondered what Terry, in the office, would have said if he had known; whether his rage would have turned murderous or whether it would simply have fizzed itself flat. What possible reaction was there after all except utter deflation? Horror, yes, and anger, certainly, but both depended wholly on conviction, on being convinced that the thing you had been told had actually happened; that contrary to everything you thought you believed about the fundamental principles of humanity, evil was unbound, unlimited – capable, easily, of excelling itself.

And his father. Gone for well over a year now but only in the most literal sense. What would he think? After Leo's mother had left them and his own career had crumbled – had failed, really, to turn into a career at all – Matthew Curtice had bet his hope on the prospects for his son. He had always been so proud of what Leo did – not of what the job in reality entailed but of his son's *profession*. A chance to make a difference, he had said; to achieve something with your life. More than he had ever managed, his father told him – just after Leo had qualified and only weeks before the first of his strokes.

What, though, would his father think now? Of Leo, of his barely concealed delight in being – how had Howard put it? – on this boy's side.

'Leo?'

Megan was leaning through the doorway. Leo moved to shuffle away the photographs.

'It's late. Are you coming to bed?'

Leo's watch had twisted face down. He jangled it the right way up. 'Lord. You should have called me. I was planning to watch the news.'

'I taped it for you. I looked but I didn't see you on it.' She said this last with a smile.

'No. I wouldn't have been yet. I mean, that's not why I . . .' He slid a smile back. 'Thanks.'

'So are you coming up? You can't stare at those all night. You'll give yourself nightmares.'

Leo moved to cover the few photographs that remained on display. His bad dreams were inevitable; Megan might escape for a few more nights. 'I'll be up in a bit. Just a couple more minutes. Maybe I should . . . I'd like to check on Ellie too.'

'Ellie? Ellie's asleep.' Megan took a step into the study. She angled her head to get a view of the file on Leo's desk. 'What are you looking at?'

'Nothing. Just, you know. Paperwork.' He prodded a protruding edge.

Megan took another step and laid her hands on Leo's shoulders. 'How are you feeling?' She kneaded and Leo exhaled, closed his eyes.

He felt something press against his ankles. The cat, he assumed, had trailed Megan into the room and was weaving her affection in a figure of eight. It was Ellie's cat, really: Rupert, 'because she looks like a bear', which to an eight-year-old had been powerful enough in its logic at the time to trump any misgivings about gender.

'Tired,' Leo said, in answer to his wife's question. 'But like I'll never be able to sleep.' He half turned and reached for Megan's hand. 'You?'

'I don't know. I don't know what to feel. Tired as well, I suppose, but more from the thought of it. I'm worried, Leo. I know, I know,' she said, when Leo smiled and squeezed her hand. 'But Ellie. That's all it is. I'm worried for Ellie.'

'Ellie'll be fine. We'll be fine. It's not like any of us did this, Meg.'

She squeezed back. 'When are you seeing him?'

Leo shifted and sensed the cat dart away. 'Tomorrow. First thing. Before they start on him again.' Megan, for an instant, looked puzzled. 'The police,' Leo said. 'They've no intention of hanging around.'

Megan nodded. She kissed his crown. 'Then come upstairs. Get some sleep.' She reached the door and held it.

'I will. I'll be up soon, I promise. Just a couple more minutes.'

He watched Megan go. There was the sound of the front door being bolted and of the kitchen light being switched off and then of his wife's leaden footsteps on the stairs. He waited until he was certain she had reached the landing and let his head fall into his hands.

3

Now, here: just say it.

But he said nothing. He allowed the Passat to creep closer to the car in front, then broke the silence by ratcheting the handbrake. He cleared his throat, with as cheerful a timbre as he could manage, then turned to face his daughter and made a sound like he had thought of something funny.

Ellie did not respond. She maintained her dead-eyed stare, one hand cupping her chin, the other a fist in her lap.

Leo again cleared his throat and this time Ellie turned. 'Can we put the radio on?' she said, reaching.

'In a minute.' Leo moved his hand to catch his daughter's but she was too quick on the withdrawal. 'I actually wanted to talk to you.' Leo let his palm settle on the gear lever instead. 'About work,' he continued. 'My work, I mean.' The traffic began to move and Leo slipped the car into gear. 'There's a . . . I have a . . .' He coughed. 'The thing is, Ellie . . .'

'I know, Dad.'

Leo turned. 'You know?' The traffic stalled and once again he applied the handbrake. 'What do you know?'

Ellie shrugged. 'Felicity. The boy.' Again the shrug – barely even that really. 'The case.'

'What? How?'

'Mum told me.'

'Your mother? When?'

'Last night.'

'When last night?'

'You were working.'

Leo considered. 'Oh.'

Quiet. Even the traffic outside seemed for a moment to be waiting on what might come next.

'So what do you think?' said Leo and the cars ahead released their brake lights. 'Are you okay with it?'

The shrug.

'You shouldn't worry, you know.'

Which, of course, had precisely the wrong effect. 'Why would I worry?'

'I said you shouldn't worry.'

'But why would I?' Ellie sat straighter. She faced her father. 'You shouldn't,' Leo repeated. 'That's what I'm saying. There's no reason for you to worry.' A car from the outside lane was moving into his. There was no cause to but Leo jabbed at his horn anyway. 'Look at this idiot,' he said. His eyes twitched towards his daughter but she was clearly not to be distracted. She looked swamped, all of a sudden, in the passenger seat: a child with a grown-up-sized furrow on her brow.

'What do you mean, though? Tell me, Dad. I'm not some little kid.'

24

'Look. Ellie.' Leo sighed and the sigh, to him, seemed clearly to convey everything his daughter needed to know.

'Dad—'

Leo lifted a hand from the steering wheel. 'It's a nasty business. That's all. It was a horrific crime and there's bound to be a lot of attention. I just wanted you to know that . . . that it's to be expected. That it's nothing to worry about. That it might be uncomfortable for a while but it will pass.'

Ellie regarded him.

'Honestly, Ellie, that's all.' Leo held his daughter's gaze for as long as he dared divert his from the road ahead. Slowly, Ellie withdrew into her seat. She resumed her vigil of the passing pavement.

Leo tried to think of something else to say that was not a condescension or a cliché or in fact an outright lie. He opened his mouth but it was his daughter who spoke first.

'Did he do it?'

Leo turned halfway, then fully. 'What?'

'Did he do it.'

'What? Who?'

'Dad.'

'Ellie, I . . . You know I can't . . .'

'You must know. Right? You're his lawyer. Right?'

'I'm his solicitor. Which means that whether he did it or not, or whether I think he did it, is entirely beside the—'

Ellie rolled her eyes.

'Don't roll your eyes at me, young lady.'

'I didn't.' She spoke to the window.

'You did. I saw you. You just did.'

'You weren't answering the question.'

'I was! I was explaining, if you'll let me, the role a solicitor, in circumstances such as these, is obliged, by professional necessity, to—'

She did it again.

'Ellie!'

'You're still not answering.'

'I was, I—'

'You sound like a teacher. You sound like Mr Smithson.'

Which, for a moment, flummoxed him. 'Ellie. There is nothing wrong with explaining, when an explanation is needed, how things—'

'You're dissembling.'

It was a word he never thought he would hear from a teenager. 'I'm what?' He had to smile.

'Dissembling. Don't laugh. It's a word.'

'I know, but—'

'It means talking shit.'

'Eleanor!'

'What? It does. Mum used it and I looked it up and basically it means you're talking—'

'That's enough!'

'– so you don't have to answer.' Ellie's voice withered into silence.

Leo was open-mouthed. He gripped the wheel and emptied his lungs through his nostrils. Dissembling. Ha. He would have to remember that at the office this afternoon.

'What's funny?'

'What? Nothing. I was just . . . Nothing. You shouldn't swear, Ellie.'

His daughter watched him as they drove. The turn-off towards Ellie's school was approaching and Leo signalled left. He hated this part of their journey. In the time it took him to make the detour, he would cede to his rival commuters all the ground he had worked so hard the past three miles to gain. It seemed so futile. Just like work, he had often thought. Every case, like every car, was as one-paced and nondescript as the next. If you managed to get past one, there would always be another. And another, just as long as you remained on the road. That, at least, is how it had been.

'Dad.'

'Mm?'

'If he did it . . . I mean, okay, you're his solicitor and whatever, blah blah blah. But if he did it . . .'

Leo was about to interrupt but was distracted by the brake lights on the car in front. They flickered and flicked off and then finally fixed on red.

'. . . why are you defending him?'

The driver ahead seemed to have stalled. There had been a gap at the junction but he – she? – had changed his mind at the last moment. The car behind Leo's blared its frustration. Leo glanced in the rear-view mirror, then dragged a palm across his eyes.

'Dad?'

'Ellie. Sorry. What did you say?'

'I said, why are you defending him?'

Finally the gap became a chasm and the car ahead peeled right. Leo accelerated in its wake and the Passat lurched clumsily to the left.

'Defending . . . What? No. I'm not defending him, Ellie – not in the sense you mean. I'm representing him is what I'm doing. There's a difference.' Leo took a breath. 'One of the great things about this country, about our legal system, is that everyone, no matter how heinous the alleged crime, has the absolute, unimpeachable right to qualified representation, to trial before a courtroom. Habeas corpus, it's called. It's a question of process. Which means, in this case, that . . .' Leo interrupted himself when he caught sight of his daughter's expression. 'Mr Smithson. Right?'

His daughter nodded. 'I know he gets to have a lawyer. I'm not stupid. What I mean is, why does he get you?'

'Me? He gets me because . . .' Leo lifted a shoulder. 'Because I was there. Because it's my job.'

'You could say no, though. If he did what they say he did, you should say no.'

Leo made a face. 'It's not that simple. I mean, there are other . . .'

'You could, though. Couldn't you? You should. I really think you should.'

Ellie wore an adult, earnest expression that did not sit easily on her fragile features. She looked pale, almost grey. She looked, in fact, as if she was close to tears – although these days it was often difficult to tell.

'Look, darling. I don't get to pick and choose who I represent. It doesn't work like that. And anyway . . .' He had not yet said it, not out loud. 'I want this case. I really think I do. You might not understand that yet but one day, I promise, you will. This is a good case, Ellie. This is good for my career.' And that was the point: for all his father's misplaced pride, what had Leo really been doing with his life except mopping up the spillage from the high-street bars? This case was something more: a chance, as his father had put it, to make a difference.

'Even though you said it would be awful?' Ellie asked. His daughter's tone was even but her expression was ominously rigid.

'I didn't say that. I didn't say awful.'

'You did. You said it would be awful and you said we should all be worried.'

Leo laughed. He could not help it.

'Could you please pull over now.'

'Ellie. Please. I didn't say awful, I said uncomfortable – that it *might* get uncomfortable, not that it would necessarily. And I said you *shouldn't* be—'

'Dad! Pull over. Let me out. Please, let me out.'

'It's raining, Ellie. We're still a block away.'

'Pull over. Just here. Please, Dad. Dad!'

'Okay, okay!' Leo braked, harder than he had intended, and swung the car to the kerbside. 'Ellie, look . . .'

His daughter had unbuckled her seatbelt and her fingers were reaching for the door catch.

'Wait,' said Leo. 'Ellie! Don't I at least get a . . .'

But his daughter was already gone.

He should have been braced for the frenzy at the police station. A twelve-year-old boy was helping the police with their inquiries; for the time being they were not looking for anyone else. For the stringers, TV reporters and local hacks, it was as enticing an invitation as an open bar.

Leo almost made it through. He was of average height and build and wore nothing more arresting than a high-street suit. Aside from his boxy, decade-old briefcase, he might have passed for an overdressed journalist or a face-man for the local news. The local newsmen, however, were all in attendance, having grabbed prime position by the doors. They knew Leo; Leo knew them. It was the crime reporter from the *Post* who spotted him first.

'Mr Curtice! Leonard! Over here, Leonard!'

'Excuse me,' said Leo. 'Thank you. Sorry. Excuse me.' He sensed the television cameras tracking him and trained his gaze at shoulder height.

'Leonard! Leo! Hey, Leo.' A hand around Leo's elbow and he turned.

'Tim. Hi. Sorry. If you'll excuse me. I really have to . . .' Leo tried to forge ahead but the scrum enclosed him. The grip on his arm tightened.

'What's going on, Leo?' Tim Cummins pressed his stubbled, fleshy face towards Leo's. 'Who have they got in there?'

'I can't comment, Tim, you know that. If you'll excuse—'

'Can't comment on what, Leo? You're not denying that this is your case?'

'Please, Tim, I really should be—'

'Who's the client, Leo? Is he local? Will he be charged?'

Leo shook free his arm. 'Excuse me,' he said, with more force this time. He shoved and the journalists closest to him stumbled. Cummins dropped his notebook. He let it lie, raising himself instead on his tiptoes.

'You have a daughter, right, Leo? How do you feel about what happened to the Forbes girl? How does your family feel about your involvement in this case?'

Leo felt himself flush. He did not look back but pressed his way onwards, leaking from the crowd and through the doorway.

Inside it was no less frantic. Exeter Police Station was an inert place, usually: a city-sized precinct for small-town misdemeanours where business was conducted with languid efficiency. Not today. Officers – some uniformed, others suited – streaked from doorway to doorway, bearing files or flapping pages and with an air that there was somewhere else they needed to be.

Leo's entrance, nevertheless, did not go unnoticed. The desk sergeant was waiting. A tall man, wide too, he had his long arms locked and his hands splayed on the counter. Leo gave a twitch in the officer's direction. It was ignored. Leo straightened his jacket and pinched his tie-knot and failed to stop himself checking across his shoulder as he started forwards. Cummins, he saw, was pressed against the glass of the door, his hands around his eyes. How do you feel? he had asked.

How does your family feel? As though Leo's family were any-one's business but his own.

Leo approached the desk. His jacket was twisted and he shrugged a shoulder. He glanced back towards the entrance, then faced the man on reception. There was no question about who would speak first.

'Good morning,' Leo said. He cleared his throat. 'I have an appointment. With a client.'

The desk sergeant drew back. 'Your name . . . sir?' The desk sergeant's was Brian and he surely knew Leo's.

'Curtice,' said Leo through a frown. 'Leonard Curtice.' He allowed his expression to settle. 'I'm sorry if I'm late but there was quite a crowd on the—'

'Sign here. Then go through there.' The desk sergeant flicked his chin towards a set of double doors.

So this would be the way of things, Leo thought as he re-crossed the lobby. Howard had warned him, just as he in turn had warned his daughter, but still he had not been prepared. It was discomfiting, he would admit. But no matter. Yes, his daughter was upset but she was, after all, only fifteen years old – she could not be expected to understand. As for the desk sergeant, the local hacks, anyone else who had assumed he had sided with Felicity's murderer: their ignorance, surely, was their problem. At least now Leo understood. At least, now, he knew the extent of the hostility he would have to deal with.

He shifted his briefcase from left hand to right and once again adjusted his tie. He passed through the set of double doors. There was an escort waiting for him on the other side.

The man nodded and the nod gave Leo heart. He called Leo 'sir' and without a hint of a sneer. He behaved properly, professionally, and Leo resolved to do the same. He would talk to Ellie and he would bear all the rest. Here, now, he had a job to do.

4

They were being watched. It was part of the agreement. The investigating team – the police – were excluded but the social worker, the boy's parents: they were watching and listening to everything that was being said. Which, in practical terms, was very little: questions but no answers; prompts but no replies; a lopsided conversation, then, that had toppled, momentarily, into silence.

Leo glanced again at the security camera. He wanted to stand and to pace but standing and pacing was what the police had done, what Daniel's parents had done, what the social worker had, after more than an hour alone with the boy, finally resorted to. So Leo sat. When his foot tapped of its own accord, he forced it flat. When his fingers took up the beat instead, he wrapped them in a fist. He was, would be, patience personified. He and Daniel: they had all day.

They had, in truth, a deadline that was fast approaching. Leo did not want to look again at his watch because the boy had caught him last time and that single glance, Leo estimated, had cost him far more than the split second it had taken. Instead, on a blank sheet of notepaper and with the pen Meg had bought for him for Felicity Forbes's final Christmas, he drew.

A stick figure, at the base of the page. He considered giving the figure more substance but the fleshless lines, given the boy's build, seemed appropriate. He gave it shoes, which became trainers when he added the swoosh: blue on white, just like Daniel's. He gave it ears and on one of them he planted a full stop. The head he left hairless, except on top: here he drew a succession of spikes – sharp, as the boy's would have been had he not spent seventeen hours without access to a tube of hair gel. Knowing how sensitive his daughter was about the freckles that spotted her own fair skin, Leo resisted dotting the stick-boy's cheeks and ignored, too, the silvered scratch lines around his throat. Instead he drew a mouth: a line, straight across, which he stitched shut with a string of smaller lines a pen-nib apart.

'Not a bad likeness,' Leo said and spun the page so Daniel could see. He caught the boy's eyes as they leapt from the piece of paper to a point on the table beside it. 'This is you: now, here,' Leo said. 'And this . . .' He turned the page again and worked quickly. He drew a man beside the boy: the same earring and fastened mouth; the same hair but with a gap this time on the crown. 'This is you in twenty years' time. Here,' he repeated, and directed his chin around the interview room. 'Or in a cell a bit smaller.' To make the point he drew a box around both figures, so that the stick-man's head brushed the ceiling, and sectioned the box with bars. Then he turned the page once more and thrust it across the table. He clicked his pen and stared at the boy. Daniel ignored the picture. With his chin tucked against his collarbone, he kept his rinsed-denim eyes fixed on the tabletop.

'You need to talk to me, Daniel. This – ' he used his pen to tap the picture ' – is what will happen if you don't talk to me.'

Nothing.

'I'd like you to trust me, Daniel. I'd like you to trust me but it's not important that you do.' He paused. 'Shall I tell you why?' Again he waited but the boy, unsurprisingly, gave no answer. 'Because I couldn't tell anyone what we discussed even if I wanted to. If I did, they'd put me right in here with you.' He gestured once more to the page he had ripped from his notebook. 'I'm on your side, Daniel. Not because I want to be. I'm on your side because I *have* to be.'

The table that divided them was drainpipe grey: unmottled, unmarked but perhaps it was that absence of anything at which to stare that continued to draw Daniel's focus. Leo was reminded of his first impression of the boy: that Daniel, despite everything, seemed timid, almost shy – not like a killer at all.

'You could tell me . . . I don't know. That you'd robbed a bank. The NatWest on the high street, say. You could tell me and I'd have to keep it secret. Or that you'd stolen a car. A Porsche, say. A Lexus. You . . .' Leo was about to carry on but something about the boy stopped him. He had moved. Had he moved?

'What?' Leo said. He waited. What, he was about to say again but the boy spoke first.

'No way.'

Leo fought an impulse to lean forward.

'No way? What do you mean, no way?'

'No way I'd steal a Lexus.'

Leo swallowed. He nodded. 'Fair enough,' he said. 'A Porsche, then. Would you . . .' steal, he was about to say, but the word – the direct question – did not seem appropriate '. . . how about a Porsche?'

Daniel rolled a shoulder.

'Not a Porsche either?' Leo slowly shook his head. 'You're a hard man to please, Daniel.' And this, the 'man' Leo would have bet, earned a twitch of Daniel's pale, cracked lips.

'So what would you drive? Free choice. You're in a forecourt with every car ever made and you get to take one home. What would you choose?'

The boy did not hesitate. 'Subaru Impreza.'

Again Leo nodded. 'In blue. Right? Like . . .' Like? Like whom? The rally driver. Scottish bloke. Or was he Irish? 'McRae.' It came to him. 'Colin McRae.'

Daniel, though, made a noise. 'In white.' He seemed to contemplate, then bobbed his head. 'Yeah, white.' He gave Leo a fleeting, bashful look. Leo, in response, picked up the drawing and crumpled it into a ball.

'Just another half an hour.'

Detective Inspector Mathers strode on. Leo skipped to keep pace.

'Inspector, please. He's talking to me.'

'He told you – what was it, Mr Curtice? The car he'd most

like to steal. What next, would you say? His favourite serial killer? His top ten genocides?'

'That wasn't . . . That's not what . . .' Leo dropped back to avoid a phalanx of uniforms. He caught up with the inspector at a fire door. 'The point, Inspector, is that he said something. His first words in seventeen hours. That's progress, wouldn't you say?'

'I'm sorry, Mr Curtice.' Mathers stopped mid stride and Leo's soles screeched. 'That's not the kind of progress I'm looking for. Either he co-operates now or we proceed right away to pressing charges.'

'But half an hour, Inspector. That's all. What's another half an hour when you've already told the world you've caught the killer?'

'Come now, Mr Curtice. We've hardly—'

'Oh no? Shall we ask the mob on your front steps and see how they interpreted your announcement?'

The detective inspector, a chiselled man far too ruddy for the season, made a motion with his mouth like he was sucking a boiled sweet.

Leo stepped close. 'Be frank with me, Inspector Mathers, and I'll be frank with you. This boy, my client: we both know the truth. You've got DNA that will turn out to be a match and you've got a witness – a fine, upstanding PhD student – who saw him fleeing the scene. He did it. We both know he did it.'

The policeman could not quite hide his satisfaction.

'What we don't know is how it happened,' said Leo. 'And we won't, not until Daniel starts talking to us. Wouldn't it be easier – for me, certainly, and for my client, yes, but also for your investigation – if someone could get him to open up? To give an account of himself?'

'Mr Curtice. I hardly need remind you how time-sensitive this operation is becoming. It's been four weeks since Felicity went missing; two weeks since the body was—'

'Half an hour, Paul! That's all! I don't want Daniel to fight you any more than you do because we both know how that will end. It's in everyone's interests that he talks to me, that he trusts me. At the moment he's tired and he's scared and—'

This time it was Mathers who leaned close. 'Do you think I give a fuck how scared he is? Do you think I give a fuck if he had a sleepless night?' He pressed a fingertip to Leo's chest. 'How much sleep do you think I got last night? Or the night before? Or the ten, fifteen nights before that? How much sleep do you think the Forbes family got, or every other officer working this case?'

'Look, Paul, all I meant was—'

'You're damn right we know the truth, *Mr* Curtice. You're damn right we caught the killer and the world, as far as I'm concerned, deserves to be told.' The detective inspector paused: a dare, seemingly, for Leo to fill the silence.

Leo said nothing.

'Have your half an hour,' said the inspector, waving a hand. 'Come up with some story if you can. Just don't try and kid me. You're not here to do the world any favours. You're on nobody's side but your own.'

*

They were back, it felt like, where they had started. Yet Leo, this time, let his fingers drum.

'Daniel?' Leo watched, waited. 'Daniel, please. They will charge you. You understand that, don't you? You understand what I've told you? Unless you give an account of your version of events, they'll decide for themselves what they think happened.'

The boy sat with his shoulders hunched. He shrugged, as much as his posture would allow – which was communication, at least, of a kind.

'This refusing to speak. It does you no favours. I thought I'd made that clear. Did I not make that clear?' His tone would not help, Leo knew, but it was becoming harder to resist. He looked at his watch, openly.

'I can't help you if you don't let me. Your parents – ' Leo tipped his head to the security camera ' – they won't be able to help you either.'

A noise this time: something between a sniff and a snort.

Leo stood. He turned away and clutched his forehead. He turned back, a rebuke half formed, but Daniel was now sitting upright.

'What's . . .'

Leo waited.

'What's . . . that thing.' The boy, for an instant, met Leo's eye. 'That thing you said. The thing with the letters?'

Leo shook his head. 'I . . . DNA? You mean DNA?'

The boy did not say no.

'It's a genetic . . .' Leo stopped himself. 'It's us. It's tiny pieces of us. It's incontrov . . . It's proof, Daniel. Like fingerprints.

They take samples at the scene and try to match it to their suspect.'

'But it doesn't mean . . .' The boy glanced at the camera. 'It doesn't mean anything. That . . . that I did anything.'

'It . . . No, not in the sense I think you mean. But unless somehow—'

'And no one saw me. Like . . . there. Doing, you know. What they say I did.'

'No,' Leo said. 'No, that's true. But the DNA—'

'She was my girlfriend.'

Leo stared. 'Sorry?'

'She was my girlfriend. She, you know. Loved me and that.'

For ten, twenty, thirty seconds, Leo made no sound. Then, 'Were you there, Daniel? Is that . . .' He breathed. 'Is that what you're telling me?'

'I . . . Yeah. Sort of.'

'Sort of?' Leo stepped towards the table. He held the back of his chair but did not sit down. 'What happened, Daniel?'

The boy shuffled. 'We . . . we kissed and stuff.'

'You kissed. Meaning, she consented?'

Daniel frowned.

'Did she let you kiss her?'

'I told you: she was my girlfriend.'

'Daniel, I—'

'We did it all the time. And other stuff. Proper stuff. Like in films.' The boy's expression was a challenge but as he spoke he seemed to flush.

'Proper stuff? What do you mean by that?'

Daniel, this time, looked away. 'Sex,' he said and he slid a little deeper into his chair.

This time it was Leo who glanced towards the camera. 'Did you have sex with her, Daniel? Is that what you're saying?'

The boy took a moment to answer. 'Loads,' he said, concentrating now on his hands. 'But, um. Not this time. She . . . she was worried. She didn't wanna kid.'

'She didn't want to get pregnant?'

'Right. So instead, this time, we did other stuff. Like, with sticks and that.'

Leo covered his mouth with his hand.

'But . . .' Daniel shifted straighter. 'There was someone watching. A perv or whatever. She spotted him. The girl . . . er . . . Felicity, did. She told me to get off and when I didn't cos I didn't see the perv she did this.' The boy pointed to the marks on his neck. 'By accident.'

'By accident.'

There was a silence.

'And then?' Leo sighed. 'What happened then, Daniel?'

Daniel jerked a shoulder. 'I left.'

'You left.'

The boy nodded.

'And this man. The one you saw—'

'I didn't see him.'

'You didn't see him?'

'Uh uh.'

'What then? Only the girl did. *Felicity*. Is that what you're saying?'

Daniel nodded again.

Leo dragged his chair further from the table. He lowered himself onto it and caught his elbows with his knees. He looked at the sole-stained linoleum. 'You said you left.' He raised his head. 'Why did you leave, Daniel?'

Once again the boy shrugged.

Leo waited. 'Okay,' he said, after a moment. 'What about Felicity?'

The boy, this time, turned away.

'When you left,' Leo persisted, 'was Felicity . . .' He coughed. He tried again. 'In what state did you leave her?'

Silence.

'Was she alive, Daniel? Was Felicity alive when you left her?'

This time the boy spoke but Leo did not catch the words. 'I'm sorry, Daniel, I didn't hear what you—'

'She was alive. Okay? That's what I'm trying to tell you.' There was something in Daniel's expression that reminded Leo all of a sudden what the boy was capable of.

Leo backed slightly away. 'No, I know, I just wanted to—'

'You don't believe me. Do you? You're just like all the rest of them.'

Their time was almost up. DI Mathers and DC Golbas would by now be gathering their notes, their props, their wits, ready to settle things one way or another but quite unprepared, Leo suspected, for what they were about to hear.

'Look,' Leo said, 'Daniel. All I can say, as your solicitor – as someone who is here to help you – is that if you did what the police think you might have done, it would be better . . . it would be better for you to admit it. If you lie, and they catch you in that lie, the consequences – the punishment – will be all the greater.'

'I'm not lying.' The boy's voice was taut to the point of tears.

Leo showed Daniel his palm. 'I'm not saying . . . No one's accusing you of that. Not yet. But things get confused. They get mixed up. It's perfectly natural that you should be worried, that you should be scared, that you should be looking to find some—'

'I'm not scared either!' Daniel's hands, Leo saw, were curled and bloodless. His cheeks were blotched with red.

'I'm sorry,' Leo said. 'I'm not putting this very well. What I'm trying to say is, when they come back in here, the police are going to charge you. It's either that or let you go and they're not going to let you go. They have evidence, Daniel. Solid evidence. And your story . . . This story . . . It will only make things—'

'You asked me what happened. Didn't you? And I told you. Didn't I?'

'I did. You did. But—'

'So why can't you just tell *them*?' the boy said and the door behind Leo clicked open.

5

Something detonated against the glass and Leo dived. He peered up and saw only sky, as well as what looked like a bleeding sun.

'Jesus!' he said and someone, somewhere within the car, echoed it. The driver? Daniel's stepfather?

Leo straightened and tried to see beyond the haemorrhaging egg yolk. The street, a somnolent sequence of shops until the corner before, had rounded into a throng. Young men mostly, Leo thought at first, and clearly in the wrong place, directing their ire in the wrong direction. These were anarchists, anti-capitalists, fascists, anti-fascists. Something was happening, obviously, that Leo had not known about – surprising perhaps that it should occur in Exeter of all places but unsurprising that Leo was so out of touch. He had not looked at a newspaper in days; not at a story that was not somehow connected to the case. And yet, here, there: a pushchair. A mother chanting as she held her son. And over there: schoolchildren. Three, four of them; two girls, two boys; his daughter's age and – yes – in his daughter's uniform.

Not, like Leo, caught up inadvertently but bawling and baying like the rest of the crowd. Schoolchildren. Just schoolchildren. And as Leo looked it was one of the schoolboys who threw another egg.

Again Leo ducked but the missile, this time, missed by a car's length. Something else hit, on the roof it sounded like. In the seat behind Leo's, Daniel's mother screamed: a counterpoint to the baritone boom of the impact. And, 'Jesus!' said the voice again. It was not the driver: a policeman and trained, Leo hoped, for this sort of thing. Daniel's stepfather, then, in the back beside the boy's mother. Leo turned, hugging his cheek to the velour upholstery.

'Who are these people?' said Stephanie Blake. With her eyes drawn wide, Leo could see gaps, like wrinkles, in her makeup. She had slouched in her seat and her skirt, too short already for a visit to court, had risen halfway up her nylon-trussed thighs. 'Vince? Vince! What's going—'

'What the hell is happening?' said Vincent Blake. 'Where the hell are you taking us?' He was seated behind the driver so had no choice but to focus his outrage on Leo.

Something hit Blake's window and he spun. His pinched face turned pale. The man had a nose crooked like a brawler's and a crease, across it, extending below his eye but there seemed nothing intimidating – nothing tough – about his appearance now. He slid towards his wife, forcing her closer to the nearside door.

'Sit tight,' said the driver and Leo turned back to face the front. The policeman, a youthful, earnest constable, was doing his best to appear stoical but there was tension in his grip, ten to two, on the steering wheel. 'This might get rocky,' the young man said.

It was an understatement. The crowd through which they had already passed was only the fringe of the mob outside the courthouse. There was a cordon of yellow-clad officers along the kerb but their line was bedraggled and beginning to fray. Just as the van – Daniel's van – turned to make its final approach, the string of policemen snapped.

The protesters swarmed. There must have been two, three, four hundred people gathered and the men in front – and it was, here, mainly men in front – led the charge. The convoy – a police car, the van, another marked unit and finally Leo with Daniel's parents   had been moving at a brisk speed but now the lead driver had no choice but to press his brakes. The procession slowed, then stopped, and the protest turned into a siege.

A dozen men, then a dozen more, surrounded Daniel's van. They launched kicks at its bodywork and threw fists at the glass as though the pain they would be feeling in their toes and knuckles would somehow disseminate towards their prey. Someone swung a placard but in slow motion because with the sign it would have been like trying to swing an oar through water. The man turned it instead and used the pole end as a club.

'Daniel!'

The boy's mother had wedged herself between the two front seats. Her scarlet nails were clawing Leo's shoulder but when he winced she paid no heed. Her attention was on the scene ahead: on the van, which was beginning to sway. Just lightly but the momentum was building, the efforts of the protesters coalescing. They would tip it. In a moment, the van would be on its side.

Leo tried to picture the boy. Seated between two policemen, would he be reaching for one of their hands? Would he be crying, like a twelve-year-old ought?

'For Christ's sake!' Blake had displaced his wife between the seats. 'Why aren't we moving? Just drive, will you? Just go!'

'Vince!' Stephanie was trying to pull her husband to her side. 'Sit down, Vince, please!'

'You!' Blake said, prodding the driver. 'Put your foot down. Just drive through them – it's their own damn fault!'

The policeman turned. 'Sit down, Mr Blake!'

Blake fell away. He swore. He was starting forwards again when another impact tipped him back. It was not a missile this time but a body, splayed across the windscreen. Even the driver recoiled. His hands were locked to the wheel but his head was tight against his seat as he stared at the face confronting his. It belonged to a kid: a student, Leo guessed – hair bedraggled, skin pitted, expression ecstatic in righteous fury.

'Move!' the driver hissed. 'Bloody move!'

He was talking to his colleagues, Leo realised – the drivers in the vehicles ahead. It was the student who obeyed. He slid from the bonnet until he was standing and then seemed somehow to convulse. His body curved and whipped forwards and something splattered against the windscreen. It was a bilious, viscous green. Leo heard himself sound his disgust.

Their car became engulfed. Leo could barely see the van now, although he could tell it was still, somehow, upright. That explained, perhaps, why the mob had transferred its attention along the fleet. The student, for instance, had gathered his friends. There was a group of five or six of them on the driver's side, all teeth and fingers and flob. One in particular seemed enraged by Daniel's stepfather. He was bawling, pounding against Blake's window.

'Is this reinforced?' Blake said, scrabbling for safety. 'This glass! Is it bulletproof?'

He received no answer. Beside him, Daniel's mother was hunched and sobbing, fists bunched below her chin and knees tight to her belly. Someone – Leo could see only a thick, bare forearm – had attached themselves to the handle of her door and was tugging to try and prise it open. The door, though, held firm and the arm, its owner, seemed to fall away – until Stephanie shrieked and Leo saw, through his window, what she saw: a man growling through the glass and grasping in his reddened knuckles a piece of wood the shape and length of a baseball bat.

Leo jerked back as far from the window as his seatbelt would allow. He fumbled for the catch to free himself. He found it, or thought he did, but when he pressed it his seatbelt held firm. He looked, finally, at what he was doing and saw he was pressing the wrong button: the driver's belt had come free but Leo's remained clipped in place. He struggled, wrenched his body, but the more violently he moved, the tighter the seatbelt held him. And the man outside, filling the glass now, had the wood raised level with his shoulders. He had his torso turned and his feet set: ready, Leo realised, to swing.

He pressed himself deeper into his seat. He closed his eyes. He braced himself for the sound of shattering glass, for the shards to pierce his skin – but instead he heard a shout.

'Finally!'

Leo looked: at the policeman beside him, then back at the window. He expected to see his assailant, the plank of wood on its downward path. The man, though, was gone. In his place was a curtain of yellow, drawing itself around the car. There was space, too, up ahead. A metre, then two, then road – clear road – where the car in front had pulled away.

Theirs was the last vehicle into the courtyard but the first to reach a stop and immediately Leo was out, on his feet, pacing and puffing and pressing at his temples with his palms. He could hear echoes of the scene outside the gates and the bellows of officers within. Someone nearby was swearing: at subordinates, perhaps; at a situation they had collectively failed to expect.

Daniel's mother emerged next, followed by her husband. Stephanie was silent but Daniel's stepfather was, indiscriminately, making his fury plain.

Leo offered Stephanie his arm. She staggered, then took it.

'Are you okay?'

Daniel's mother made no reply. Her head was in her handbag, a cigarette already hanging from her lips. She was shuffling manically – for a lighter, Leo assumed, and though he no longer smoked, he frisked himself for something that might help.

'Jesus, Stephanie.' Daniel's stepfather, from his stance, seemed finally to have found himself a target. 'Your family's almost torn to pieces and all you can think about is getting yourself another fix.' He sneered and Leo stared, until the driver stepped between them.

'Here,' he said, a match in his fingers aflame. Stephanie lurched but her cigarette fell. The driver lit his own and passed it to her and she dragged as though coming up for air.

'Okay?' said the driver this time. He looked at Stephanie, who managed a nod, and then at Leo.

Leo could only shake his head. 'Who were all those people? Surely they weren't all here for—'

'Daniel!'

Leo saw the boy, beside the van and struggling against a policeman's grip. A second officer touched his colleague's shoulder and Daniel, with that, found himself free. Once again his mother called his name and he hurtled across the court-yard towards her. He was sobbing, Leo saw. Snot-stained and streaming, he streaked past his stepfather, who was lighting up himself now, and into his mother's arms. The force of him nearly toppled her but she caught him, her balance too, and she squeezed as though to smother him. As she did the boy spoke but Leo could not make out the words. A single phrase, more than once, stifled by his mother's embrace. It was only when she held him away – to wipe his eyes, to scour him for sign of harm – that Leo was able to hear.

'I'm sorry,' Daniel was saying: again and again and again.

6

'Leo.'

He could not stop pacing. Out of habit he had removed his shoes but he still had on his coat and even his scarf and he was explaining, or trying to, but the difficulty was knowing where to start.

'Leo. Leo!'

He jiggled his head, held up a hand. 'And honestly, Meg. They brought pushchairs. Pushchairs! One woman, she had her toddler with her. She was holding him up like . . . like, I don't know . . . like he was a placard. Ha! Right, just like that. She had him here, like this, and in her other hand she had an actual placard, a sign, and it said—'

'Leo, please. Just listen for a moment.'

'– it said shame, just shame, just that single word: shame. And there were others too, like this one I saw that said, what was it, it said—'

'Leo!'

Leo stopped. He stared at his wife, who covered her mouth with her hand. She shut her eyes.

'Meg?'

'Please, Leo,' she said, opening them. 'Please, just listen. Just for a moment.'

'What? What is it?' Leo frowned. He reached for his wife's hand.

Megan pulled away. 'It's Ellie.' She folded both arms, then let them drop.

'Ellie? What about Ellie? Is she okay? Where is she?' Leo spun towards the hallway but Megan reached and anchored him in the kitchen.

'She's fine, Leo. I mean, she's not hurt. They didn't hurt her.'

'What? Who hurt her? Where is she?' Again Leo made for the stairs.

'Leo! I said they didn't hurt her. She's not hurt. She's just upset, that's all.'

'Upset? Why is she upset? What happened, Megan, tell me!'

'For pity's sake, Leo!' Megan glared until Leo fell still. 'She came home without her coat,' she said. Leo was about to interrupt but his wife held him off. 'Her blouse, her white school one, it was covered in . . . I mean, it looked like she was covered in . . .'

'In? In what?'

'Blood. It looked like blood.'

'Jesus Christ! I thought you said she—'

'She's fine! Honestly, Leo, she's not hurt.'

'But the blood! What then? Are you saying it wasn't hers? Whose was it? Jesus, Meg, why didn't you—'

'It wasn't hers. It wasn't anyone's. It wasn't blood, Leo. It was ink.'

'Ink?'

'That's what she told me. Ink. Red ink. But honestly, when she walked in that door . . . I mean, she was crying, or trying not to, and her shirt, her hands, her face: she was covered in this . . . this *stuff*. It was like . . . a dream. A nightmare, rather. Like every nightmare I've had since you came home with this blasted . . . Since, probably, that poor girl . . .'

Leo shook off the digression. 'How did it get there? Why the hell was she covered in ink?'

'She wouldn't tell me. Obviously someone threw it at her but—'

'Someone *threw* it at her!'

Megan made a face. 'Of course someone threw it at her. What did you think? That she tripped in the stationery aisle at WH Smith?'

'No. I mean . . . No. But who . . . Why the hell . . .'

'I told you, she wouldn't say. But they stole her coat, I'm guessing, and they must have been teasing her and somehow, for some reason, she ended up covered in ink. Or maybe it was just – ' Megan shook her head, disparaging already what she was about to say ' – just an accident or something. Teenagers being teenagers and things getting out of hand.'

Leo scoffed. 'An accident?'

'Maybe! I don't know! I haven't exactly got a lot to go on!'

'Well we can put that straight for a start. Where is she? Is she in her room?' Leo made to move but Megan was quicker. She darted past him and pressed her shoulders to the door.

'Leo, no.'

Leo felt his lips form a humourless grin. 'What do you mean, no? We need to talk to her, Meg. Come out of the way.' He took a step. Megan gripped the architrave.

'I mean it, Leo. Not until you calm down.'

'What the hell are you talking about? I am calm!'

'You've still got your coat on. You're flushed and you're sweating and you're shouting. You don't seem calm.'

'Oh for heaven's sake.' Leo tore at his scarf and wrenched off his coat. He spread his arms. 'Satisfied?'

Leo listened at Ellie's door before he knocked. He heard nothing – no music, no television – so he rapped with a single knuckle. He reached for the door handle, expecting the door to be locked, but the catch clicked and the door opened.

'Ellie?'

The room was dark but for a lamp on Ellie's desk that had been angled upwards to spotlight the wall. The desk itself was otherwise clear but for Ellie's computer, a parade of reference books and a bright yellow pen holder: only the masticated ends of the items it contained tarnished the overall sense of order. The rest of Ellie's bedroom was similarly neat. Her posters – souvenirs from London art galleries, mainly – were, even to Leo's wonky eye, regimentally aligned; her clothes were shut where they should be; her CDs were stacked and, probably, categorised. The books on the set of pine shelves seemed, at first glance, more of a jumble but Leo suspected that these were arranged, too, to satisfy some taxonomical urge. The overall impression, Leo had once pointed out to his wife, was of a bedroom auditioning for an IKEA catalogue. It wasn't normal, he had insisted, not for a teenager. Neither, Meg had countered, was a parent bemoaning having nothing to complain about. It was just their daughter's way: her space, her choice. Leo's appetite for disarray, meanwhile, was surely sated by the condition of his office.

'Go away.'

Ellie was a corpse on the bed. With her back to the door and Rupert a tabby bundle in the crook of her knees, she made no movement. Her words, for all the signs that she was otherwise sentient, might have been carried on her dying breath.

'Darling, we just want to talk to you for a moment.' Leo squinted. 'Do you mind if I switch on the—'

'No!'

Leo recoiled from the light switch. He looked at Megan, who said, without saying it, what did I tell you?

Leo hesitated, then forced a smile. He stepped towards his daughter's bed and attempted what he hoped was an empathic-sounding sigh. 'It seems we've both had quite a day,' he said. He regarded his daughter's back, cast in the light from the hallway. Ellie's fine, fragile spine jutted through her vest-top towards him. Her shoulders, heartbreakingly slender, were drawn in a self-protecting pinch. Her hair seemed damp – washed but not combed – and Leo could sense the chill of its touch on her bare shoulders. He had an urge to sweep the hair from her skin, to tuck his daughter beneath the bed sheets on which she lay. He sighed again. The mattress was pressing his knees and he thought about lowering himself onto a corner. He brushed it with his fingertips instead, trailing his touch across the balled-up cat. 'I'll make you a deal,' he said. 'I'll tell you about my day and then you can tell me all about—'

'I don't want to hear about your stupid day!'

Leo flinched. 'Ellie, I—'

'Go away! Just go away!'

Leo parted his lips. Ellie, listen, he was about to say but when Ellie turned towards the light he was distracted by the flush to her skin. It only covered one part of her face: a raging red that extended down the left side of her neck and to her collarbone, too lopsided and vivid to be explained by Ellie's anger. Leo could not stop himself reaching.

'Leave me alone!' Ellie wrenched her chin from Leo's touch.

'Switch on the light.' When his wife did not respond, Leo turned. 'Meg. Switch on the light.'

This time Megan obeyed. Ellie winced and Leo stared. Once again he reached and this time Ellie allowed her face to be turned.

'I couldn't get it off,' she said. She began to cry. 'I scrubbed but I couldn't get it off.'

Leo heard his wife's exclamation. He felt Megan draw to his side. His attention, though, was on his daughter's skin: blotched from the ink but scoured, too. Along her jaw line and below her cheekbone there were sketches of blood, as though she had been dragged along tarmac.

'Ellie,' Leo said and barely heard himself. His fingers gravitated towards his daughter's wounds. This time Ellie flinched and Rupert, reluctantly, stirred.

'Don't!' Ellie shuffled towards her headboard. She was sobbing now. 'Just go,' she said. 'Please. Just leave me alone!' And she thrust her face into her bloodied pillow.

They pieced it together. In the living room and with barely a discussion they worked out what, when, why. Who, they did not tackle. In one respect, they could hardly hope to. In another, they both already knew.

Ellie's coat was taken from her just as Felicity's had been. The ink: it was Felicity's blood. They might have used fairy lights, had they found any. They might have threatened to drag her to the river.

'I'll talk to the school,' Leo said. He glanced at Megan, who was beside him on the sofa, staring at the blank television screen. 'Her teacher. The headmistress. I'll go in first thing.' Although, as he spoke, he was struggling to see how he could afford the time. After the riot Daniel had changed his story, had admitted what everyone else had already known. So there was the confession to get on record and the remand hearing to discuss and the boy's parents to deal with because everything was moving at such a pace that Leo had not really had a chance yet to—

'First thing,' Leo said. Megan sniffed and fiddled with her tissue and seemed not to have sensed his vacillation.

Leo shuffled closer and reached an arm around her shoulders. 'It's kids, Meg. It's kids being cruel like only kids can be.'

His wife pulled away from him.

'Meg? What's wrong?'

Megan hesitated before answering. 'I was spat at,' she said.

'What?'

'We were. Ellie and me. Yesterday, at the supermarket. I wasn't going to tell you but . . . after today . . .' Her voice seemed colder all of a sudden.

'Spat at? By who?'

'By a woman. A mother. She was my age, younger. She had a shopping trolley and two children and as she passed me she turned and spat.'

'What? Are you sure? I mean—'

'I'm sure, Leo. I'm perfectly, one-hundred-per-cent sure.'

'No. I know. I just meant, why? Did you say something to her or—'

'It wasn't my fault!'

'Calm down, Meg. I'm not saying it was. I'm just trying to understand what happened.' He shook his head. 'Why on earth would someone spit at you? Do you think . . . Are you saying . . . You think it was because of the case?'

'The thought occurred to me.'

'Why though?' Leo said again. 'How did she even know who you were?'

'Your secret's out, Leo. You're a big name, suddenly, in a small town. No.' She corrected herself: 'You're a small name in a smaller town full of even smaller-minded people. That's why, Leo. That's how.'

Megan shuffled round to face him. She took his hand and held it. 'The point is, it's not just kids. What happened today, what happened at the supermarket: it's not just kids.'

Leo looked down. He felt Megan's plaintive stare and turned from it.

7

What more was there to say? The whole episode: it was deplorable. Entirely contrary to the ethos of the school and not, Ellie's head teacher had assured him, behaviour that would be tolerated. The culprits would be identified and punished. Mr Curtice could no doubt understand, particularly given his profession, that it was difficult at this stage to say how exactly but the school – she, personally – would not let Eleanor down. It would help, of course, if Ellie could be encouraged to come forward – to name names, as it were. But no, yes, of course, it must be extremely difficult for the poor child and yes, indeed, just as you say, the onus must of course fall on the school to get to the bottom of things. And they would. Of *course* they would.

Ms Bridgwater was a slight, suited woman washed in scent and smeared in make-up. She had deflected Leo's anger with the practice of a politician. Leo, having expected a twelve-round brawl, had felled his opponent with a single swing – and was left as dazed as he would have been had he lost.

'Well,' he said. He sat straight, gave a firm nod. 'Good. I

appreciate your cooperation. And I . . . apologise if perhaps I seemed a little – ' he rolled a hand ' – upset. Before.'

'Not at all, Mr Curtice. You have every right to be upset. As a parent myself, I can fully appreciate the distress you must be feeling.'

'Yes. Well. Thank you.'

'And of course,' Ms Bridgwater added, 'there is the pressure of your work.'

'My work?'

Come now, the head teacher did not say. 'The case, Mr Curtice. The Forbes case.'

'Oh. I see.'

'Forgive me for mentioning it but, well' Ms Bridgwater pinched a smile. 'I saw you on the news. You're quite the local celebrity.'

Leo fumbled a laugh. 'Oh, I wouldn't go that far.'

'There is no need for modesty, Mr Curtice. And besides . . .' The head teacher's smile turned gluttonous. 'Doing what I do,' she said, 'being in the position that I am, I cannot help but take an interest in these matters.' She raised her arms from her lap and settled them on the edge of her desk.

Leo, this time, returned a frown. 'Ms Bridgwater. You appreciate, surely, that I cannot discuss—'

'Oh, please don't misunderstand me, Mr Curtice. I wouldn't dream of putting you on the spot. My interest is not so much in the case itself. It is, rather, in . . . the boy. The accused.'

Leo made to stand. 'I'm sorry but I'm really not comfortable . . .'

The head teacher leant across the desk, reached an apologetic hand towards Leo. 'I thought perhaps I might help. That's all. I thought I might offer *you* some information – not the other way round.'

Leo drooped into his chair. 'Me?'

The head teacher tipped her head. 'The boy,' she said and, perhaps noticing Leo stiffen, quickly raised a palm. 'I know, I know – his identity has not been disclosed. But this is a small town, Mr Curtice. There is a limited number of secondary schools and a very active branch of the National Association of Head Teachers. We talk, just as you talk, I'm sure, with your fellow professionals.' Again Ms Bridgwater smiled.

'Well, naturally, but—'

'The boy. The accused. If it is whom I – we – suspect it is – ' the head teacher gave a twitch that was almost a wink ' – then, as I say, I would perhaps have some insight that you might find instructive. He is not, I am sure, the most cooperative of clients.'

Leo resisted his instinct to agree. 'I'm still not sure I follow. I don't want to sound ungrateful but what insight could you offer?'

'We taught him,' the head teacher said. Then, when Leo began to dissent, 'Not most recently, I concede. But he was here, for about as long as the boy has spent anywhere.'

'Here? But . . .' But this was his daughter's school. It was a good school. A state school but as reputable a state school as a parent could hope for. Leo shook his head. 'When?'

'He started his secondary education here. We excluded him after a term. This is all on the assumption, of course, that we are indeed talking about the same boy.' The head teacher studied Leo. She gave him seconds to respond. 'But you will have access to the boy's records,' she said when Leo did not. 'You will be able to confirm the precise dates, I'm sure.'

Ellie would have known him. No, not necessarily. It was a big school, one of the biggest in the county. She will have seen him, though. She will have passed him, brushed against him. He will have seen *her*.

'Did you teach him?' Leo said. 'Why was he expelled?'

'I am denied, in my role, the pleasures of classroom contact.' The head teacher twitched her lipstick. 'But certainly I had dealings with the boy. He was, shall we say, a regular visitor to my office.'

'He caused trouble?'

'When he was present, Mr Curtice, yes, he certainly did. We'd heard about his reputation before he started here so we thought we were prepared. But when a child will simply not allow himself to be taught, there is very little that we can do.'

'Not allow himself . . . What do you mean?'

'I mean he was abusive, disruptive, entirely lacking in deference. A real attention seeker. Our strategy was reduced to restricting the impact his presence would have on the children around him.'

'He was isolated?'

'He isolated himself. His attendance record was woeful, as I say. When he was present, he may as well not have been.'

The head teacher shook her head and her hair, sprayed rigid, moved not a jot. 'Such anger. Such visceral, unaccountable rage. He attacked a teacher, Mr Curtice. That's why, in the end, he was excluded. An unprovoked attack, by all accounts but the boy's.'

Leo frowned again, waited for Ms Bridgwater to continue.

'The teacher, Miss Dix: she asked him to read aloud. Just a simple passage from a text the class was studying. The boy was subdued that day, which for him amounted to his best behaviour, and poor Josie sensed an opportunity to involve him.' The head teacher made a face, like really her colleague should have known better. 'She asked, gently, and the boy refused. She persisted and the boy insulted her. He called her an s-l-u-t, Mr Curtice. Josie was admirably restrained in her response – far more restrained than I would have been, I assure you – but when she approached the boy's desk and set an open book in front of him, the boy hurled it aside and flung himself at Josie's throat. He throttled her – or would have, had the other boys in the class not restrained him.'

'So he was excluded?'

'He was excluded.'

'Permanently?'

'Permanently.'

'But after a term, you say? A single term. Is that, I don't know. Is that not unusual?'

'Ordinarily perhaps but not given the boy's history. And we were warned about him, as I say. We expected trouble. We were prepared, all along, to take extreme measures should they be called for.'

'Well,' said Leo, 'clearly. But expulsion, I'd always assumed, is a last resort. Isn't there a process? A gradual escalation in sanctions?'

'Sanctions escalate in line with the behaviour that warrants them. It was not his first offence, by any means, and the boy, after all, attacked a teacher. How could we do anything thereafter but exclude him?'

'I understand but would not a suspension have sufficed? Or, I don't know . . .'

Ms Bridgwater did not wait for Leo to finish. 'I have staff to protect, Mr Curtice. I have children under my ward. In view of the reason for your visit, I must say I struggle to comprehend your disapproval.'

'Disapproval? No, I . . .' Leo moved in his seat. Ms Bridgwater was watching him and he looked towards the window to avoid her eye. The head teacher's office was on the first floor at the front of the main building – a squat Sixties structure assembled from shades of grey and pupils were beginning to appear in the playground below them. There was a boy, alone, rummaging in his rucksack and weaving towards the entrance. In his wake whirled a gossip of girls.

'You've met Daniel, Mr Curtice. You know the kind of boy he is. You know, more to the point, what he is capable of. We acted with alacrity and I can only be thankful, for the sake of our school, our pupils, that we did.'

Leo turned to face her. His nod started slowly and gathered pace.

'As much as it pains me to say it, Mr Curtice, some children are beyond help. They are born bad, plain and simple.

I have seen many, in my time, though few quite so wicked as Daniel Blake.'

Leo, again, gave a nod. He looked towards the clock on the office wall. He reached for his briefcase and stood. 'I should get along.' He gestured towards the window, to the trickle of children that was becoming a torrent. 'I expect you must too. Thank you for your time, Ms Bridgwater.'

The head teacher pressed the desk until she was standing. 'Please send Eleanor my very best wishes. She should of course take all the time she needs to recover from her ordeal.'

'Thank you. I will.' Leo shifted his briefcase and accepted the woman's grip. He nodded, turned and pushed at the door until he realised he needed to pull. In the corridor he walked slowly, and was slowed further on the stairs by the tide of children. It was only when he reached the car park that he realised what Ms Bridgwater had achieved. Confirmation. A name to toss to her peers and renown, no doubt, for having won it. All she had really hoped to, then.

Some children are born bad. Isn't that what the head teacher had said? They are born bad and there is nothing that anyone can do. The teachers: they tried their best. The parents: they did too. It is not as though the boy was denied opportunities. It is not as though he was not shown right from wrong. So how else can you explain it? He was born bad, Mr Curtice: bottom line, end of story, case closed.

8

'Case closed. Right?'

Leo looked up from his open briefcase. Daniel's stepfather was the only one standing. He had his feet hip-width apart and his arms across his pectorals. Stephanie, his wife, was seated to Leo's right, her chair as far from the table as the wall behind her would allow, her chin offset and her bloodshot eyes on the floor. Daniel, across from her, faced his knees. His hands were pinned between them, his shoulders drawn inwards. He seemed a slight, feeble thing – though so, Leo reminded himself, might any wild creature that had been caged.

'Right?' Blake repeated. 'Sounds to me like a no-brainer.'

Leo took out his files and set his briefcase beside his feet. 'It's not quite that simple, Mr Blake. As with any of the options open to us, there are risks.'

Blake showed his incomprehension through a sneer.

'The sentence,' said Leo. He glanced at the boy. 'The sentence, if the argument is rejected, might still be . . . harsh.'

'Harsh? How harsh?'

Again Leo looked towards Daniel.

'Never mind,' said Blake, flicking a hand. 'It's his best bet, that's the point. That's what you're saying. Right?'

'Not necessarily. All I'm doing, at this stage, is laying out some of the—'

'I'm not mental.'

They turned to the boy. His voice had been a whisper. His face, like his manner, was downcast.

'No one's saying that you are, Daniel. We would simply argue that you were not responsible for your actions, on the grounds that—'

'What would you call it then?' interrupted Daniel's step-father. 'Why the hell else would you have done what you did?'

Daniel's mother gave a whimper.

'Mr Blake,' said Leo. 'Please.'

'Well?' the man persisted. He was leaning towards his step-son but not, Leo would have said, as close as he might have. When Daniel raised his eyes – full of misery; fear, too, though checked by his obvious resentment – Blake backed slightly away. He disguised his retreat with a grunt. 'Not mental, he says. Like that makes everything all right. Like anyone's gonna think less of him if he ends up in a loony bin instead of in prison.'

'Mr Blake—'

'Talk to your son, Steph, for Christ's sake. Don't just bloody sit there.'

Daniel's mother did precisely that.

'You saw what happened outside the court,' Blake persisted.

'They'll tear him apart if he goes to prison. Ask your ex, Daniel's father: ask him. He's inside, he knows what it's like. Daniel won't last five minutes. They'll rip him to pieces, even before they find out what he's done.'

Stephanie, this time, choked back a sob.

'Oh Christ. Here we go.' Blake looked at Leo, as though expecting him to mirror his rolling eyes. 'Power up the sprinklers: that'll help. Sit there feeling sorry for yourself when it's your son – *your* bloody son – who's just confessed to murder, who's gonna spend rest of his worthless life, probably, in some stinking, piss-stained—'

'Mr Blake! That's enough!'

At the sound of Leo's raised voice, the guard outside the door framed his face in the security glass. When Leo raised a hand, he returned a frown – then reluctantly, it seemed, revolved away. Blake, meanwhile, had settled his snarl on Leo. He made a gun shape with his fingers and spoke down the barrel.

'You listen to me, Curtice. This is my family, my business. You're just the hired help. Do you get me?'

Twerp. Obnoxious, poisonous, vicious little twerp.

But: 'I get you, Mr Blake.' There was a hint of a challenge in Leo's tone but he let it fade. 'And I apologise for raising my voice. The purpose of this discussion is to lay down some options. That's all. We do not need to make any decisions right away.'

With a snort, Daniel's stepfather made plain what he thought of Leo's options.

'Also,' Leo said, 'I had hoped to clarify where things stand. From a procedural perspective, I mean.' He turned to Stephanie. 'A lot's happened in the past few days and I thought ... Well. I thought you would probably have some questions.'

Daniel's mother, after a pause, gave a nod. She did not look up, however. She did not speak.

'The remand hearing, for instance. The court visit. Did you understand the implications?'

Still Stephanie said nothing.

'Daniel? Did you understand what it meant?'

Daniel, too, avoided Leo's eye.

'It meant he's not getting out. Right? It means they're keeping him locked up.' Blake, as he spoke, seemed to smirk.

'You're to be transferred, Daniel,' said Leo. 'To a . . . facility. A place like this but closer to home. You'll be able to visit,' Leo added, turning to the boy's mother.

Stephanie swallowed. She took a breath, seemed to taste the words that were forming on her tongue. 'What about . . .' She cast a glance towards her son that did not quite reach. 'What about bail? Is it not worth trying? I know you advised not to but . . . later, maybe? Will they . . . will they let Daniel come home?'

The boy made a sound, something between a murmur and a moan.

Leo nodded, in understanding rather than affirmation. 'It would not, I think, be wise. Daniel's well-being has to be the priority and he'll be safest, I'm certain, where they're taking him. Also,' he added, 'in view of the alleged offence, of the publicity surrounding the case . . . It is doubtful that an application would be granted, at any stage.' More than doubtful: it was certain, though he did not say so.

'The court visits,' said Leo, shifting. 'They will become a regular occurrence, I'm afraid – at least in the short term.'

Stephanie's eyes drew wider and Leo raised a hand.

'Things will settle down. There'll not be the . . . trouble . . . there was last time. It's just routine, I promise you. Part of the remand process, that's all. And soon Daniel will be . . .' committed, he was about to say '. . . referred to the Crown Court. He'll be arraigned, formally, and depending on what plea we enter, the judge will set a trial date. For the autumn, I expect. Late summer at the earliest.'

'That long?' said Stephanie, her expression aggrieved once again. 'Why so long?'

Leo made a face: there was nothing he could do. 'We'll push for sooner, naturally. It won't be in anyone's interests to drag this out.'

Daniel's stepfather parked his hands on the surface of the table. 'Hang on,' he said. 'A trial date, you said. As in, for a trial?' He bent upright and jabbed a thumb towards his stepson. 'He did it. He's said he did it. What the hell do they need a trial for?'

Leo, for a moment, struggled with whether it should be necessary for him to answer. 'To present the case, Mr Blake. To allow us to mount our defence.'

Blake sniffed. 'Sounds like a waste of money if you ask me: taxpayers' money, *my* money. Sounds like a bloody publicity stunt too. They want a show trial, is that it? They want to string the boy up and make sure the newspapers are there to take pictures.'

'Vince!'

'Just tell them. Can't you? He's nuts, insane, Looney Tunes: whatever term you want to use. He did it but he didn't mean it and he's sorry. Case closed, just like you said.'

Leo was transfixed. He sensed Daniel squirming beside him. 'That's not what I . . .' He shook his head. 'Diminished responsibility. That's the term, Mr Blake. And I can't just *tell* them. The Crown, probably, will dispute any defence we present. If we argue for diminished responsibility, we would have to enter a plea of not guilty. And Daniel will need to be evaluated. He'll need to talk to a psychiatrist and they, in turn, will—'

'Wait a minute. You can stop right there. There's no way Daniel's talking to a shrink.' Blake looked to his wife. Stephanie, at the prospect, seemed terrified, appalled – ashamed?

'He would have to, Mr Blake. The psychiatrist's findings would be the basis of the entire defence. Really, there's no disgrace in it.'

'I said, no.' Again Blake turned to his wife and she gave a twitch of something like affirmation. 'No means no, Curtice. End of discussion.'

'With respect, Mr Blake, I'm afraid it's not your decision to make. It would be up to Daniel.'

'What? What are you talking about? I'm his stepfather. Steph's his mother.'

'And Daniel is my client. I work for him.'

Blake belched out a laugh. 'He's twelve years old!'

'He is. You're right. But he's old enough to be charged with murder, which means the law considers him old enough to instruct his solicitor. If it is Daniel's decision to plead not guilty, to argue for diminished responsibility, then the first step would be to—'

'I'm not mental!' The boy, all of a sudden, was on his feet. 'I'm not and I'm not saying it!' He slid behind his chair and backed away, dragging the seat with him as a ward. His eyes were blooded and his cheeks damp.

Blake saw Daniel's hands on the chair and braced himself as though readying for it to swing. 'What the hell do you think you're . . . Put that down!'

'Mr Blake, I don't think . . .' But Daniel had indeed raised the chair slightly, if only to keep his stepfather at bay. Blake lunged and ripped the chair from the boy's grip. Daniel staggered backwards, into the corner of the room, sobbing now but snarling at his stepfather too.

'Get away! Get away from me!'

Blake held the chair, posturing like some circus lion-tamer. 'Calm down! Do you hear? Calm down or so help me I'll . . .' Blake glanced at his wife. He shifted the chair in his grip but did not seem at all sure about what it was, actually, that he might do.

'Leave me alone!' Daniel swiped at the tears in his eyes. He looked from Blake to his mother to Leo. 'All of you!'

Daniel's mother gave a wail.

'Sit down, Daniel,' said Leo. 'Please.' Like the others, he was now on his feet. It felt like there was something in his throat, squatting on his voice box and preventing him from swallowing. 'Please,' he said again and he held out a hand. The boy, in response, batted at the air.

'Get off me! Don't touch me!'

There was the sound of a latch and the door to the cell swung open. The guard appeared in the doorway and at the sight of him Daniel reared. He squealed and, as the man started to advance, backed himself further into the corner.

'Settle down!' The guard had one hand on his holstered truncheon and the other splayed in front of him. 'Okay? Just settle down.'

'Leave me alone! Please!' Daniel threw a glance towards Leo. 'Make him leave me alone!'

Leo took a step. 'Officer. It's all right. It's just a misunder—'

'Grab him!' said Blake. 'For Christ's sake just grab him!' Daniel's mother started forwards but Blake barricaded her with his arms.

'No,' said Leo. 'Don't!' He reached to the guard's shoulder but the man just shoved him away. Leo tried again. He stepped forwards. He came between the boy and the guard, facing the man's fury and conscious of Daniel's terror at his back. 'He's fine. Leave him be.'

The guard lunged. Daniel howled. Leo spun, stumbled and grabbed instinctively to still the baton. He held it, briefly, and hung his weight on the guard's arm. The man was stronger, though, and Leo staggered. He reached once more, flailing now, but just as he made to grab again he spotted something on an arc towards his face. And then he felt it: a searing, slashing pain – followed by the cold of the concrete floor.

It was glorious. There was a fragility to the light and a preciousness about the warmth. Here, behind the building and beyond the wind, it might have been spring. A sample exclusively for him. An atonement.

He had his eyes closed and his chin high. To catch the sun. Also, to slow the bleeding. He had a paper towel pressed to his cheek and he dared not take it away because it would stick and the anticipation of the pain was worse, almost, than the pain itself. A proper gouge, the guard with the first-aid kit had said, with a kind of awestruck revulsion that had stung as much as the antiseptic. His nails? he had asked, angling his head. The boy did this just with his nails? Then, little shit. What a proper little shit.

At which point Leo had reclaimed his personal space. Shrugging off the man's concern, as well as his incitement to press charges, he had made his way to the lavatories and escaped, after that, through a fire door. He was not quite sure where it had led him. Behind the car park, he reckoned: a concrete expanse walled by road noise and infused with the odour of the industrial-sized bins. Yet calm, too; calming. Wherever it was, it would do.

I'm not mental, he had said. I'm not and I'm not saying it.

There was a house, a hall, in the area of Reading in which Leo had grown up. It was flats now: overpriced and underoccupied, he had heard, which to Leo was hardly surprising. The building, before the renovation, had been an asylum.

The high gates and imposing walls that now served to keep people out had been installed, initially, to keep them in. Who – in their right mind – would want to live there? Leo, his mates: when they were kids they would try to break in. Not *really* try because breaking in, actually, was the last thing they wanted to do. It was a terrifying place and that was the thrill: fear of what lay beyond. Manic laughter and swinging light bulbs. Baby-eaters, shit-throwers, shrinks. There was a prison close by too but the lure was barely as great. Prison, after all, was no big deal. Not compared to the alternative.

Leo tested the paper towel. It was stuck, just as he had feared. He tugged, gently, then harder, and winced the tissue from his face. He touched his cheek. His fingertip came away red. He tore a strip from the paper towel and applied it to the wound, as he would have had he sliced himself shaving. Would he get away with that, he wondered? Old razor, he could say. Ageing face.

He inhaled and pursed his lips and puffed until his lungs emptied. He felt, all of sudden, in violation, though of what he could not have said. There was work to be done, apart from anything. Yet he had no desire to return to the world, to forsake this unlikely oasis. And so he sat, alone, on a wall, wondering what on earth had just happened and failing, despite everything, to blame the boy.

9

They watched on the television. Megan, probably, would have liked to have gone. Ordinarily, at least. Leo, on the other hand, would rather have forsaken even the coverage. He had suggested it – started to – but it was not, apparently, up for debate. This was part of it, his wife's expression had conveyed.

And so they watched, side by side but as far apart as their three-seater sofa would allow: Leo with paperwork balanced on the arm on his side, Meg with a box of tissues on the arm beside her. The curtains were drawn and Leo had resisted the urge to ask why. It seemed needless; superstitious, almost. Tokenism, in the harshest terms, much like the funeral itself. A ceremony for the sake of the living that would help, in Leo's experience, only if one did not truly hurt.

He switched on the side light.

The anchor, on the television, was reaching for the weather. Already, only minutes into the broadcast. It was befitting, apparently, that it was so unseasonal – just as, Leo suspected, rain would have been, or a shroud of snow, or a furious, anguished wind.

It was a strange decision, he would have argued. Letting the world in when he, in the Forbes's place, would have done what he could to shut it out. It seemed improper, somehow: turning the day into a public event. Although perhaps, given the attention their daughter's death had received, they no longer had any choice. Even his father's funeral, after all, had snowballed into something less than private. There had been relatives that Leo barely recognised, friends who had long since moved away – no one, other than Leo and his family, who had attended other than because they had felt obliged to. So maybe, in the circumstances, what the Forbes family was doing was brave. Maybe, actually, it was generous. More so, in retrospect, than Leo had managed to be.

The cortège, to the anchor's commentary, diverted from the Exe and towards the High Street. There were even more onlookers along the route than had been expected; the pavements were clogged from doorway to drain. So much for the pundits' predictions, that most would choose to mourn in private, in the consoling surround, as they had put it, of their homes. Probably they would prove wrong about the viewing figures, too. Six million would follow the coverage, they had estimated, in living rooms from Truro to Thurso.

Leo saw Megan glance over at him. Just a glance but he knew what it meant. Look, Leo. Look at the enormity of this.

It was astonishing, he had to concede, that one life should impact on so many. One death, rather; one manner of death. Twice now the anchor had made reference to the 'depth of feeling' and though Leo would have taken issue with the first aspect of the sentiment, there was no denying that the feeling was there. The weight of numbers, after all, was hard to ignore.

'Is he watching this?' said Megan. She spoke to the screen. 'He should be made to.'

Leo glanced again. He said nothing.

The coverage cut from the procession to an air shot of Exeter cathedral. The building, a Gothic colossus that might have been constructed with just such an occasion in mind, was sited in a large open area behind the High Street, ringed by a cobbled lane and a grass verge that was popular, on a normal day, with sandwiching students. Today only a cordoned-off strip of ground was visible beneath the throng.

Leo reached for his paperwork. He set it on his lap. He felt Megan gauging him and stared at the topmost page as though reading it. He flipped over to the next sheet.

'Who is this character?' he said, not looking at the television but failing not to hear the talking head. 'He sounds like he's swallowed the *Daily Mail*.' Every word spoken, every image cast, seemed also somehow a condemnation. They did not name names, of course. But the point was, they did not have to.

Megan gave a sob and Leo raised his head. What? he was about to say but then he saw.

Felicity's family. The cortège had reached the cathedral and the passengers were unfolding from the cars. The uncles were out first, the voice-over said, fastening their jackets and fixing their expressions into frowns. They formed a perimeter, and only once it was secure did the aunts, under hats, follow. Next came the cousins and the grandparents, the children in unwashed black, the pensioners in fades of grey. They drew together, the generations, and moved with the cameras towards the foremost car.

There was a delay, long enough to cause a ripple. This – those within – was what everyone watching had been waiting for. The page in Leo's hands drooped into his lap.

The door cracked and a foot appeared: a man's lace-up, polished to a patent black. The gap widened and Felicity's father followed. He was not a tall man but he unfurled himself to his full height, raising his chins and marshalling his shoulders. He faced out, and for a moment found the camera, but his expression did not alter and he turned back towards the car. He dipped and then withdrew and his sons, Felicity's brothers, joined him on the cobblestones.

Even the youngest was a clenched fist taller than his father. The boys were fifteen and seventeen, Leo seemed to recall. Frederick, was it? And Francis? Names beginning with F, anyway, because it was one of the Forbes family's idiosyncrasies that all the children had names that began with F. Both boys were blond, unlike Felicity, and Leo was reminded of an image from a few years before, of the princes beside their father at Diana's funeral. The boys, like their royal counterparts, appeared composed but heartbreakingly so. Even the commentator seemed struck, for he fell silent. Not a conscious choice, Leo supposed, but the appropriate reaction nonetheless.

On screen there was confusion, briefly, until someone approached the group and guided them with an outstretched arm. The camera, though, floundered. Someone was missing. The picture panned left, then jerked right, before settling, it seemed, on a target. A woman and a girl, hand in hand, rounding the lead car from the passenger side. Felicity's mother and Faye, Felicity's sister, had emerged off screen, under cover of the mother's improbably wide-brimmed hat. Again the camera jerked, as though jostled, and the picture switched to a different angle. The girl's face – a more fraught, less rounded version of Felicity's – became visible but the picture passed her by. The director, the cameramen: they wanted the mother. Anna Forbes's hat, however, had clearly been chosen for a reason. Tipped towards the cameras, it masked all but her pale chin, until the aunts and the grand-parents drew around her, her daughter too, and curtained their passage towards the church.

The commentator found his voice and Leo switched off to it. He looked at his lap again and only caught sight of the coffin from the corner of his eye. Was that Felicity's father bearing it? Alongside her uncles? Megan gave a whimper and Leo decided he did not want to know. He tried to concentrate on the task he had set himself but there was silence again from the screen and the silence, in a way, was more of a distraction than the punditry.

He set aside the paperwork and picked up the mail he had collected that morning from the office. Grateful for some-thing that required physical engagement, he inserted his finger into the topmost envelope and tore.

'Leo. Please.'

Leo met his wife's tear-smudged frown.

'The post,' she said. 'Do you have to deal with that now?'

'I'll do it quietly,' Leo said. He lifted the letter, acting as though studying it but focused, rather, on the television screen.

The coffin was three-quarter size. He could not, at first, work out what seemed odd about it but that, he realised, was it. Three-quarter size and a pure, lustrous white. Felicity's family members bore it towards the cathedral entrance as though it were a tray of crystal. The two men at the rear – the girl's uncles, it looked like – had their adjacent arms wrapped around each others' shoulders, whether to help keep their burden steady or to give each other comfort, Leo could not tell.

The images on screen were transmitting now from inside the cathedral. The pews, needless to say, were full. The coffin, being threaded so carefully along the aisle, was a stark contrast to the collective pall of black. Some mourners tracked its advance, Leo noticed. Others looked conspicuously away. They stared at their hands or their feet or the backs of their eyelids.

'You can watch, you know. You don't have to pretend you're not.'

Leo hastened to pick up another letter. 'What? I know. I'm not pretending.' He turned the envelope and acted as though intrigued by it.

'Just watch it, Leo. I won't tell anyone, I promise.'

This time Leo scowled. 'What's that supposed to mean?'

Megan sighed. 'Nothing. I . . . Sorry.'

Leo glared for a moment. He looked again at the envelope he was holding and tossed it without bothering to finish opening it. There was quiet: in the room, on the television.

'Leo.'

He did not look.

'Leo.'

He did.

'Don't be angry,' Megan said. 'I was only . . . I only meant . . .'

Leo waited.

His wife sniffed and gathered herself. She shuffled to face him. 'I only meant . . . that no one would blame you. I wouldn't. Certainly your daughter wouldn't.' Megan tipped her head to the ceiling, a gesture towards Ellie shut away in her room.

'Blame me?' Leo set his head at an angle. 'Blame me for what?' They were clearly not talking just about the funeral any more.

Megan shook her head: not an answer but a dismissal. 'Look, Leo. Just look.' She pointed to the screen. Neither of them turned to it. 'And your face. Have you seen what he did to your face?'

Leo brushed his fingertips across the scores on his cheek. 'It was an accident.' He let his hand fall. 'I told you how it happened.'

Megan frowned.

'What?' said Leo.

'Nothing. It was an accident. Fine. But I'm just saying. That's all. If you handed over the case. If you decided it wasn't worth it. I'd understand.'

'Not worth it? What do you mean, not worth it? This is about the only thing I've ever been involved with that feels remotely worthwhile!'

Megan bridled. 'I'll ignore that, Leo. I'll pretend you didn't say that.'

'Professionally. I meant professionally.'

'You mean you're bored. Is that it? You're putting your daughter, your wife, yourself through this because you're tired of the same old commute?'

The commute. Leo thought again of the processions of cars, the parade of drunk and disorderlies. He thought of his father, of his bitterness at his cigarettes-and-TV existence and his hope that Leo would achieve something more. Yes, he wanted to tell his wife: that's it exactly. Because how else to put it? How else to admit that a year . . . No. More. Almost two years. How else to admit that almost two years after his father's death, he was yet to move on? Was yet to see a means to.

He said nothing. He picked up another envelope.

'You have a family, Leo,' said Megan after a moment. 'You have a daughter. Ever since Matthew died you've been—'

'I've been what?' said Leo. He snapped. He did not mean to.

Megan hesitated. 'You don't want to talk about your father,' she said. 'I get it. But Ellie's terrified. Can you not see that? About going back to school. About leaving her room.'

'Megan, please. Ellie will be fine. I went to the school, didn't I? I spoke to the headmistress.' Inside the envelope was a query about an invoice that should really have gone straight to admin. Leo flipped the folded page in the direction of the floor.

'Well,' said Megan. 'That's okay, then. If you went to the school. If you spoke to the headmistress. That makes the fact that someone threw blood at your daughter perfectly all right.'

'It was ink! For Christ's sake, Meg.' There was a final envelope to open and Leo started his assault on the seal. On screen a eulogy had begun. Felicity's death, the minister was saying, had not been in vain. Justice, apparently, would prevail. Over whom, he did not elucidate.

'What do you think, Leo? That they would have resisted throwing blood if they'd had any? That the fact it only looked like blood made your daughter any less upset? That she came away any less traumatised?'

Traumatised. Jesus Christ. Leo's head juddered. He tugged at the sheet of paper caught inside the envelope.

'Do you know what I don't understand?' Megan leant towards him. 'What I can't – ' his wife splayed her hands, gripping something solid but invisible between them ' – what I can't grasp?'

Leo did not ask for the answer. He focused on the note in his hands.

'It's that he did it. It's that you know he did it. He's told you he's guilty and still you insist on putting his well-being above your daughter's.'

It was a prompt for him to rile and he almost took it. The note, though. He could not stop looking at the note.

'He killed an eleven-year-old girl, Leo. He doesn't deserve

you. Maybe he doesn't deserve to be defended at all, by anyone!'

Leo felt for the empty envelope he had discarded. It was ripped now but the address, like the words on the note itself, had been typed or printed and gave away nothing more.

'Leo. Talk to me! Don't just ignore me. Don't you dare just ignore what I'm saying!'

Two sentences. That was all. Barely that, grammatically speaking, but enough to make their point. Enough, in the gloom, to make clear their intent.

'Leo!' Megan grabbed at his arm and forced him to turn. 'Answer me!'

But Leo, facing his wife, did not know what to say.

She trails, though she knows she is expected to lead. It is not, she imagines, what the boy is used to: this salesman, essentially, who every day must put up with being sold to. Look here, young man, at the flooring. And here, in the bathroom – we put that in ourselves. Megan, in comparison, must seem almost hostile. Uncaring, at least, though she does not mean to be. It is uncertainty. Bewilderment, rather. She is in a barrel, it feels like, on a hill – aware that she has set things in motion but too dazed to wonder where they might stop.

'Cracking kitchen,' the boy says. His head bobs as he surveys it. 'Large,' he says and he makes a note.

Megan moves from her position in the doorway. Her toast is rubble on the worktop and some instinct, at the sight of it, reasserts itself. 'Sorry,' she says. She stacks the honeyed knife on the plate and slides the plate to the side of the sink, the half-full ashtray too. With her hands she makes an attempt at sweeping up the mess.

'The units.' The boy points with his pen. 'Are they new?'

'Um.' Megan considers them. They are not. They came with

the house. But the boy, before she can answer properly, has moved on.

'What's through here?' he says, disappearing into the utility room. 'Cracking!' comes a voice and the boy emerges with his pen working in unison with his head. 'Great space,' he says. Then, earnestly: 'Useful.' He looks to Megan for agreement and she makes a noise like she should probably have spent more time thinking about it. She gestures for the boy to lead into the hallway.

'So what's the story?' the boy asks as he bounds up the stairs. His head is turned to the ceiling and his mouth, between words, swings unhinged. He is like a tourist beneath the dome of St Paul's.

'The story?'

The boy has stopped to make another note and Megan, reaching the landing, is grateful for the chance to draw breath.

'The house. Have you got something else lined up? How soon would you be ready to push the button?'

It seems an apt turn of phrase. Megan thinks of the films Leo always used to like to watch, of buttons controlling bombs.

'Soon.' She realises, as she says it, that she means it. 'Immediately, actually.'

The boy turns. 'Oh,' he says. He smiles. 'Cracking.'

'Would that be a problem?'

'No. Not at all. It's just . . . when we spoke on the phone . . .'

'I know. But, well. Circumstances have changed.'

The boy, finally, exhibits an expression that does not employ his teeth. In half a morning? he is thinking.

She did not follow the boy into her daughter's room but she returns there once he has left. She perches at the foot-end of the single bed, a notepad on her knees and Leo's antique Casio beside her. She taps, reckons, taps. The calculator is straining in the dim light, displaying figures as faded as the pattern on the bed sheets. She has deducted all she needs to, though, and the important thing is that there are numbers still showing. Enough to pay off what she owes. Enough for rent. Enough, if things work out, for something permanent. And this, if the estate agent is to be believed, is worst case. Best case is . . . She taps the keys again. She shakes her head. Why on earth, she wonders, has she been deaf for so long to her own advice?

The answer comes unbidden: circumstances have changed. Isn't that how she put it? I have awoken, she might have said. Or, I was caught in a barrel on a hill and it has shattered, finally, and thrown me into glorious freefall. She laughs. She thinks she is laughing but it turns out she is crying. Worst case, best case. The money has nothing to do with it. Or perhaps it did, when she did not think she had enough. The point is, it does not any more. The money, now, is the least of things.

She drags a hand across each eye and she stands. She straightens herself, as though there were someone there to straighten herself for. She glances around her daughter's bedroom and she gathers her things as though to leave.

She lingers.

A shrine, her mother called it. She did not mean it in a good way. You can't mourn forever, darling, she said. You should clear things away. I could help. It would be less painful. Wouldn't it? To take down the curtains and box up the CDs and cover the wallpaper with just plain white. But Megan would not let her, so a shrine it remained: one Megan worshipped at, in the earliest days, but only ever visits now to clean. Or so she tells herself.

She sets down her notepad and the calculator on the bed. She lets her hand graze the bed sheets. She would grip them, hold them, clutch them tight to her face and inhale – but she has done it before and it has never helped.

Her eyes sweep the bookshelves and the CD spines, ordered to a code she has long since cracked. The music, by mood: melancholy, for the most part, through angry and then outraged and thinning, at the furthest end, towards joy. The books, by worth. Not simply most preferred, a teenager's top forty, but by her daughter's estimation of their content. On the top shelf, in prime position, *To Kill a Mockingbird*, the creases on the spine repaired to black with a Magic Marker. Beside it, T.H. White, L.M. Montgomery and *L'Etranger* by Albert Camus. A school copy, it looks like, read and re-read and requisitioned. There is more Montgomery on the bottom shelf, alongside C.S. Lewis and Enid Blyton and a re-issued hardback of *The Catcher in the Rye*, which for some reason her daughter took against. Also, beside it, *Lord of the Flies*, which to Megan has also never seemed quite right. Her daughter, though, was categorical: only a *Beverly Hills, 90210* annual has been afforded a less esteemed spot.

From the pen holder on the desk, Megan plucks a pencil. She studies the gnawed end for a moment, then sets it within the cradle of her tongue. She sits, on the floor, and she sucks.

It is where she would often find Ellie: on the carpet, in the space between her desk and the foot of her bed, a pillow against the wall behind her and a book, often, propped on her knees. Other times she would simply be sitting, as Megan is, to a soundtrack perhaps and with her eyes lidded or to the ceiling. What are you thinking about? Megan might sometimes dare to ask from the doorway. Her daughter would rarely answer. Or, if she did, her response would in no way be formulated to reassure a worried mother. Nothing. Just things. Shut the door, Mum – please.

A piece of pencil comes away in Megan's mouth and she dabs to catch the scrap of sodden wood. It sticks to her fingertip and evades her flick so she uses the handle of one of the drawers beside her to dislodge it. Her grip, once she has, returns to the handle. She hesitates, then pulls, and the drawer expels its contents.

The drawer, the topmost of three, is full of clippings. It was Leo's idea to save them. He was in the habit, Megan would have said, but he claimed too that they might help. They might, he insisted, yield some clue. That he was wrong gives her no satisfaction. She would have sacrificed any part of her – her pride, a limb, her very life – if it would have meant that Leo was proved right.

She did not read the clippings then and she has no desire to read them now. She makes to shut the drawer but pauses with it halfway closed. Well? she thinks. Why not? She opens the drawer more fully once again and begins taking out the clippings by the handful. She makes a pile. For recycling, is her citizenly instinct, but there are better options, surely. Shredding, say. Or burning.

When the first drawer is emptied she shuts it and opens the next. She shifts herself onto her knees, taken suddenly by the decisiveness of the task. Her daughter's waste-paper basket is beside her and she hoists the discarded clippings into it and scrunches them down. From the second drawer she takes out a folder and frowns at the absence of a label. She lifts the flap and, swallowing, shuts it again. Posters, a sheaf of them, with the sketch of the suspect beside a picture of Ellie, A4-size and copied by the ream at Leo's office. They ran out of lamp posts.

Below the folder is another, again unlabelled and this time empty. The ancient cardboard rips easily and she stuffs the pieces on top of the posters and the newspaper clippings. The bin, already, is halfway full.

The next three folders she cannot bring herself to throw away. They are stuffed with letters, removed from their envelopes to save space. Leo counted them once. Megan cannot remember what figure he reached but she knows it was over two hundred. There were others too, less support-ive – vicious, in fact; vindictive – but those are elsewhere. The police asked for them, as she recalls. She does not think they ever gave them back. They were welcome to them, as far as she was concerned, though she would take a certain pleasure in adding them to the kindling pile now.

She starts to read and has to stop. The letters were sent to help but they remind her only of how much they made her hurt.

I simply can't imagine.

It must be awful.

They'll find her.

They'll find *him*.

You must not give up hope.

Platitudes, the least of them. Lies, the worst. Nothing at the two extremes or between them that made anyone feel any better but the person who wrote them. Not that she was permitted to say as much. Not that she was able to voice, at any stage, what she was truly feeling. Even to Leo, as things turned out, which was almost the hardest part.

Sod it. Sod *them*. She stuffs the letters into the bin and keeps stuffing until the folders are empty and the bin is almost full.

Her momentum regained, it quickly stalls again. She has reached to open the final drawer but her fingers curl from the handle. She has remembered the part she had forgotten. The part she willed herself to forget. They are inside. They must be. The police have the originals but Leo, being Leo, took copies. So surely they are . . .

They are. She has opened the drawer the way she would peel away a plaster and there, all alone, is a plastic wallet. Inside, sealed as though in an evidence bag, are the notes.

Again Megan hesitates. She dares herself. More than a dare, it would be a penance. Not like reading the newspaper clippings, which would be detestable mainly because they are so emotionally amiss. The notes, in contrast, would drag her through the way she felt. Even just lifting out the wallet, for instance, reminds her of the weight of her shame. At their failure. At *her* failure. Because she blamed him for so long but who, really, was in a better position to know the truth? To see past the deceit and the misdirection and to act – *act* – before it was too late?

I AM WATCHING

YOU WILL BE JUDGED BY YOUR LIES

She can see the first note quite clearly through the plastic and the first note, tame enough compared to what followed, is more than enough. The shame is one thing but she is not prepared to relive the terror. Of the memories. Of her imaginings. Of the sick, morbid fantasies of her masochistic mind. Nor is she prepared yet to reconcile the way she felt with what is to come. Equally terrifying, in a way. Her fresh new start. Her brave new world. Her attempt to rediscover what was lost.

The notes go in the basket. The contents, downstairs, go in a sack. The sack goes in the dustbin and Megan shuts the lid. Before she can stop herself she picks up the telephone. She will call the agent, first, as she promised she would. Go ahead, she will say. Press the button. After that she will call her husband. Not because of Daniel Blake but because she should have called him long ago. She has a confession to make.

10

It might have been a school: modern, characterless, crouched amid the office blocks and council flats and camouflaged to the colour of slabs. It was mainly the fencing that gave the building away. The security signs, adorning it, were discreet enough until you noticed them but once you did you noticed other things too. Cameras, for instance, trained inside and out. An intercom at the entrance, higher-end even than the system in the city's courthouse or gaol. And the windows on the building itself appeared barred – discreetly, again, in window-frame white, but still barred.

He was unsure, at the gate, for whom to ask. Leaning through the car window, he offered his name to the expectant static. It seemed to have no effect and he started to explain himself – clumsily, warily, trying to avoid explaining anything – but then the static gave a surge and a buzzer buzzed. The gate, with a jerk, beckoned him in.

This was it, then: the place Leo had read about just that morning in the tabloids. Here were the cushy, five-star surrounds in which Felicity's killer was being made to feel at home – at the taxpayer's expense, in case readers needed to be reminded. It was like Butlins, apparently, this facility the newspapers had shied from naming but had spared no adjectives in describing.

There were two empty visitor bays sectioned off in the expanse of tarmac and Leo pulled into the first of them. He gathered his things from the passenger seat and, out of habit, lifted his chin to check his teeth in the rear-view mirror. His eyes caught instead on his cheek. The wound, it felt like, was taking an age to heal. Beneath it, he noticed, there was a patch of stubble he had skirted when shaving. Above it, his eyes were recessed and bloodshot.

His teeth were fine.

A neat, narrow pathway led him through bark-topped flower beds and he arrived at the main entrance. He considered the windowless door and looked about for another intercom. As he was searching, the door buzzed.

Inside, it was a school once more. Leo had expected a lobby: guards, a desk, something to sign. The area, unmanned, was more an entrance hall, with a set of double doors in each wall. The linoleum-tiled floor seemed polished, the walls recently painted. Through one set of doors he saw a figure approaching. The man ducked and gave a cheerful, inefficient wave through the glass, then moved to one side as though to punch a code. The door clicked and then opened and the man bore his smile into the entrance hall.

'Mr Curtice?' The man's smile broadened and he covered the hall in three emphatic strides. 'I'm Bobby. Hope you found us okay.'

Bobby wore a suit that shone and shoes thirsting for polish. He was younger than Leo but carried with him a certain authority: the confidence and depth of voice of an out-of-work actor. Or a schoolteacher; or social worker. Someone who would inspire suspicion in most adults but devotion, probably, among children.

'Just about,' said Leo, accepting Bobby's enthusiastic hand. 'Although I came close to missing the turning.'

'Cool,' said Bobby, bobbing. 'That's kind of the idea.' His smile had not faltered but somehow it seemed to reassert itself. 'Come through. This way. Daniel's waiting for you.'

Leo hesitated and Bobby seemed immediately to realise why.

'We use the boys' real names,' he said. 'We think it's important they face up to who they are. To why they're here.' He winked and tipped his head. 'Come through.'

They left the entrance hall through a different set of doors and were immediately confronted by another. Bobby waited until the first set was sealed and then, as he had a moment before, prodded a code into the adjacent keypad. 'You get used to this,' he said. He gave one of the doors a hearty shove and held it open. 'After you.'

There was a man waiting in the next corridor, wearing a name tag and dressed in a shirt and trouser combination that might, or might not, have been a uniform. His biceps, ham-like, were straining the seams. The man did not speak but fell into step behind them as they passed. 'This is Garrie,' Bobby said. 'He'll be your escort today.'

Leo, as they walked, checked behind. He nodded but Garrie said nothing. Leo turned back and Bobby shrugged, gave another wink. 'Not a big talker, our Garrie. But he'll watch your back.' Bobby's eyes dipped towards Leo's cheek, then glanced away.

They had to wait for the next set of doors to be unlocked from the other side and beyond, finally, was a desk at which Leo was expected to sign. Two more guards watched as he fumbled with the pen. They checked inside his briefcase and showed what they found there to Bobby, who returned a nod. A guard handed Leo his pass and Leo clipped it to his breast pocket. Bobby clapped him on the shoulder.

'Ready?'

He had put on weight. It had been barely a week but Daniel had definitely managed to grow a chin. He had been lacking one before so it was a good thing in terms of the boy's health. Leo, though, could not help but think immediately of the jury. Waif-like was good. Emaciated better. Ruddy, well fed, portly: each suggested slobbery, contentment – a lack, above all, of contrition.

He was well turned out, though, and that was something. Much like the guards tacked to the common room walls, the boys all wore smart shirts and trousers, and Daniel looked respectable, as though his mother had assembled him for a family occasion. His posture needed work – he seemed cast, by default, in a slump – and his hair would look better rinsed of gel but with a few minor adjustments he would seem almost . . .

Leo touched his cheek. He was getting ahead of himself.

'Daniel?' said Bobby.

The boy was seated in the corner of a sofa furthest from the wall-mounted television. There were several older boys around him, their eyes pinned slackly to a nature documentary, and Daniel seemed more watchful of them than of the programme. He had set himself at a distance, his knees drawn to his chest and his arms wrapped around his shins. At the sound of his name, he gave a start.

'They're allowed thirty minutes in here before lessons,' said Bobby as they watched Daniel slide to his feet. 'Another hour in the evenings but no TV after eight. They can read, play board games, listen to certain music. No cards, though. No gambling.' Tough but fair, he seemed to want to imply, but Leo thought again of the morning papers. The tabloids, he suspected, would have blown their budgets for an image of the scene before him, irrespective of the type of programme and the ennui of the boys who watched. They would have had these children breaking boulders, even before they had been convicted of a crime.

Bobby fell silent as Daniel approached. The boy shuffled. He seemed conscious that the other inmates were watching him and managed, somehow, to make himself seem smaller standing up than sitting down.

'Mr Curtice is here to see you, Daniel. You have something to say to him, I believe.'

Daniel had stopped several paces away. He flushed, glanced across his shoulder at the boys around the television. He muttered a sentence that Leo did not catch.

'Again please, Daniel. Express yourself clearly.'

There were sniggers. Daniel's flush deepened. 'I'm sorry about what I did to your face,' he said, his gaze reaching no higher than Leo's chin. Another boy had drawn close and Garrie, Leo's guard, stepped forwards to usher him away.

'Better,' said Bobby and he looked expectantly at Leo.

'Oh,' Leo said. 'It's fine, Daniel, really. It was an accident. There's no need to apologise.'

Someone, from somewhere, made kissing sounds. Several of the older boys laughed.

'That's not quite the message we're hoping to get across, Mr Curtice,' said Bobby, 'but I'm sure Daniel appreciates your good grace. Don't you, Daniel?'

Daniel seemed to realise that he was not, this time, expected to answer.

'We've set out some sandwiches for you,' said Bobby. He turned and held out an arm and Daniel sloped into the lead. 'Daniel helped prepare them. We no longer allow hot drinks outside the staff areas, I'm afraid, but I'll have someone bring in a jug of water. Unless you'd prefer orange squash?'

The sandwiches – crustless corners on a tray – were waiting for them in Daniel's bedroom. The room, to be fair to the papers, was a long way from being a cell. It was larger than Leo would have expected: maybe two thirds the size of Ellie's bedroom. The space was Daniel's own – there was just a single bed in the furthest corner – and included what the newspapers would have described as an en suite bathroom, though the washing facilities were basic and boxed off by barely more than a screen. There was a built-in desk, on which the sand-wiches had been set, as well as a CD player and an armchair and a pile of thumbed magazines: *Top Gear*, *Autocar*, *Bike*. There were bars outside the window but the window itself was ajar. The view was of the building's hollow centre: air-conditioning units, mainly. The impression Leo had was of a cheap hotel room. Not fancy but a long way from what he had feared.

'This isn't so bad,' he said, peering around the screen at the lidless toilet. On the sink there was a tub of hair gel, some toothpaste without a cap and a Buzz Lightyear toothbrush. The mirror on the wall was polished metal.

The boy, when Leo emerged, had sunk into the chair, the only one in the room. Garrie was waiting in the corridor through the open door, which left Leo to pick his perch. He settled himself on the edge of Daniel's bed and felt be-neath him the unmistakable crinkle of rubber sheets. Stand-ard issue, he wondered, or only for those who had shown a need?

'So,' said Leo. 'How are you finding things?' He tried to keep his tone light; tried not to worry that he had allowed Daniel to position himself in the path towards the only way out. He glanced at Garrie, who had his eyes averted but his attention, surely, on his ward. 'It's a nice room,' Leo found himself saying. 'A good size. It's got to be at least as big as your room at home, right?'

The boy's eyes snapped to his. 'You went to my house?'

'What? No. I mean, I was only guessing.'

A silence.

'What are the people like? The other boys. And Bobby? Bobby seems . . . er . . . cool.'

Daniel, hunched, twitched a shoulder. 'He's all right.'

'And the other boys? Are you getting along okay?'

Again a twitch. 'They're older mostly. Bigger.'

Leo nodded. There were boys here as old as eighteen and Daniel, at twelve, would not normally have been admitted. The choice, for the magistrates, had been between sending Daniel here or keeping him further from his family.

'But you're getting on okay?'

Leo waited for an answer but the boy did not reply. Leo tapped his fingers on his briefcase.

'Where's Mum?' said Daniel. He jerked upright and Leo flinched. 'Is she coming?'

'She is, Daniel,' said Leo, recovering himself. 'She'll be here this afternoon. I thought it might be helpful, though, for you and I to have a chance to talk alone.'

'Alone,' Daniel echoed. 'Without *him*, you mean.'

Right. Without *him*.

'He told me . . .' Daniel looked up, as though wary of whether to continue. Leo gave the faintest of nods. 'He told me to get rid of you. After last time. He said . . . he said you were a . . .' his voice dwindled '. . . a waste of space.'

'Who did? Your father?'

Daniel glowered. 'Step.'

Leo held his thumbs against the catches of his briefcase. 'Step,' he repeated. 'Sorry.'

'He said . . .' Daniel shuffled slightly straighter in his seat.

'He said he'd pay for someone better. Said he'd get a loan if he had to.'

Slowly, Leo nodded. 'What about your mother? What did your mother say?'

The boy just shrugged.

Leo hesitated. 'And you? What about you?'

Daniel looked down. 'You're here, aren't you?'

Leo almost smiled. He pressed and the catches clicked. 'Let's get started, shall we?' He took out his pad and his pen and set them beside him on the bed. He was about to close his case again when he remembered. 'I brought you something,' he said, digging beneath a clutch of papers. 'Here,' he said and he held out a box no bigger than a soap dish. Inside was a Subaru Impreza, exactly to scale apparently and far too expensive for what was in essence a child's toy. 'They didn't have one in white, I'm afraid. Just the rally version.'

Daniel eyed the car. He eyed Leo and his outstretched arm.

'It's fine. I cleared it on the way in. Take it, it's yours.'

'What for?'

'You like cars, don't you? I thought you'd appreciate it, that's all.'

'What do I have to do? I'm not doing anything for it.'

Leo, for an instant, could only stare. He glanced towards the guard outside the door, who was watching the exchange but without expression.

'It's yours, Daniel. It's a gift. You don't have to do anything for it.'

The boy raised a thumb towards his teeth and gnawed for a moment at the nail. Then, with something like a swipe, he plucked the car from Leo's hand. He clawed open the box and lifted the toy to the tip of his nose. He turned it, studied it.

Leo waited. He set about fastening his briefcase.

'Thanks.'

Leo raised his head. Daniel looked anything but grateful. He looked suspicious, rather; sceptical. Leo, though, smiled. 'You're welcome.'

'We can't just ignore it.'

'I'm not ignoring it.'

'It won't go away, Daniel. We have to address it.'

'I don't want to talk about it, that's all.'

The boy was running the car up and down his thigh. Leo was pleased with how his gift had been received but was beginning to wish he had waited until the end of the session before giving it. Although perhaps it would have made no difference. The boy was looking for a distraction and the car was simply the closest thing to hand.

'Look, Daniel—'

'Just tell them. Can't you? Like *he* said. Just tell them that I did it and that I'm sorry.'

'I will. That's just what we'll say. But there are ways of saying it. There are ways of *explaining* it. All I'm asking is that you help me decide how we do that.'

'Me? How am I supposed to help? Aren't you supposed to tell me?' Daniel turned the car onto its roof and flicked one of the wheels.

'Okay. Fine. Then it's my decision that we will consult with a psych—'

'No!'

Leo recoiled. He looked at Garrie, who lifted his chin. Leo, with a hidden hand, held him off.

'You only need to talk to her, Daniel. Just to start with. There's a woman I know and she's really friendly. You'd like her, I know you would.'

Daniel, this time, said nothing. Leo eased himself forwards.

'It wouldn't mean anything. Not unless we decided we wanted it to. No one would even know. Honestly, Daniel, I really think—'

'I said, no!'

Daniel stood. Leo did too. Garrie entered the room and the three of them, for a moment, were cowboys waiting for the draw.

Leo lowered himself onto the bunk.

'It's okay, Garrie. Really. We're fine. Aren't we, Daniel?'

The guard, beside the boy, was a behemoth. Daniel would have barely outweighed one of his arms. The boy showed no fear, though. At this – the prospect of a confrontation he had no chance of winning but could at least comprehend – he did not flinch. But then whatever emotion was holding him up seemed suddenly to subside and he dropped his eyes to his toy. He sat.

Leo busied himself until Garrie retreated – not quite to the corridor, this time, but far enough that he was out of Daniel's eye line. Leo closed his pad and clicked his pen, then shut them in his case and shifted himself further onto Daniel's mattress. He hooked one ankle over the other and set his hands in his lap.

'You're right.'

The boy looked up.

'I'm rushing things. I'm sorry. We don't need to decide anything right away.'

Daniel's eyes narrowed and Leo hurried on.

'Why don't we go for a walk. You could show me round. What's outside?'

Daniel shrugged. 'Grass, mainly.'

'I'd like to see. Will you show me?'

'It's just grass. And anyway they follow you like you've just walked into Asda with a sack.' He gestured with a glance towards Garrie. 'Three of them do.'

Leo met Garrie's eye. 'Three of them?' The guard looked away.

'I get three. The others just get one. Except for Stash. He's eighteen. He's . . . he's scary. He gets three like me.'

'I see,' said Leo. 'Well.' He searched the room for inspiration. 'What else, then? Is there anything else we could do?'

'There's a games room.'

'A games room? Terrific. Why didn't you say so? What do they have?'

Daniel looked blank.

'What is there? In the games room? Darts or something?' There wouldn't be darts. Christ, Leo.

'There's board games. Monopoly but they've taken all the money. And table tennis.'

Leo set his feet on the floor. 'What are we waiting for then? Table tennis. It's been a while but I think I remember how to score.'

Daniel shook his head. He slumped.

'What? What's wrong?'

'I'm rubbish. I can't do it.'

'Nonsense. It's fun. Come on, I'll show you how it's—'

'No!'

Leo sat down again, on the edge of the bed. He waited for the seconds to soothe the air.

'There's a PlayStation.' Daniel's words were a mutter.

'A what?'

'A PlayStation. You know. Computer games. I never get a go but we would if you told them we had to.'

'Told them? Told who?'

'The others. The bigger boys.' Daniel looked down.

'Fine.' Leo stood. 'The PlayStation it is. You'll have to show me. I probably can't even remember how to hold a joystick.'

Daniel, briefly, gave Leo a look that would have suited Ellie.

'On your feet, then,' Leo said. 'Lead the way. I mean . . .' Leo turned to Garrie. 'Assuming it's okay?'

The guard, finally, showed he could smile. He stepped into the corridor. Daniel went next and Leo trailed, his gaze on the boy's narrow shoulders. At the door Leo stopped. 'Wait,' he said, thinking: sod the jury. He turned back into the room. 'We might get hungry.' He reached for the plate of sandwiches.

11

He paced. Sitting was out of the question. He felt like a nervous father – or a father soon to be. Although that was probably down to the surroundings: the off-the-peg void of the public-institution canteen. There was nothing to distract him, that was the problem. No *one* either, not even behind the counter. If Leo had not been alone, he would have busied himself with at least a pretence of looking busy. As it was he simply paced, his shuttling between cutlery and condiments interrupted only by a glance, every ten steps or so, towards the door.

He would have liked to prepare her. He had briefed her on the telephone barely twenty-four hours ago but a dozen things had occurred to him since that she would, he was sure, have found useful. Things, more to the point, that might prove useful to their case – and that Karen, without forewarning, might overlook. It would be Leo's fault: if an insight were bypassed that should have been signposted; if the answers that Daniel gave were to the wrong questions – or if the boy, at the last, failed to answer at all. Karen, though, had been insistent. That's fine, Leo. That's all I need to know. She had made her own way here and would have been making her way straight home again, had Leo not pleaded for a first-impressions debrief before she left.

But it was taking an age. Seven more minutes and he could start to reckon in hours. Daniel gets restless, he should have said. Don't push him or you'll push him away. And he's only twelve. Just remember he's only twelve. Even the police kept their sessions to less than an hour and most of those were thirty minutes too long. He's not used to sustained conversation. He's not used to conversation, full stop.

Not that Karen would have needed telling. She was a professional, after all. And that it was taking so long was probably a good sign. Wasn't it? Unless it was taking this long because they had barely started. It was entirely possible, given Daniel's record with such things. The police, the boy's parents, the social worker, even Leo: they could all testify to that.

'Not talking to yourself are you, Leo?'

The voice was at Leo's shoulder. 'Karen.'

'It's one of the things we look for, you know. That and hairy palms.' Karen tilted her head to get a view of Leo's hands.

Leo looked too, then offered one for Karen to shake. 'How did it go? Was Daniel okay? Did he speak to you? What did he say?'

'I need coffee. Is there coffee?'

'What? Oh.' Leo peered towards the counter. 'Probably. I don't know.'

'Want one?' Karen aimed herself towards the coffee machine in the corner. The pot on the hot plate was empty so she started filling it. Leo followed and loitered by her side.

'No,' he said. 'Thanks.' Then, again, 'How did it go?'

Karen peered at him across the frames of her glasses. She rolled her eyes and resumed her search for an on switch. She found it, flicked it, then stood upright and began with a sigh.

'He needs help, Leo. Counselling at the very least. What he's been through, what he's going through: it's clear he isn't coping.'

'Not coping? What do you mean? I thought he seemed okay. Given the circumstances.'

'He's twelve, Leo. He's doing his best to act tough but tough is only ever a shell. It's what lies beneath that concerns me.'

The coffee machine gurgled and started to dribble. Karen reached for a cup. She brandished a second at Leo. 'You sure?'

Leo waved away the offer. 'So . . . what? He wouldn't speak to you, is that what you're saying?'

'He spoke to me.' Karen filled her mug and raised it level with her chin. The steam from the coffee misted her glasses and she blew.

She was making him wait. They had not spoken to each other in years and now Leo had finally got in touch, it was only because there was something from her that he needed. So she was punishing him. This is what you get, she was telling him. This is what you get when you assume that friendship doesn't deflate when you neglect to fill it once in a while with a little air.

'We should get a drink,' Leo said. 'Or I'll buy you lunch. Because I know it's been a while and I know we haven't even caught up but really, Karen, this is important. I called you because I knew I could trust you and because I didn't think you would mind if—'

'Leo,' Karen said. 'Calm yourself. I'm thinking, that's all. I'm digesting. I didn't even stop on my way from seeing Daniel to visit the ladies'. I didn't dare.'

Leo made as though to answer.

'Ordinarily, you know, we wouldn't even be talking. Not yet, anyway. I don't work like this, Leo. I don't like to work like this.'

Leo looked to the floor. This was Karen, he recalled. This was why, when they had had their fling at university, they had reverted to friendship after barely a week. Not because they did not enjoy each other's company but because they were configured to function at a different RPM: Leo at forty-five, Karen a more considered thirty-three.

Again Karen sighed. The sigh, Leo thought, was new. Probably it was one of the things she had acquired in qualifying for her profession. That and her oversize jewellery.

'You're right,' he said. 'I'm sorry. I should give you some time.' He considered the room. 'I'll wait over there. You finish your coffee.'

Karen gave a gee-thanks snort. She winced through another sip then gestured for Leo to tag behind as she made her way towards the seats. 'It's fine,' she said, taking one. Leo slid into the chair opposite and propped his elbows on the table, his chin on his interlinked hands. 'Just so long as this conversation is about what we agreed it would be: first impressions, nothing more. Okay?'

'Absolutely,' said Leo. 'First impressions.'

Karen, briefly, tightened her gaze. 'Daniel,' she began and she paused. 'Daniel is suffering from post-traumatic stress disorder.' She met Leo's eye. 'And that's not a first impression, Leo. That's a diagnosis. He's not sleeping. He's eating but only because he's bingeing. He has nightmares, flashbacks, repressed memories that are refusing to stay that way. And he's enuretic. Did you know that?'

Leo recalled the boy's rubber sheets. 'I had an idea.'

'Not that it means anything necessarily. He may well have been so before. The point is, he needs help. Skilled therapeutic input. Something he is categorically not receiving here.'

Leo frowned and Karen rattled a hand.

'It's not their fault,' she said. 'The staff here – and Bobby, is it? The bloke in charge? – they seem competent enough, caring enough. I'm certain, if they were permitted to, they would ensure Daniel got all the help he needs. But they're not permitted to. Are they, Leo?' It was not a question; it was an accusation. As though Leo, facing her, were representing the entire legal system. Which in a way, he supposed, he was.

'He'll get treatment, Karen. Once the trial is over, there'll be no end of doctors through his door.'

Karen drew her chin towards her collarbone. 'Right. Once the trial is over. Although by then, of course, he could be permanently damaged. But what the hell. He stands accused so his rights hardly matter. Forget about the presumption of innocence – it's the evidence against him we need to protect.'

'Look, Karen, I—'

Karen held up a hand. Her jewellery jangled. 'I know, I know. I'm sorry. But you asked me for first impressions and that's the issue that made an impression first. If you wanted to avoid an earful, you should at least have let me finish my coffee.'

Leo smiled, looked down.

Karen, after a moment, smiled too. 'But your case. You want to talk about your case.'

'We need something, Karen. He did it; he said he did it. We're not trying to get away from that. But you've met him now. You've seen him. He's just a kid.'

Karen, slowly, nodded. 'He is that. But he killed. He . . .' She shifted. 'He did more than kill. If you're asking me to find something that will excuse it . . .'

'Not excuse it. Explain it. He's twelve, Karen. He has fifty, sixty, seventy years of life ahead of him.'

'There you are then. He's twelve. That's an argument. Isn't it?'

'It's an argument,' Leo said. 'It's not a defence. It would have been, a year or so ago, but the law, now, is definitive. You only need to be ten. If you're ten, you know right from wrong. That's the line.'

'The line. As in, the point of no return. If you weren't yet ready to cross it, you shouldn't have been reckless enough to celebrate another birthday.'

'Something like that.' Leo stared at the table, drummed with his fingertips. He looked up. 'What about that, though? He's twelve but could we argue, say, that his mental age was lower?'

'Three years lower?'

'It would have to be.'

Karen puffed. With a look, she showed her answer. 'I've only met him once, Leo. And I'm on your side. But he's bright, he's emotionally developed. You should test his IQ but it will be there or thereabouts. He's of his age. There's not a psychiatrist I know who would go on record disputing that. None I respect, rather.'

'You mean you wouldn't?'

'I couldn't. How could I? I'm not going to lie for you, Leo. I mean, I hope that's not why you asked me here because, really, you should know—'

'Karen. Please. That's not what I meant. I'm just . . .'

'Thinking aloud?'

'Exactly.'

There was a silence.

'What about this . . .' Leo rolled his hand. 'This post-traumatic stress thing. Is there any chance he could have been suffering from that at the time of the attack?'

Karen was already shaking her head. 'None.'

'Why not?'

'The clue is in the question, Leo.'

'Yes, no, I realise that but could he not have been suffering from something else first? Something that led to whatever he has now?'

'He killed a girl. That's why he has post-traumatic stress disorder. You don't just kill someone and not suffer some emotional backlash. Not unless you're a psychopath.'

Leo raised his head.

'Bloody hell, Leo. Don't look so hopeful. He's not a psychopath. You surely don't need a shrink to tell you that.'

'No.' Leo slumped. 'No, of course not.' He slid his hands across his face. He exhaled again, audibly.

'What about you, Leo?'

Leo blinked.

'How are *you*? I mean, you look tired and I'm sure you are but apart from that. How are things?' Karen's mug was in front of her and she turned it. 'I heard about your father,' she added, tentatively. 'It must have been hard for you.'

Leo felt the weight of her stare. 'I'm fine,' he said. 'Honestly. I mean – ' he laughed; he had to force it ' – is business that bad? Because even if you're offering me mates' rates, I'm not sure I could afford you.' He laughed again, grinned – and felt a burn building in his jaw.

Karen, for a moment, made him suffer it. 'You can't fool me,' she said. And then she smiled. 'A celebrity lawyer like you?' She gestured. 'That tie,' she said. 'That suit. They're just a disguise to throw off all the gold-diggers. Right?'

Leo looked down at what he was wearing.

'What about Megan, though,' Karen persisted. 'And Eleanor. This whole thing must be quite a strain for you all.'

'A strain?' Leo, involuntarily, thought of the note. It was a prank, he had decided. Whoever wrote it: a crank. Which was the reason he had not yet mentioned it to his wife. 'Why do you say that?'

'Come on, Leo. Don't be disingenuous. This isn't exactly a drunk and disorderly you're dealing with here.'

No. Exactly. Karen, if no one else, understood. 'That's the

thing, though,' said Leo. 'It was always going to be outside our comfort zone. We expected that from the start.'

'We?'

Now Leo, in spite of himself, bridled. 'It's important, Karen. Daniel needs my help. I'm not going to forsake him just because everyone else seems to think he should be left to rot.'

'No. Of course not. I understand that completely. I just . . .' Karen seemed to contemplate saying something more. 'I didn't mean to pry,' she said instead. 'You looked tired, that's all.' She smiled until Leo mirrored it.

'I'm fine,' he said. 'Meg, Ellie: we're all fine.'

'Good. I'm glad to hear it.' Karen slid her mug to the centre of the table. She smiled once more and she stood.

'Wait,' Leo said, standing too. 'You're not going? What about Daniel?'

'We agreed, Leo: first impressions, that's all.'

'I know but there must be something. Mustn't there?'

'Something? You mean some reason why a boy of twelve murders a girl he barely knows?' Karen, all of a sudden, looked weary. She sighed once more and her strength, with her breath, seemed to leave her. She propped herself against the table. 'There's always a reason, Leo. Sometimes there are a thousand reasons.'

'I just need one. Just to start with. Diminished responsibility, Karen: it's the only chance Daniel's got.'

Karen made a face. 'You're looking at this backwards. Aren't you? I thought the idea was to consider the evidence and then decide your plea.'

'Maybe. Sometimes. But you said it yourself: there's always a reason. Right?'

Karen regarded him. She stood straighter and buttoned her coat.

'Daniel's family,' she said. 'Is there any way I could meet with them?'

'Maybe.' Leo looked up. 'Why? What did he say about them?'

Karen came close and kissed Leo's cheek. 'Take care of yourself, Leo. Try and catch up on some sleep.'

Leo tracked her progress towards the door. 'Karen?'

She turned.

'What did he say about them?'

Karen twitched a shoulder. 'Nothing,' she said. 'Nothing at all.'

12

It had not worked. It always worked. Think of an outcome: the worst thing that could happen or the most unlikely or even, sometimes, the thing you most wanted to take place – and it would not. That was the rule. So sometimes it worked to spite you and sometimes it worked as a ward but it always, one way or another, worked.

Except it had not.

The envelope had been tucked amid the pile of letters. Leo had been late after spending most of the day out of the office, so he had carried the pile into the meeting room. He had shuffled and shuffled again and as he had backed himself blindly into his seat, there it was. Just where he had expected it to be and just, therefore, where it should not have been.

'Leonard?'

'Mm.'

'Leonard.'

Leo looked up. 'What? Yes. Sorry, I . . .'

Howard smiled his concern.

'Sorry,' said Leo, more decisively. He slid the pile of mail below the table and into his lap, his thumbs pinning the top-most envelope in place. Beneath them, and beneath its outer skin, the note seared.

'So what do you think?'

Leo could not resist peeking. The question, though, registered and he glanced up to see who would answer. Alan, John, Terry, Howard; even Jenny, seated between Leo and their boss and jotting minutes on a notepad: everyone present had their gaze fixed on him.

'Me?'

There was laughter, not all of it kind.

'You are fairly central to the proposal, Leonard. But if you feel it would make you uncomfortable . . .'

'What? No. Of course not. Um. If what would make me uncomfortable?'

Terry turned and muttered. Howard spoke over him.

'The feature, Leonard. The interview.'

The words resonated. On their way into the room, some-one had been talking about an article. For a newspaper – or a magazine? *The Lawyer* was it? The *Law Society Gazette*?

'Well,' Leo said, as though considering. 'What would be the focus, exactly?'

Jenny looked down at her notes. Howard simply stared.

'Honestly, Leo,' said Terry. 'I hope you pay closer attention in meetings with clients.'

More laughter. A 'quite'. Leo felt himself flush.

'Let's recap,' said Howard. 'Shall we? It's exciting news so I'm not exactly loath to repeat it.' He turned to Leo. 'Although I do hope once more will be enough.'

Leo, in spite of himself, was slinking another glance at the envelope. He pressed it flat with his palms, tweaked his frown and aimed it at his boss.

'The *Gazette*, Leo, has approached us with a suggestion for a feature. Small firm, big case: that sort of thing. They won't mention anything too specific, of course, but they'll want to talk to you. They'll want to photograph you. As well as the rest of us, naturally. We wouldn't want you stealing all the glory.' Howard twinkled and Jenny tittered. Terry, from his expression, seemed not to appreciate the joke.

'Well,' said Leo. 'I see.'

Howard extended a finger. 'It's only the *Gazette*, I realise, but you know how these things tend to get picked up. It would be an excellent opportunity for this firm, Leonard. And for yourself, of course. A clipping for the curriculum vitae.'

Terry did not miss a beat. 'Watch out, Leo. It's not a good sign when your boss starts mentioning your CV.'

There was laughter. Leo ignored it. 'It sounds great, Howard. It really does. Although I think perhaps I should check with Meg. It's only the *Gazette*, as you say, but this case . . . It's . . . Well . . . There have been certain . . . pressures.'

'Check with Megan,' said Howard. 'By all means. But it would be a shame to pass up the opportunity.' His boss, suddenly, looked like a child denied Christmas.

'No, of course. I mean, I'm not saying she'll have a problem with it. Not at all. Quite the opposite, probably.'

'Well then,' said Howard, once again displaying his ivory. 'That's settled then. Is it? Provisionally, shall we say.'

'Provisionally. Yes. Okay.'

'They'll be here a week on Thursday,' said Howard. 'At ten o'clock.' And he flipped to the next page of the agenda.

'That's not what I'm saying, Terry.'

'It's what I heard, Leo. It's what everyone – ' Terry turned left, right ' – in this meeting room heard.'

Leo regarded the faces regarding his. He's right, they seemed to say: that is what we heard.

'Well, it's not what I meant. What I meant was—'

'You remember what he did, Leo – don't you? This "kid".' He pronounced the inverted commas. 'This "child" you keep mentioning?'

'All I meant was—'

'Because it sounds to me like maybe you've forgotten. Like maybe you've lost track of—'

'*All I meant was,*' said Leo and his volume commanded a silence. 'There are other considerations. He's twelve years old. It complicates things.'

Terry made a noise.

'I'm sorry, Terry, but it does. We have different options. We have different priorities. Different problems, too,' Leo added, more quietly.

'We?'

'Yes, Terry: *we*. I am his solicitor, you know.'

'His solicitor. Right. Because all I'm saying is, it sounds to me like maybe you've convinced yourself you're more than that.'

Leo felt his back stiffen. 'What's that supposed to mean?'

'Gentlemen,' said Howard, reaching both hands towards the

centre of the table. 'Perhaps we could try and keep this civil. Let's remember there's a lady present, shall we?'

Jenny looked down.

'And anyway,' Leo persisted. He had the stack of letters in his hand and the envelopes were crumpling in his grip. 'What's so contemptible about feeling sorry for him? It doesn't mean I condone what he did. It doesn't mean I'm looking to excuse it.'

'Diminished responsibility, Leo? What's that if not an excuse?'

Leo affected astonishment. He cast his expression around the table, then settled it on Terry. 'Am I missing something?' he said. 'Is there something about representing a client I've fundamentally misunderstood?'

'Gentlemen!'

'You tell us, Leo,' said Terry. 'Think about it, then come back and tell us.'

'Gentlemen,' said Howard again. He pressed his teeth and his jaw bulged. 'Let's move on, shall we?'

Something about paper. Re-using it, not using it, the dream – impossible though it might sound – of a paperless office.

Leo tuned in, out. Out, mostly, but he was wary of being caught not paying attention again so he was making an effort not to lose pace entirely with the drift of the discussion. The lecture, rather: Howard's rant. The theme was familiar, though, and the message predictable so while the others bobbed their accord and doodled, meanwhile, on paper they were meant to be conserving, Leo worked slowly, soundlessly, on the seal of the envelope.

Except he was getting nowhere. The envelope was gummed as though with superglue and there was no opening into which he could work his little finger. He picked with his nail but in truth, since the start of the case, he had no nails left – just raw, fleshy pads that were about as much use in this situation as his toes.

Except maybe . . . He had a corner. Did he? It was difficult to tell without looking but it definitely felt like . . . He did. An opening. Just big enough to—

'Shit!'

'Leo?'

'Shit!'

'What?'

Blood.

'Ow!'

Shit. Blood. Ow. Ow!

He stood. The others stared: at him; at the blood, when they noticed it, that was flowing from his fingers.

'Shit,' said Leo again. 'Jesus, ow!' He had dropped all the envelopes except the one that had bitten him. And it had felt exactly like that: like a mouth with razor teeth had taken a bloody great bite.

'Christ, Leo,' said Terry.

Jenny was standing at Leo's side. Howard was standing, barely, at hers. From the colour of his face, the blood on the floor might have been his.

'I'm fine,' said Leo, turning away. 'It's just, I don't know.'

He lifted the envelope. 'A paper cut or something.' The hole he had dug into the seal was the colour of an open wound. It sparkled, though. It grinned.

'That's quite a paper cut,' someone said.

'Here,' said someone else and a handkerchief appeared in Leo's eye line. 'Let me take that,' the same voice said but Leo snatched the envelope away. He stuffed it, blood and all, into his trouser pocket.

'It's fine,' he said. 'Thanks. I'll just . . .' He bundled his bleeding fingers in the handkerchief and tipped his head towards the door.

'Go,' Howard managed. 'Please.'

Leo went. Through the doors and past the empty desks and into the nearest toilet. He spun the tap and winced as the water sunk into the wound.

His finger was shredded. There was not one cut but several: a mesh of interlinked scores that seemed colourless beneath the water but bulged red as soon as he withdrew his finger from the icy flow. Leo reached across himself for a strip of toilet paper and had to tug twice, three times, to snap it from the roll. He ended up with far more tissue than he thought he needed but it quickly became sodden around his finger. With his good hand he squeezed. He counted, waiting until the blood and the pain subsided, then shifted. Gingerly, he pulled the crumpled envelope from his pocket.

The grin was glass: crystals the size of sea salt dusted along the envelope's rim. Incongruously, Leo thought of Ellie; of the pictures, not so long ago it seemed, that she would often bring home from school – seascapes stuck with sand or Christmas cards sprinkled with glitter. The glass on the note had been applied using the same technique, Leo realised. There was something juvenile too, it struck him, about the way the note writer had chosen to demonstrate his malice.

He had keys. He unsnagged the bunch from his pocket and used his latch key to work an opening in the envelope's closed side. The paper seemed thick, toughened somehow – chosen, perhaps, to disguise the glass – and yielded reluctantly. Leo hacked and gained an inch, another. Blood began seeping through the toilet paper and glass fragments pattered from the envelope onto his lap. Leo ignored them, ignored the throbbing too, and finally had the note free. He shook it, unfolded it, turned it and stared

HOW WOULD YOU LIKE IT LEO
HOW WOULD YOUR DAUGHTER?
THE BOY IS GUILTY
LEAVE HIM TO ROT

13

The lobby smelt of leather and centuries-old tomes, and was infused with a luxurious hush. There was artwork on the walls and copies of *Country Life* and *Vanity Fair* fanned meticulously on the side tables. Leo, doing his best not to slump on a deep-tan, button-backed Chesterfield, felt obliged every so often to straighten his tie. His suit, wrinkled from the train journey, seemed tattier than he remembered and shapeless. Nothing like those that drifted past once in a while atop hand-made, leather-soled shoes. Leo looked, he imagined, like a wide-eyed yokel, which was exactly the way he felt. Out of his depth: that was the phrase. And it was apposite in so many ways.

'Leo!'

Leo, tapping his fingertips on his knees, had not even realised the lobby housed a lift. He raised his head and saw the wooden panels across from him had drawn stealthily apart. Beyond them was a sparkling brass interior, out of which stepped the man Leo had come to see.

'Dale.' Leo got quickly to his feet. He buttoned his jacket

and aimed his hand at the one being propelled towards him.

Dale Baldwin-Tovey should, by rights, have been a tosser. It was the word Terry had used to describe him the last time the barrister had been engaged by their practice but, unsurprisingly perhaps, Leo had felt obliged to demur. Dale was younger than Leo and Terry both. In financial terms he was considerably more successful. He had more hair than they did in the places it mattered and less where the lack of it mattered double. His teeth were almost as impressive as Howard's but his grin was less ostentatious. The man seemed embarrassed by his good looks and was openly so of his double-barrelled surname. Leo found him humble, engaging and almost disconcertingly bright. A tosser then, as Terry would have it, precisely because he was not.

'You found us okay? How was the journey?' With his hand on Leo's shoulder, Dale guided him back towards the lift. The barrister pressed the call button and kept pressing it, as though unwilling for his guest to be kept waiting.

'It was fine. Thank you.'

'Good. Great. Thanks again for coming up. Sorry you had to bother but there was just no way I could leave London this week.'

Leo made a face. 'It's fine. Really.' Although the truth was, he had almost cancelled. Ellie was refusing to return to school and Meg had asked Leo to speak with her. Not only had Leo not had the chance, he had barely spent more than a few snatched seconds this past week talking to Megan. His wife, he knew, was less than happy. But the case – Daniel – could not wait, which was something Megan did not seem to understand. Plus, of course, there were the notes. Leo did not trust himself not to show them to his wife and doing so, given her obvious anxiety, would not be fair, at least until Leo could decide for himself whether they were worth worrying about. Which, actually, was another reason why Leo had decided in the end to make the trip.

The lift arrived and Dale gestured Leo inside. The doors closed and Leo found himself surrounded by an army in his own likeness. The floor, a dark-wood parquet, was the only surface that did not gleam. It was Leo's first visit to a set of London chambers and his astonishment must have shown on his face.

'Don't be fooled,' said Dale. 'The decor's as contrived as the whiskey barrels in your local Irish pub. They want you to like coming here, that's all – they want you to enjoy spending your money.'

Leo did his best to return Dale's roguish grin.

They got out on the fifth floor and Dale led Leo along a corridor that did nothing to undermine the impact of the lobby. Elegant wall lights and walnut panelling channelled them into a meeting room and they sat across from each other at a table worth more, probably, than Leo's car. There was coffee and a tray of pastries and Dale offered Leo both. When Leo declined, Dale slid the trays to one side. He clicked his pen.

'So.'

It sounded ill-considered. More than that, it sounded naive. Arguing with his colleagues back in Exeter, a presumption of rectitude had allowed him to skirt the obvious flaws in his thinking. Dale, though, was not hostile. He clearly sympathised with Leo's intent. Which meant Leo could not resort to bluster, nor hide behind a moralism that was beside the point. And so he fidgeted. He cleared his throat, for the fourth or fifth time it felt like – even though it was Dale he was willing to speak.

'What about his IQ?' the barrister said at last.

'Ninety. He was tested last week.'

Dale responded by twisting his lips. Low, he did not have to say – but not low enough.

'And the psychiatrist . . .'

'Karen.'

'Karen. She doesn't feel there's anything compelling we might use?'

The 'we' was reassuring, until Leo considered the context.

'Nothing obvious. He's of sound mind, capable of rational judgement. He knows right from wrong. He has posttraumatic stress disorder but no sign of anything underlying. She has her concerns, though.'

Dale raised an eyebrow but Leo could only disappoint.

'They're just concerns,' he said. 'Nothing concrete. He's clearly damaged in some way but . . . Well. We knew that already.'

Dale clicked his pen again: a double beat, followed by another, and then another in a metronomic rhythm. 'You could use someone else, you know.' He held still as he spoke, as though wary of Leo's reaction. 'Assuming Karen left us

room for manoeuvre in her report, we could always find someone who would be more . . . sympathetic.'

Leo shifted. He had considered it, of course he had. But,
'He's on legal aid. We wouldn't get the funding. And it was
hard enough convincing him to see Karen in the first place,
let alone someone new.' Again Leo shuffled in his seat. 'Besides.
This is about doing what's right for the boy. It's not about
fabricating a lie.'

'No one's suggesting we lie, Leo. But truth, in this field, is
hardly absolute.'

'Of course not. But there's the matter of consensus. And
I trust Karen's judgement. She's not wrong. She was never
wrong. For every expert we find who disagrees with her findings, the Crown will find ten who concur.'

Dale shrugged an eyebrow. There was quiet for a moment.

'Let's go back to the victim.' Dale moved his weight to the
opposite armrest, set his legs at a different angle. 'What was
the boy's connection with her?'

'They went to the same school. They lived in the same city.'

'That's it?'

'It seems to be. The first time I spoke to Daniel, he could
barely recall her name.'

'She didn't bully him? Taunt him? She didn't provoke him
in any way?'

'Not that anyone has suggested. Not even Daniel. And to
be honest, she didn't seem the type.' An image of Felicity's
hands, bloodless and bound in fairy lights, flickered in Leo's
mind. 'She was in the wrong place,' he said, forcing himself

to focus on Dale. 'At the wrong time. Or Daniel was: physically, mentally.'

'So provocation, self-defence . . . ?'

Leo shook his head.

'And he's not an alcoholic? A drug addict? He wasn't drunk or anything at the time?'

'He's twelve years old, Dale.'

Again Dale twitched his eyebrows. 'You'd be surprised.' He frowned at his leather-bound notepad. His pen, between his fingers, seemed to whirl of its own accord. Leo watched it spin, grateful on the one hand that a man with such dexterity was on his side; terrified, on the other, that having Dale as an ally might not make the slightest bit of difference.

'I think you're right,' Dale said. 'Diminished responsibility, if Daniel decides to plead not guilty, would be about his only option.'

Leo tensed. He sensed a but.

'But, with the evidence we have, I just don't see how we could make the case.'

The 'we', now, seemed generous. A consolation, that was all. Leo waited for something more.

'When's the arraignment?' said Dale, after a pause. 'A month, you said?'

'Just over.'

'And your client. Daniel. He's insisting on this, regardless of your advice?'

Leo had been waiting for this. Waiting – but not ready. 'He's not insisting on anything in particular.'

The pen in Dale's hand came to a stop.

'He trusts me.' Leo spoke to the table but realised as he uttered the words that they yielded a certain pride. He looked up. 'Daniel's instructed me to do what I think is best.' He paused but the silence that followed felt like a condemnation. 'He's a boy, Dale. How can he be expected to understand the complexities of—'

Dale nodded, held up a hand. 'What about the boy's parents? What do they say?'

'They seemed in favour of diminished responsibility until they realised what it would involve. Now they think Daniel should plead guilty. Throw himself on the mercy of the court.' Tell them Daniel did it and say he's sorry – isn't that how Blake had put it? As though sorry was the magic word; as though uttering it would be enough to salvage a future for his stepson.

'The boy has a record. Doesn't he?'

'He does but the infractions are minor. Just kid stuff, really, and some time ago. They might even help us. Mightn't they? If we paint them as cries for help. Like his school record. Couldn't we use that too?'

Dale gave Leo a weary smile. 'You don't believe that, Leo.'

And it was true. Leo did not.

'What about the schools?' Dale said. 'Daniel's teachers? Might their testimony help us in any way?'

Leo thought of Ms Bridgwater, Daniel's former – and Ellie's current – head teacher. He thought of the younger teacher Daniel had attacked. 'What could they say?'

Dale considered. He shook his head. 'You're right. It would hardly matter.'

Leo straightened. 'There's plenty to show Daniel was troubled. His father's in prison, walked out on the family when Daniel was eight. And Daniel must have been to, what? Four? Five schools in the past three years? All his life he's been shunted from one place to the next. He needed help but he was never offered any. I mean, he's not stupid, his IQ tells us that, but he's a year behind where he should be.'

'They kept him down a year?'

Leo nodded. 'And he's bottom of his current class too.'

'Any learning difficulties?'

'None that have been diagnosed. One of the schools made a tentative diagnosis of hyperactivity. If you ask me, though, it was just a guess. A dismissal, rather. The only label that seems to have stuck is that Daniel was a troublemaker. A "low achiever" – isn't that the term they use?'

'What about social services? Was he on any lists?'

'Not at the time. There was an investigation when he was a toddler because he kept showing up in A & E. It didn't come to anything, though. Accident prone, was the verdict. One of those kids who'd find a knife in a drawer full of spoons.'

Dale resumed his pen spinning. He nodded his head as though to a beat. 'Useful background,' he muttered. Leo could not quite tell if he was talking to himself or offering some half-hearted encouragement. Either way, background would not be enough. Leo felt his posture deflate. He looked at his hands and, glancing up, realised that Dale was watching him. The barrister, caught, looked away. Then he set down his pen and tested the air with a cough.

'Have you considered,' he said, 'mitigation?'

Leo felt his expression harden.

'There's no reason you can't make the argument you're making now in the pre-sentence report,' said Dale. 'Plus, if he pleads guilty, Daniel could benefit from a reduction in his tally.'

Leo was shaking his head. 'But then he's guilty. It's not just about the sentence, Dale. If he's guilty, he's guilty for the rest of his life: on registers, databases, lists. And anyway, there's no guarantee that he'll be any better off. Not given the attention on the case.'

'Possibly not. But it seems to me it's the boy's best option. I mean, his parents . . . Something tells me you don't think much of them but . . . well . . . they might, in this case, be right.'

'It's not right. How can it be right? Someone needs to consider why. Don't they? Whoever judges him needs to understand what led Daniel to do what he did. They owe the boy that much. *We* do. At least my way he has a chance.'

'He took a life, Leo. An innocent child's life.'

'He took two lives. He took his own at the same time.'

'Not in the sense that matters. And anyway it's not about why. It's never about why. We need to condemn a little more and understand a little less. John Major – remember? This is England, Leo, not Scandinavia.'

'So we leave it to the newspapers. Is that what you're saying? We let the *Sun* and the *Mirror* and the *Mail* take care of why?'

'I'm saying that it's not our job. That's all.' Dale paused, then added, 'Especially when we don't even know the answer.'

Leo opened his mouth, then clamped it tight. He was leaning forwards, he realised, reaching towards the centre of the table. He slid his hands into his lap and sat back.

Dale sighed. 'Don't get me wrong. I'm on your side. But you should consider as well the effect the trial would have on Daniel. Whether dragging this thing out is really, from his perspective, the right thing to do.'

'What do you mean?'

'Think about it. Think about what would be involved. You've been to a murder trial, I'm sure.'

Leo had. Two of them. One as an observer, the other as part of the defence team. Neither had been as dramatic as he had expected but they had been long, gruelling, even for someone just watching from the sidelines. 'It would be different, though. Wouldn't it? Given Daniel's age.'

Dale shrugged. 'The barristers might take off their wigs. The judge might sit a little lower. But no, actually – it would be exactly the same. A little slower. A little more drawn out. It would be an ordeal, Leo. There's no getting away from that.'

Leo moved in his chair. 'Well. As you say. There's no getting away from that.'

Dale, charitably, ignored Leo's tone. 'Would Daniel be up to it, do you think? If he had to testify, how would he come across? Would he stay calm? Would he seem contrite? Would he remain quiet, pay attention, sit straight: all those things he seems so rarely to have managed at school?' The barrister's gaze seemed to have settled on the scratches on Leo's cheek.

Leo turned away, dropped his chin. 'I think,' he said. 'I think maybe we're getting ahead of ourselves.'

Dale said nothing. He watched Leo for a moment, then smiled and pulled himself straight. 'Perhaps we are. I'm sorry, Leo. It wasn't my intention to make this harder.'

'No,' said Leo. He looked up and said it again, this time displaying a brightness he did not feel. 'Really,' he added, 'it's fine. You've been a huge help. You really have.'

Dale smiled, in a way that said they both knew that was not true. He closed his folder. Leo, for a moment, stared at the table. Then he set about gathering his belongings.

'How much youth work have you done, Leo?' said Dale, after a moment. He was tucking his pen into his jacket pocket, not looking at Leo as he spoke.

Leo had, once, attended a seminar. He rescued himself from saying so. 'Some,' he said instead. 'Not a lot.' He had a daughter, too. That was the other reason, as Leo recalled, that Howard had appointed him their practice specialist.

'It's tough,' Dale said. 'Isn't it? It can get to you. Affect your judgement.' He was standing now, facing Leo across the table. 'It can be hard, sometimes, to remain objective, to distinguish what we need to do from what we feel we should.'

Leo focused on fastening his briefcase.

They were almost at the lift. Leo cleared his throat and Dale glanced. 'Do you . . .' Leo said. 'Have you ever . . .' And now Dale was smiling and frowning both. 'Have you ever been threatened?' Leo spoke quickly. 'Because of work?'

They stopped at the elevator. Dale pushed the call button and gave a puff. He folded his arms. He looked suspiciously at Leo. 'You mean by a client? Are you talking about Dan—'

'No, no, no. Not at all. I mean generally. By someone else. Because of a case you were involved with.'

Again Dale considered. 'Well, I . . . Yes. I suppose I have.'

Leo, ludicrously, felt a surge of relief.

'More than threatened, actually,' said Dale and he seemed to brighten at whatever recollection was forming in his mind. 'I was attacked. When I was a pupil. By the girlfriend of this bloke I was defending.' Dale grinned. 'She didn't like my advice. She wanted to testify, you see, tell the judge what an upstanding man my client was, when the whole point was this bloke, my client, was married – twice, concurrently – and charged with bigamy. We were in chambers, just downstairs in fact, and what happened was . . .' Dale fell silent. He had noticed the expression on Leo's face. 'It didn't end well,' he said, dismissing the story with a gesture. 'I had scratch marks for a while, just . . . er . . . just like yours.' He twitched a smile, then coughed and looked down. He reached once more for the call button.

Leo raised his fingers to his cheek. 'I was thinking more about . . . you know.' He let his fingers fall. 'Members of the public. People not directly involved.'

'Like protesters, you mean? Like that mob outside the Magistrates' I saw on the news?'

'Well. Yes. Sort of, I suppose.'

'I've battled my way through a few crowds in my time.

Dodged the odd egg; even got hit by one or two. The dry-cleaning bills, I would say, come with the gown. Should really be tax deductible.'

Leo smiled politely. He nodded, as though that was the sort of thing he had in mind. 'What about letters. Notes. Things like that.'

'Letters?'

'Like, um . . . poison-pen letters.'

'Hate mail, you mean?' Dale, incongruously, grinned. 'We get it by the sackload, my friend. Human-rights protesters, environmentalists, animal-rights campaigners, you name it. When they're not writing to the *Guardian*, they're writing to us.' Dale glanced across his shoulder, made a show of leaning in close. 'I'll let you into a secret,' he said. Then, in a whisper: 'Lawyers, in this country, aren't very popular.' He held up his hands, backed away. 'It's crazy, I know. I, for one, feel misunderstood.'

Leo mimicked the barrister's grin. There you had it. Exactly as Leo had suspected.

Dale turned and reached again for the call button but almost as he pressed it the lift arrived. There was a ping and whisper of wood and Leo, facing inwards, was greeted by an image of his smiling self. He stepped to meet it, his briefcase a little lighter in his grip.

14

Their house was on fire. In the midnight dark that had swallowed the evening, that was how it seemed. The bedroom, the kitchen, the hallway, the study: each of the windows at the front of the house was ablaze with light. It was as though every curtain had been hauled back and every bulb angled to fend off the encroaching darkness. The effect, truly, was that the house was being consumed; that Leo would open the front door and be blinded, burned. And it was Megan at home. The woman who had been parentally programmed to turn out the light in the kitchen if she were popping upstairs to use the bathroom. Had Leo come home to find flames feasting on the mock-Tudor timbers, he did not think he would have been any more alarmed.

He did not wait for his change. He spilled from the taxi and hurried up the driveway and rang the bell at the same time as fishing for his key. He found it, found the lock, but when he turned the key the door clung tight to the frame. It had been bolted on the inside, top and bottom it felt like. He rang the bell again and rapped with his good set of knuckles. 'Meg?' He listened, rapped again. 'Meg, it's me.'

Shuffling, scrabbling – the sound of the bolts sliding back. The door opened, on the chain, then shut again to allow the chain to be unhooked. Finally Megan showed herself, pale and looking frayed in the unrelenting light.

'Leo. Where have you been!'

'What? I was . . .' He had told her, surely, about his trip to London. 'In a meeting,' he said. 'What's going on, Meg? You look . . . Why are all the lights on?' The question did not come out as intended. It was the tone he might have used with Ellie had he discovered that his daughter had left a tap running or the television blaring.

'Come inside,' Megan said. She peered into the outdoors and kept watching until she had sealed them both inside the house.

In the hallway, Leo sniffed. 'What's that smell?' He angled his nostrils towards his wife. 'Have you been smoking?' Again, the tone. Christ, Leo.

'I'm fine, dear husband. Thank you for asking.' Megan turned away from him and towards the kitchen. Leo followed but lingered in the doorway. He watched Megan set herself behind the counter. On the worktop was a wine glass, half full, and a bottle of red, half empty. There was a saucer beside the bottle containing the charred filter of a single cigarette, and a Zippo, next to the saucer, that Leo had long since assumed lost. Neither Megan nor he had smoked a cigarette in over a decade – since Megan's thirtieth birthday. So Leo had thought.

'Megan? What's going on?'

His wife, to Leo's surprise, replied with a laugh. She shook her head, picked up her wine and spluttered as she took a sip. She wiped around her mouth with the hinge of her thumb.

'Where's Ellie?' said Leo, casting round. 'Is she upstairs?' He took a step into the room. 'Megan? Will you please just tell me—'

'Ellie's at Sophie's house. I rang and checked. She wouldn't talk to me, of course. She's still angry because I made her go to school.'

'You made her go to school?' Every question Leo asked seemed to come out as an accusation.

'What else was I supposed to do! You said you'd talk to her, Leo. Today, you said: two days ago. Yesterday you said the same and then this morning you were gone before dawn and all she's been doing is sitting and moping in her room! I just . . . I thought . . . I just thought it would be better for her . . .'

'Meg. Calm down. It's fine. She went to school. She's at her friend's house. Everything's fine.'

'Everything's not fine, Leo! Everything's far from bloody fine!'

Megan turned. She clumsily set down her wine glass and reached to open the cupboard above the cooker – the cupboard no one in their family ever used. Leo watched, wondering what on earth Megan would produce that would explain things, but the object she brought down solved another mystery entirely. It was a tin, barely big enough to contain a packet of cigarettes. Megan plucked a cigarette from the box. Her fingers shook as she lit it and her face, when she dragged, puckered.

'Meg? You're smoking. I mean, why are you smoking?'

Megan exhaled. She glared as though daring him to go on. When he failed to, she propped an elbow on her wrist and dangled the cigarette level with her chin. She started forwards, trailed by smoke. 'In here.'

Leo watched her go. He looked at the tin, the cigarette packet – and then he followed. In the hallway again he noticed a chair in front of the door to the living room. Not just in front of it: the seat back was wedged under the handle.

'What is it? What's in there?'

'Nothing,' Megan said. She reached for the chair and scraped it free. She did not open the door, however. She stood aside as though waiting for Leo to go first.

'Meg?' He looked at her. When she did not answer he faced the door. He grasped the handle but kept it at arm's length. The door opened and he held it ajar, then gradually eased it wider. The space beyond was black. It was surely the only room in the house in which Megan had neglected to turn on the light. Leo submerged his hand in the darkness and frisked the wall for the light switch. He found it, flicked it, and braced himself for what he might see.

He turned to Megan, who was peering now across his shoulder. 'Meg?' he said and stepped into the room. 'There's nothing in here.'

Megan continued looking. 'That's what I said.' She did not, though, sound convinced.

Leo spread his arms and glanced about. There was just the sofa, the television, the piles here and there of everyday clutter. The only thing amiss was that the curtains, like those in the rest of the house, would normally by now have been drawn. The bay, with the light on, was a span of impenetrable blackness. Leo moved to cover it.

'Leo!'

He stopped halfway to the window. 'What? I was just going to—'

'Don't. Leave it. Can we . . . Let's go back into the kitchen.' Megan waited for Leo to follow her.

'Megan. Honestly. What on earth are you so frightened of?' Now it was Leo who sounded uncertain. He looked again at the window.

Megan raised her cigarette but it had burnt already to the filter. She looked for somewhere to dispose of it and settled on the soil beneath the Kentia palm beside the door. When she unbent she folded her arms.

'There was a man.' She spoke across Leo's shoulder. 'There. At the window.' She shuddered and wrapped herself tighter.

'A man?' Leo looked where his wife was looking. 'I don't understand. What man?'

'I don't know what man! Just a man! Staring at me! Pressed against the glass and . . . and . . . leering!'

'Leering?'

'Leo, don't!'

He had started again towards the window and this time he made it across the room. He pressed his face to the glass. 'There's no one out there, Meg. There's no one there.'

'Of course there's no one there! He's hardly going to sit around waiting for you to come home!' She sniffed. 'He'd be there all night.'

'What was he doing?' Leo said. 'What did he want?'

'It completely slipped my mind to ask,' Megan said, sounding dangerously reasonable. 'Maybe he just needed directions. Maybe he got lost delivering pizza.'

'What? You think he was just—'

'No!'

The word pealed. It took an age, it felt like, to fade.

'He was in the bushes, Leo. In the dark, at the back of the house.'

Leo struggled for something to say but before he could settle on the words his wife, without warning, left the room. He trailed her back towards the kitchen.

'Meg? What then? He was looking at you. "Leering," you said. As in . . .'

Watching.

Leo stopped short at the threshold

I am watching. You will be judged by your lies.

Leo felt a tightening in his gut. Ellie. He thought again of Ellie. 'Meg, wait. Ellie. Are you certain she's at Sophie's house? You said you didn't speak to her. How do you know she was definitely there?'

Megan had a hand on her cigarettes. 'What? What are you talking about?'

'Ellie. If you didn't speak to her, how do you know—'

'I spoke to Sophie's mother. She's not going to lie to me, Leo.'

'I'll go and get her.' Leo patted his pockets, checked about him for the car keys. 'Shall I?' But Megan. The man at the window. Fetching Ellie would mean leaving Megan on her own.

'They'll bring her over, Leo. Sophie's father will, after dinner. Don't you dare leave me here on my own.'

'No. No,' Leo said again. 'Of course not.'

'Leo?' Megan was studying him. 'What is it? Why are you suddenly acting so strangely?'

'What? I'm not.' Except: the notes. He should tell her about the notes. Shouldn't he? A man at their living-room window, ground-up glass with the most recent note. Leo looked at his bandaged finger. It still hurt when he tried to bend it but the pain, apart from that, was fading.

He covered the injury with his other hand. By the sack-load. Isn't that what Dale had said? And if he told Meg while she was in this state – if he told her, actually, any time at all – there was no question she would insist he drop the case. And he couldn't. He just could not.

Besides. A man at the window. It could have been anyone, no one.

'Tell me again,' he said to Megan. 'The man. At the window. Did you see his face? What did he look like?'

'He had a beard,' Megan said. 'He seemed big but maybe just because he was standing so close to the glass.' She shivered, shook it off. 'And his eyes were . . .' She narrowed hers. 'Bright. Light, I think.' She made a gesture: that's all. Rather: that's enough.

'But . . . You said it was dark. Didn't you? How did you see him if—'

'I'm not lying, Leo! I'm not making things up!'

Leo raised his hands. 'I didn't say you were. I'm just trying to understand, that's all.'

'He was smiling at me, Leo. Like he was gloating. Like me seeing him, being frightened by him, was the point.'

There was a rhythm in Leo's chest and he breathed to try to settle it. 'And then? What happened then?'

'Then? Then he went,' Megan said, her expression fierce. 'Down the passageway, I assume.' She looked at her wine glass on the counter. 'I ran around checking all the windows, all the doors, but everything was locked. After that I shut the curtains. But that was worse, somehow, so I opened them again.'

'And turned on the lights.'

Megan did not answer.

'What about after that? Did you see him again after that?'

'No. I didn't. The first time was enough, I promise you.'

'But you didn't call the police? Why did you not call the police?'

'I thought about it. I called your office instead. No one seemed to know where you were.' She tipped her head. 'Where were you, Leo? Were you with *him*?'

'I . . . I should get a mobile,' Leo answered, to distract her. 'They're expensive but if it means you're more at ease. That you're able to contact me in . . . When there's an . . .' He did not want to say the word.

Megan made a noise: something between a scoff and a sigh. 'It was hardly an emergency, Leo.'

He looked at his wife in surprise.

'I was scared,' she said. 'Probably he was just . . . just some . . .' She shook her head. 'I was on edge. After arguing with Ellie, after not knowing where you'd gone. And, anyway, there's a less expensive solution. If you're so worried about cost, I mean. If you're worried about putting me at ease.'

And here it came. Exactly as Leo had predicted. Was this, really, what this whole thing was all about?

'We've discussed this, Meg.'

'No, Leo, we haven't. Not properly.'

'We've said all we need to. Don't you think? I know how you feel, you know how I feel. At the end of the day, it's my decision. I'm not going to be swayed just because you . . . because of some . . .' He gestured loosely towards the living room.

'*Your* decision?' Megan seemed to wrestle for a moment with her fury. She closed her eyes and clasped her forehead. 'Can't you see?' she said at last. 'Don't you realise how this is hurting us? You, me. Ellie above all. And why? For some evil little . . .' She shook her head in lieu of the noun.

'Evil? How do you know he's evil? Christ, Meg, you haven't even met him!'

'I don't want to meet him! That's the last thing I would want to do! And what's evil, Leo, if not what he did? What's evil if not *him*?'

Leo directed his disgust towards the floor. 'You don't understand,' he said. 'You can't possibly understand.'

'I understand perfectly. Better than you do, clearly.'

'Meaning what exactly?'

'Meaning why you're doing this. Meaning what it is you're trying to prove!'

'Trying to prove? The only thing I'm trying to prove is that this boy – this child – needs help, not a life in prison.'

Leo shook his head, forgetting for an instant that he was in the middle of an argument. 'You should meet Daniel's parents, Meg. In their way they're as messed up as he is. I mean, it's no wonder, when you think about it, that—'

'I don't care!' Megan gripped the air. 'I don't know why *you* care! Why you seem to care more about a murderer than you do about your family!'

'That's not true! And he's not a—'

Leo stopped himself. Megan stared. She did not speak but she did not have to.

Leo coughed. 'That . . . that's not true,' he said. 'You and Ellie come first. You know you do.'

Megan moved from her position by the counter. 'Then *put* us first, Leo. Please.'

15

The track curved and the train tipped and the ground beneath them seemed to fall away. Out of one window reared a ragged cliff face; in the other, the bucking sea. A wave lunged and clawed the track, then slid back into the writhing mass. The water, in the winter sun, sparkled like a lunatic's grin. It seemed joyous, heedless, unconstrained in its dementia. It launched itself again and this time lashed the carriage but the train seemed barely to judder. It sped on – lungs full, head down – and dived for the approaching tunnel.

The world turned black.

It had been Leo's idea. A day out, just the three of them. To the coast. How about Dawlish? Megan had been averse, initially; suspicious, though of what specifically she probably could not have said. Leo had remained steadfast, however, acting as though her objections were grounded in the purely mundane. Agreed, he said: the weather wasn't perfect but when, in this country, was it ever? The sun was out; it was just a bit windy. So let's just go. Shall we? It would be good for Ellie. It would be good for all of us. Please, Meg. What do you say?

Ellie, it had turned out, had been even more reluctant than her mother. She had argued, to the point where Leo had nearly given up, when Megan had brought her convert's zeal into the fight. Together they had convinced her – dragged her – and here, now, was their collective reward. Fun, part one: the train ride.

And it was spectacular. In this final section of the journey from the city, the Riviera Line laced itself along the country's edge. The ocean was beside them – beneath them, it felt like – and only the tunnels offered intermittent shelter from waves that were rising to the season. Even Ellie, in her withdrawn, anxious way, seemed – almost – thrilled. Seated on her own and facing sideways, her breath was steaming the glass. As they emerged from the tunnel a wave pounced and she recoiled in imitated terror. She even squealed, just as any child might. But then the wave receded and Ellie turned to Megan with a display of something more like genuine fear.

'Isn't this dangerous?'

Leo looked from his daughter to his wife. 'Dangerous?' He turned back. 'What do you mean?'

Ellie answered but addressed her mother. 'The waves. The train. What if we get knocked off the rails?'

There was a woman, Megan's age, on the seats across from theirs and she caught Leo's eye and offered a smile. Leo forged one back.

'We'll be fine, darling,' said Megan. 'They wouldn't let the train run if they didn't think it was safe.'

But then another wave broke and this one, Leo would have sworn, wrapped itself over the roof. Megan gave a start and, perhaps forgetting herself, turned to Leo with a schoolgirl's grin. Leo was too surprised, in the instant he had, to react. He thought belatedly about reaching for his wife's hand but hesitated and lost his chance.

'Mum.'

Megan crossed from Leo's seat to Ellie's. She slid an arm around her daughter's shoulders and Leo felt a pang. Even though it was with her mother that Ellie had argued, Leo remained the focus of her ire: his punishment, as far as Leo had deduced, for having complained to his daughter's school.

'It's fine, darling, I promise.' Megan smiled and Ellie sunk into her mother's embrace. Leo smiled too and waited for Ellie to look towards him – to include him. She did not. The stranger was still watching and Leo turned away to conceal his flush.

He had not expected it to be so busy. The village, he had assumed, would be deserted. One or two hardy tourists, perhaps; local dog-walkers moseying along the beach. But crowded cafes, packed-out pavements: they were not part of Leo's plan.

They had stopped at the corner of the central green. Leo had, rather. Megan and Ellie were already several paces further on.

'What?' Megan said, turning.

'All these people. It's just . . . I thought the idea was to get away for the day.'

'The idea was to have a day out. The three of us.' Megan glanced at Ellie, who was staring anxiously at her father. 'Leo,' Megan said, when Leo did not answer. Her tone – her expression – was a warning.

Leo considered the crowds. He considered his daughter. *How would you like it, Leo?*

'Fine,' he said. 'Let's just stay together, that's all. No wandering off.'

They wandered off.

Leo twisted, turned on tiptoe – and finally spotted them at the window of a clothes shop. He snapped and Megan scowled and proceeded, in retribution, to lead their daughter inside.

Leo made to follow but settled on waiting outside the door. He studied the people passing by. They were grouped in families mainly, just like theirs. But cheerier, less uptight. Some bore ice creams, others shopping bags, others just a flush on their cheeks from the winter wind. There were people by themselves, too: an older woman, a younger man, two black-clad teenagers in quick succession. None, though, seemed a threat. None seemed even to notice that Leo was there. It was just this breeze, that was all; the expanse of sea. He felt exposed because they were not locked away at home. Which was foolish too, in a way. Illogical, because if someone really wanted to find them – to watch them – their home was the obvious place to come looking. Here, amid the crowds, was about the safest place they could be.

By the sackload, Leo. Remember?

He was on edge but there was no need to be. Had he not already decided that? When Ellie and Meg came outside he would see about setting this day of theirs back on track.

'Ready?' he said as they emerged. He noticed they each held a bag. 'You bought something.' Naturally they had. Something, no doubt, they would never wear. But, 'Great. What say we find somewhere to get ice cream?' Somewhere quieter, he did not add, wondering in spite of himself how much of the day a day trip was supposed to take up.

Leo led and the girls trailed. Megan seemed cheered by her purchase and that was something. She did not speak directly to Leo but she attuned herself to his enthusiasm. She seemed, if nothing else, to remember the reason they had come.

'Ellie.' Megan nudged her daughter and pointed across the square towards the beach. The waves were storming the sea wall, breaking with the force of a battering ram and hurling up a spray that crackled, as it landed, like sparks. 'Look at that. Look at those people!' A crowd had gathered along the promenade but had ventured too close to the shore. Another wave broke and there was screaming, bodies diving for the dry.

Ellie watched but without any evident delight. 'Will the train still be running?' she said. 'Will we still be able to get home?'

Their daughter, this time, had turned to Leo. He started to respond, to reassure – but his words, barely formed, withered. He cast his attention over the top of his daughter's head.

Who was that?

A man, standing on his own in the square, watching them

– was he? – when everyone around him was watching the waves. He seemed young but from Leo's distance it was hard to be sure. The man was slight, and slightly stooped. He held his chin level with his shoulders, as though his overcoat was leaking the chill. There was something around his neck – a camera? – and a baseball cap covering his crown. Leo raised himself onto his toes to get a view of the man's face but, as he did so, the man tucked himself into the crowd. Leo shifted but a hand on his wrist tugged him round.

'Dad? Will they close the line? What'll we do if we can't get home?'

Leo stared at his daughter, conscious of the question but unable, at that moment, to associate it with an answer. He looked again towards the man but the man, this time, was gone.

'They won't close the line, darling.' Megan slid an arm around Ellie's shoulders. She coaxed her daughter towards her. 'If they do, your father will just have to pay for a taxi.' Megan led her daughter along the street. Leo, with a final glance behind, could only follow.

'And marshmallows. Can I have marshmallows?' Ellie looked left, right, and met assent on both sides. The lady behind the counter garnished the tub of ice cream and speared it with a plastic spoon. She offered it across the counter and returned Ellie's smile.

'And for you, madam?'

Megan drew a hand to her waistline. 'Nothing for me. Thank you.'

'Sir?'

Leo checked again through the glass door. There was a man in a windcheater blocking his view, moving one way, back again, so that Leo had to shift in unison to try to find a gap.

'Sir?'

A tug on his sleeve. 'Leo.'

'Sorry? What?' He turned and his wife was glaring.

'This was your idea, Leo. Don't you want one?'

'Sorry. Yes. Just . . .' He pointed at a tub of something yellow. 'Just vanilla. Thanks.' The man was still blocking the door.

'That's cheesecake, sir. This one's vanilla: over here.'

'What? Fine. Whichever.'

'So . . . cheesecake then? Or vanilla?'

Move! Why would he not just move?

'Sir? I . . . There are people waiting, sir.'

'Leo!'

'What?' Leo snapped as he spun. The woman behind the counter was still waiting. 'Cheesecake. Cheesecake's fine.' He dug out some change from his pocket and slapped it onto the counter. The woman handed over his cone and Leo ushered his frowning daughter from the shop. He heard, vaguely, Megan apologising to the owner in their wake.

There was no one out there. Just the same drifts of visitors parading around the square, groups here and there huddled beside the benches.

Leo trailed. Megan was up ahead and Ellie midway between them. Their daughter's enthusiasm for her raspberry ripple seemed to have abated and she prodded half-heartedly at the contents of her tub. Leo, similarly, only licked his cone once in a while when he felt the cold slipping in tendrils across his fingers.

So much for ice cream.

There was a single bench unoccupied, damp and in the shade, and Megan seemed to be leading them towards it. They were in no hurry. When they got there they would poke some more at their ice cream and shiver for a moment in silence and then one of them – Megan – would suggest that they head back home. Which was something. Better that than any more of this. Better to be home, safe, warm at least, with their own corners of the house to inhabit and no obligation to pretend.

'Hey!'

Leo's hand drooped and the scoop of ice cream toppled from the cone.

'Hey!' he said again. 'You!' He lengthened his stride and bumped his daughter as he passed her. He heard her exclamation but did not turn to it. He focused on the man ahead and continued his march. 'Stop right there!'

Leo expected the man to run and for an instant he seemed to consider it. He turned to his right but found his path blocked by the tree behind which he had been hiding. He turned the other way but there was a barrier now of people who had slowed on the pathway to watch. Leo, more to the point, was closing. Even were the man to run, there was no way he would get far. And so he waited, camera in hand, feet shuffling in a nervous dance.

'Leo? What's the matter?' Megan diverted from the bench but stopped when Leo passed her.

'Who are you? What do you want?'

The man was indeed young. Below his cap his hair was cropped and he wore his stubble the same length. His overcoat seemed too big, as though he had borrowed it from his father. Even Leo would have had to admit, the man looked more like a student than a stalker.

Even so: 'Well? Let's hear it.'

The man did his best impression of an innocent bystander. 'Who?' He looked about. 'Me?'

'Yes, you!' Leo took a step forwards. He was an arm and a half's distance now from his quarry. 'I saw you! You've been following us!'

Don't be ridiculous, read the man's expression. But there was uncertainty – guilt – in his eyes and he glanced again as though seeking an escape route. 'Why would I be following you? I'm just . . .'

Leo waited. The bystanders – a dozen strong now – waited too.

'Just . . .' The man smiled, incredulously, and gestured to the sea, the square, the sky. And then he ran.

Someone screamed. Megan? Leo tensed and almost darted but in the end there was no need. The man managed barely a second step before he stumbled, tripping on the protruding wheel of a pushchair. He fell gracelessly, his instinct to save his camera. Someone in the crowd laughed. Before the man could recover his footing Leo was looming over him.

'What's on the camera?'

The man tried to wrap the camera in his overcoat. 'Nothing,' he said. 'Pictures of the sea.'

'Give it to me.' Leo took a step and reached. The man scrabbled backwards on his heels.

'What? No!'

'Give me the camera!' Leo made to lunge but felt a hand grip his arm.

'Leo! What are you doing? What's going on?'

'I said, give me the . . .' Leo shook off his wife and swiped. The man was quicker. He rolled and staggered upright and held the camera aloft.

'They're just pictures! I'll delete them! Just mind the camera, will you!'

Leo grabbed and the man lurched. The camera floated out of Leo's reach.

'What kind of pictures? Who are you? Why are you taking pictures of us?'

'I don't know. They just said for me to get pictures!' The man's eyes darted across Leo's shoulder. Leo turned to track his gaze but saw nothing. But then he did: Ellie, standing alone and watching, listening.

Leo whirled back. 'My daughter? You were taking pictures of my daughter?'

The man took a step away. 'I'm just doing what I was told. Okay? It's just a job!'

'Leo! What's going on! Will you please—'

'You're a photographer.' Leo stopped his advance. 'You work for a newspaper?'

The man gave Leo a look, like why the hell else would he be here? 'The *Post*,' he said. 'But it's only a gig. I'm freelance really. I'll delete the pictures, I promise. I'll tell them I lost you at the station.' The man backed through the boundary of onlookers.

'Leo. Leo!'

Leo turned slowly towards his wife. He was aware, vaguely, that the people around them were dispersing, all except for a man in a woollen hat who was clearly holding out for something more climactic. But even he, when he noticed Leo glance, tucked his chin behind his upturned collar and fell into step with the rest of the crowd. Leo and Megan were left alone.

They were alone.

Leo looked left, right, then back at his wife, who was watching him with something like fear, something like disgust. Until her expression changed too, even before Leo could ask what they were all of a sudden both thinking.

'Where's Ellie?'

They found her discarded tub of ice cream atop a bin at the edge of the square. The contents had turned to soup, the raspberry ripples into streaks like blood.

From the square, at Leo's suggestion, they split up. She had gone home. Of course she had gone home. She would be at the railway station or already aboard a train. And she was fifteen, not a child: it was not like she had never caught public transport by herself. Yet Leo did not want Megan to see his rising panic. His wife, anyway, seemed happy to go her own way. She seemed delighted, in fact, at the prospect of being able to escape the sight of him.

Megan headed straight for the station. Leo, they agreed,

would retrace their route and then meet them, hopefully, on platform two. And so he rewound their day, pacing from the site of one minor failure to the next. None proved any more fruitful on Leo's second visit, which meant his first instinct had obviously been correct. And so he sprinted, as best he could around pedestrians who refused to part, and braced himself for the prospect of his wife and daughter braced for the prospect of seeing him.

He almost missed them. The train to Exeter was at the platform and there were enough bodies interlacing through the doors that Leo struggled for a moment to distinguish his wife and daughter's. Then he spotted them, finally – but even as he did, he thought for a second that he must have been mistaken. Because they were getting on. His wife, his daughter ahead of her and with Megan's hand at the small of her back: they were about to board the train.

They were leaving without him.

Leo, rooted, called out. Ellie by now was already aboard but Megan, behind her, turned. She saw him. There was no question that she saw him. She did not answer, however. She did not wave, nor gesture for him to hurry. She regarded him for half a moment, then turned her back and stepped from sight.

16

It had, she said, gone something like this.

Stephanie was seated when Karen arrived, facing the door and curiously still. Blake, behind her, seemed powered by the both of them, not muttering when Karen walked in but giving the impression he was merely drawing breath. He was pacing, or seemed to have been, because it took him a second or two after Karen entered to rein in his momentum. He came to a halt beside the armchair, partially obscuring his wife and soundlessly broadcasting his hostility. He checked his watch, as though Karen being ten minutes late were the cause of his disquiet. She should have been on time, of course. She had not intended to leave her office that morning but something had come up and it had taken longer than she had expected to deal with and the traffic, on the way back, had been . . .

Anyway. The point was Blake was hostile from the start, just as Leo had predicted he would be.

Karen apologised. Blake took her hand when she offered it, though for half a second she was certain he would not. Daniel's mother did not stand but smiled up at Karen. She seemed calm. Chemically so, Karen would have said. It was a glaze she recognised. One, sometimes, she prescribed.

Blake was not calm. He acted, once Karen was in the room, in a manner to imply he was perfectly in control but his agitation simmered below his skin.

'So you're the shrink,' he said, restating in his own terms Karen's introduction.

'*A* shrink,' Karen said and reinforced her smile. 'Leo. Leonard. Mr Curtice . . .' she was unsure, it struck her then, how they would know him '. . . asked me to help out. With Daniel. With the case.'

'Like you're not getting paid,' Blake responded. 'Like "helping out" isn't billed by the hour.'

Still Karen smiled. 'Would you like coffee? Tea? Water or something?'

'Let's just get on with this.' Blake sat on the join between the cushions on the sofa and aimed his knees at ten and two. 'Shall we?'

Karen waited for Blake's wife to decide for herself, then settled, when Stephanie shook her head, on the armchair beside her.

'I was hoping,' Karen said, impartially alternating eye contact, 'for a little background. I invited you here because I thought, by talking to you, I might glean some insight into—'

But she need not have bothered with the rehearsals.

'I have a living to earn,' Blake interrupted. 'Steph here has soaps to watch. What is it you want us to tell you?'

'Well,' Karen said, 'I'm not sure exactly. Which is why I

thought it important that we should talk. The three of us.'
She endeavoured, with a look, to include Stephanie.

'Talk. Always bloody talk. That's all any of you lot seem to
do.'

'Us lot, Mr Blake? Who do you mean exactly?'

Blake flicked a hand. 'Curtice. Social services. The do-good-
ers from that charity that keeps bugging us, behaving like
we're the bloody victims. And doctors. Don't get me started
on doctors. God knows we've seen enough of them over the
years to know they're all full of piss and air.'

Karen said nothing. She watched.

'This isn't easy, you know.' Blake's tone was a challenge.
'The waiting. The moving out, the moving in. The so-called
bloody protection. And Steph here – she's completely messed
up about Daniel.'

Blake did not look at his wife but Karen did.

'I'm upset,' Stephanie said. 'That's all Vince means. It's
Danny, obviously, but it's other things too.'

'She means her mates. *Former* mates, rather. Mates who
don't call any more, don't answer when she calls them.'

'And you, Mr Blake? Are you upset?'

'Course I am. But he's not my son, is he? It's different, isn't
it? I don't feel so constantly bloody guilty all the time. That's
Steph's trouble. She's acting like she's the one who killed that
girl, like it's her fault Daniel—'

'Vince. Don't.'

Blake gave Karen a look: you see what I mean? He patted
himself down and located his packet of cigarettes.

'I'd like, if I may,' said Karen after a pause, 'to discuss

Daniel's home life. His childhood. I'd like to establish a little background.'

'What's the point?' said Blake. 'He's not mad, he's not retarded – that's what you told Curtice. He's just screwed up. Right? So he pleads guilty. What choice does he have? How is talking about his childhood gonna change anything?'

'You want to help him, Mr Blake, don't you? You want Daniel to understand why he did what he did?'

'He has to be guilty first. That's what I read. No one can help him till he tells them he's guilty.' Blake turned aside, his voice dwindling into a mutter. 'Which, the way I see it, he already has.' He turned back to face Karen. He held up his cigarettes. 'You're gonna tell me I can't smoke in here, aren't you?'

Karen winced. 'Sorry.'

Blake gave a sniff. He tucked the packet of cigarettes back into his shirt pocket.

'We want to help.'

Karen turned to face Stephanie.

'Of course we want to help. We just don't see how we can. That's part of the problem. That's the reason we're finding this so hard.'

Karen nodded. 'I understand. I really do. We all want what's best for Daniel and the information you give me should help us establish exactly what that might be.'

'Why are you asking?' said Blake. 'That's what I want to know. What did Daniel tell you? I mean, if he's trying to sell you some sob story, blame everything that's happened on Steph . . .'

'Not at all. That's not at all why I invited you here. When I met with Daniel he was scared, above all. He was confused. He seemed to struggle with his family history and I thought maybe you could help me fill in some of the blanks.' Karen hesitated, then added, 'The truth is, I would not, in normal circumstances, be meeting with you both. But Leo and I go back a while and . . . well . . . I was hoping, I will admit, to be involved with Daniel's rehabilitation. Depending on the outcome of the case, of course.'

Blake snorted. 'So you're looking for a gig. That's what this is about. You're looking for freaks to dissect, to write about in some study.'

'I want to help, Mr Blake. Vincent. May I call you Vincent? I'm genuinely only interested in doing what I can to help your stepson.'

Again Blake sniffed. He made a face that implied it did not matter now what Karen said: he had her number.

It was Stephanie who broke the silence. 'How can we help? What is it that you want to know?'

Karen regarded each of them in turn. She spoke to Blake. 'What you said before, about Daniel blaming your wife. What did you mean by that?'

'What? Nothing. It's what kids do, isn't it? It's what everyone does, all the bloody time. It's Mummy's fault. It's Daddy's. It's anyone's fault but my own.' Blake looked at his wife looking blankly back at him. 'Back me up, Steph, for Christ's sake. You of all people know exactly what I'm talking about.'

Stephanie's jaw tightened.

'You think he blames you for something?' Karen, this time,

addressed Stephanie. It was Blake, nevertheless, who answered.

'I just said. Didn't I? It's what kids do. It's what everyone does. I didn't mean anything by it.' He began muttering again, something about something being exactly the type of thing he was talking about.

Karen watched him for a moment. She sighed. 'You can smoke, Vincent. It's fine. I'll open a window.' She offered Blake a smile.

His eyes narrowed. He wrapped his arms across his chest and reclined on the sofa. Karen looked to her lap.

'Can I?'

Karen raised her head. Stephanie pointed to her handbag.

'Of course,' said Karen. 'Go ahead.' She stood and moved to the window and struggled with the sash until it was ajar. She checked around her, then crossed to her desk and tipped some pens from a mug. She set the empty mug on the arm of Stephanie's chair, and one of the pens and a notepad beside her own seat. Stephanie exhaled towards the window but the draught nudged the smoke back the way it came.

'You were asking about Daniel's childhood,' said Stephanie once Karen was seated. 'About his home life.'

Blake was glaring at his wife, at the cigarette dangling from her hand.

'That's right,' Karen said. 'I wondered . . .' She coughed. Stephanie moved her hand, her cigarette, across her body. 'I wondered about the kind of things he might have been exposed to,' Karen continued. 'This isn't about blame, you understand. I'm not here to judge anyone. But, well . . .' She swallowed. 'Violence, for instance. Physical harm. Vincent is your second husband, Stephanie. May I ask why your first marriage ended?'

'It ended cos Frank walked out on her. That's why it ended. Steph would still be clinging to that loser if he hadn't shaken her off.'

Karen waited for Stephanie to answer.

'He didn't hit me, if that's what you mean.' Stephanie focused on her cigarette, tapping it repeatedly over the make-shift ashtray even though the ash had already fallen.

'And Daniel? What was his relationship like with Daniel?'

Stephanie shrugged. She ground out her cigarette awkwardly against the inside of the mug and started fishing right away for another. 'Normal,' she said. 'I suppose. Not like television normal, like kicking a ball to each other in the park, but normal in the neighbourhood we lived in.'

'Did he ever hit Daniel? Or . . .'

'No. I mean, not really. He'd give him a tap now and then, I suppose. Mostly when he deserved it. He was a drinker so sometimes he hit him harder than he meant to but he never hurt him. Not properly. He was always quite a gentle man, actually.'

'He's doing time for assault,' said Blake. 'That's how gentle he can be.'

Karen considered the scar on Blake's face; the boxer's bend to his nose.

'That's different.' Stephanie looked to Karen. 'Isn't it? That was business. That's not what the doctor's talking about.'

Karen made as though taking down a note. When she looked up Stephanie had a flame to her second cigarette, her eyes drawn together and trained, it looked like, on the tip of her nose.

'Is it possible,' Karen said, 'that Frank ever touched Daniel? Ever interfered with him in any way?'

Stephanie expelled the smoke in her lungs. 'None. Never. I would have known.'

'But you said he drank. Might his behaviour have been different when he was intoxicated?'

'I don't see why. And anyway I still would have known. Besides, he hated that kind of thing. It made him furious. Really properly furious.'

This time Karen did make a note. 'What about, I don't know. Uncles. Male friends. Older boys. Anyone else.' She did not look at Blake directly but she was watching for his reaction.

Blake did not move. His wife shook her head.

Karen tapped her pen against her notepad. 'When Frank left,' she said, 'Daniel was, what? Eight?'

Stephanie thought, nodded.

'How did he react?'

'Who? Danny?' Stephanie made a show of trying to recall. 'He – Frank, I mean – he wasn't around much by that time anyway.' She pulled on her cigarette and her frown deepened. She held in the smoke for so long that Karen felt sure it was not coming out again. 'Danny wasn't happy about it, obviously. But I wouldn't say he was specially unhappy either. He just . . . I don't know. Went on being Daniel.'

'Was Daniel generally happy, would you say? As a child. When he was younger.'

'That's what I mean,' said Stephanie. 'He wasn't ever, like, joyous. Is that a word?' She glanced at Karen and Karen nodded. 'Danny wasn't ever that kind of boy. It isn't his nature.'

'To be happy?'

'To be . . . I don't know. Laughing all the time. Things like that. It isn't Daniel.'

Stephanie finished her second cigarette. She adjusted herself in her seat, transferred her handbag from her lap to the floor. There was the rattle, as she moved it, of pills in a jar. Or mints in a tin, of course. Vitamins, paracetamol – it might have been anything.

'What about you, Stephanie?' Karen said. Blake, before, had been fiddling with his packet of Rothmans. The box ceased dancing all of a sudden in his grip. 'How did you cope when Frank left you?'

'Me? I . . .' Stephanie looked down.

'She coped just fine. Didn't you, Steph?' There was malice in Blake's tone; anger in the look Stephanie, in response, cast towards her husband.

'I coped,' she said.

Karen waited for Stephanie to say more. 'You coped,' she said after a pause. 'May I ask what you mean by that?'

'She means she coped,' Blake said. 'What could be clearer?'

Karen left another silence but neither of Daniel's parents sought to fill it. 'What about motherhood? More generally, I mean. Did you enjoy it? How did you cope, would you say, with being a mother?'

Stephanie glanced towards her husband. 'I don't know.

Okay, I suppose. It was hard but everyone finds it hard. Don't they?'

Karen let the question go unanswered. 'Hard in what way, Stephanie? Can you explain?'

Stephanie hesitated and Blake leant forwards, forcing himself into Karen's sight line. 'This is about Daniel. Isn't it? I thought this was supposed to be about the boy.'

'Absolutely,' Karen said. 'It's just background, that's all. It's just to help us try to understand—'

'What's to understand! What bloody difference does it make whether Steph "enjoyed motherhood"?' He said this last as though the concept were patently something to mock.

'Well, actually, Vincent, it does make quite a significant—'

'Steph didn't kill anyone. Frank, her ex: he liked a scrap but he never killed anyone either.'

Karen inclined her head. 'No. That's true. But—'

'So what's with all the questions about them? You wanna help Daniel, that's what you said. Sounds to me like all you're interested in doing is digging up the family dirt.' An idea seemed to strike him. His eyes tightened. 'Like for the papers or something.' He smiled. 'That's it, isn't it? You're digging up dirt to give the papers.' He allowed Karen an instant to respond but all she could manage was a shake of her head. 'I'm right,' Blake said, his smile spreading. 'Aren't I?'

Stephanie shuffled forwards, pressing her knees against the coffee table and reaching half-heartedly across it. 'Vince. Please. I'm sure that's not what this is about.'

Blake stood. 'This is over. We've said all we're going to.'

Karen rose to face him. 'Mr Blake. Vincent. I promise you.

This entire conversation is completely confidential. There is simply no way I would—'

'Let's go, Steph.'

Stephanie looked up at Karen.

'Stephanie!' Blake was halfway across the room. 'I said, let's go!'

His wife looked down. She started gathering her things.

Blake waited with his hand on the door handle. There was an unlit cigarette jutting from his lips, a lighter sparking in his grip. He tapped his trainer on the floor as he watched his wife, pointedly avoiding Karen's gaze. Karen started to speak, to make one last attempt to stop them leaving, but Blake was quicker to find his voice.

'We just want this over,' he said and he glowered. 'Understand? All your prodding, your poking about – it's not gonna help.'

Karen could think of nothing to say.

'Leave things alone. Leave us alone. All we want is our lives back to normal.'

And then, of course, Karen could have answered. Your lives will never be back to normal, she might have said. This, the way things are – it's how they're going to be.

'And then they left.'

Leo was stirring sugar into his coffee. There were two empty cups in the centre of the table, a steaming one in front of each of them. Leo stopped stirring and allowed his spoon to drip. He settled it noiselessly on the saucer.

'Leo? Did you . . . Are you okay?'

He looked up. 'Sorry? What? Yes, I . . . Sorry,' he said again. 'It was a long weekend. That's all.' He sat straighter. 'So what do you think?'

Karen peered at him before answering. 'To be honest,' she said, 'I found it quite upsetting. Not that these things aren't always upsetting but . . . well . . .'

'Because of Blake, you mean? He's like that with everyone. He's a moron, I told you. Doesn't give a damn about anyone but himself.'

Karen shook her head. 'Not because of him. On the scale of obnoxiousness among the people I have to deal with in this job, he barely scrapes a seven. And anyway,' she said, turning her cup, 'I'm not sure that's true.'

'That he's a moron?'

'No. He's definitely a moron. I mean the bit about him not giving a damn.'

Leo frowned. He started to ask Karen what she meant but she was dangling her arm into the bag at her feet, looking the way she was reaching. She glanced briefly at the tables around them – empty but for two mothers with their babies and an elderly couple crossing forks over a slice of carrot cake – then slid an A4 envelope alongside Leo's cup of coffee.

'What's this?'

'Just something I found. Something I obtained, rather. Take a look.'

Leo lifted the flap and pulled out the sheets that were inside. 'What is this?' He turned from the first page to the last. 'There was an investigation?' He turned back again. 'Why weren't we told about this?' He noticed the date and pinned it with his finger. 'This was after. This was since Daniel's arrest. Why weren't we told about this?'

Karen raised a shoulder. 'I'm guessing they don't have to tell you.'

Leo read, gobbling the words too quickly for them to properly register. He looked at Karen. 'How did you . . .'

'I have a friend.'

Leo looked again at the report. 'She took a risk, giving this to you.'

'We're close,' said Karen, 'he and I.'

Leo raised his head. Karen lowered hers.

'And anyway,' she said, 'it doesn't help particularly. Not in the way you might expect.'

Leo read aloud: '"No evidence of abuse is established."' He skimmed. '"Daniel's name will not be entered on the Child Protection Register."'

'And here. Look.'

Leo tracked Karen's fingertip. '"No connection has been established between any abuse and the alleged offence."' He looked up. 'In other words . . .'

'"It wasn't our fault. There's no way they can pin this on us."'

Leo sniffed. 'Well. That's all right then. So long as social services have got their own arses covered, nobody has anything to worry about. Their jobs are safe.'

'From what my friend told me, the investigation wasn't exactly comprehensive. But that was the point,' Karen said. 'It was an exercise in self-exoneration.'

Leo tossed the report onto the table. 'They still should have told us. Even if it doesn't help Daniel's defence, they are morally obligated to—'

'Not so fast.' Karen gathered together the sheets and started flicking. 'It doesn't help in the way you might expect. That doesn't mean it doesn't help at all. Read here.'

She thrust the pages towards him.

'But we knew about this,' said Leo after a moment. Daniel, as a toddler, had a history of visits to the emergency ward: twice following 'falls', once after swallowing household bleach, a fourth time after ingesting tricyclic antidepressants. He thought they were sweets, Daniel's mother had explained at the time; he must have done. 'They investigated,' Leo said. 'It says so right here. "Concerns were raised but were demonstrated to be unfounded."'

'Unfounded,' Karen echoed. 'Please. A baby has four near-fatal accidents in his first thirty-six months and social services see no cause for concern.'

'They must have looked into it, though. They must have asked questions.'

'It's where they looked that's important. It's what kind of questions they asked, of whom.' Karen shook her head. 'I'm not blaming social services,' she said, not entirely convincingly. 'They're underfunded, understaffed, underappreciated. The point is, something was clearly going on. Maybe we knew the facts before but we didn't know the context. Daniel's medical record, tied with his mother's depression . . .'

'Her depression? How do you know she was depressed?'

'Not was. Is. You don't need to be a doctor to diagnose that. I'm guessing about when it started but it certainly predates the murder. My hunch would be post-natal. The pills Daniel swallowed could have been anybody's but most likely they were Mummy's or Daddy's.'

'You think Mummy's.'

'I do. Who gave Daniel the pills, though, is another question.'

'Who *gave* them to him?'

'Gave them to him, left them out for him to find – it amounts to the same thing.'

'But it could have been an accident. Couldn't it? You don't think you're jumping to conclusions?'

'It could. And yes, I am. But that's what I'm here for. Isn't it?'

Leo puffed his cheeks. He stared at the pages, not seeing the words.

'Okay,' he said. 'Let's say you're right. So what? How does what happened to Daniel as a baby have any connection with the crime he's accused of now?'

'It doesn't,' Karen said. 'Not if you're looking for a direct link. Indirectly, though, it explains everything. It sets a pattern. It establishes the nature of Daniel's relationship with those closest to him and by extension with everyone around him. Depending on who you believe, Leo, it's what happens to us in our formative years that most influences our behaviour as adults.'

'Show me the child and I'll show you the man. Who said that? John Lennon?'

'Stalin, actually. Also, the Jesuits. But yes, that kind of thing. And it's doubly true in the case of sexual abuse.'

'Sexual abuse? Jesus Christ, Karen.'

'What? You're surprised?'

'No. I mean, I wouldn't have been. But the pills: that's one thing. You're saying he was sexually abused too?'

'I'm saying it's likely. More than likely. For a start, eighty per cent of abusers have themselves suffered abuse. Daniel was moulded, Leo – he wasn't manufactured.'

'But the report.' Leo lifted the pages, knocking his coffee cup. 'What did it say. It said . . .'

'It said they found no evidence. But it only dug as deep as it needed to, remember – mainly into the past few years. As far as I'm concerned, it skirted the most interesting period of Daniel's life.'

Leo looked again at the pages, searching for what Karen meant.

'There's nothing to see,' she told him. 'And that's why it's interesting. Apart from when he was a toddler and the two years just passed, there isn't any detail at all. Except here,' she said, pointing to a paragraph barely three lines long. 'There was a sustained phase of truancy, noted but never explained. It coincides with Daniel's father leaving home, with his mother . . .'

'"Coping". Whatever that means.'

'Exactly. So in the most traumatic period of his life – not counting the actual physical trauma he seems to have suffered – Daniel barely gets noticed. He was sexually abused, probably. His father hit him, then left him. His mother – his only carer – was clinically depressed. But through all of that Daniel was . . . well . . .'

'He was alone.'

Karen nodded. 'He was alone.'

The coffee in Leo's cup had spilled onto the saucer. There were puddles, too, on the wooden tabletop and Leo dabbed at them distractedly with a napkin.

'Can we use this, do you think?' He was talking to himself as much as Karen but she answered anyway.

'You're the lawyer, Leo. It's a narrative but there's very little in the way of evidence.'

Leo frowned and raised his head. 'Why now, though? Why, if Daniel was so damaged, did it take so long for the damage to show?'

'A seed has to grow. Throw on enough manure, sprinkle a few hormones sooner or later you reap what you sow. And probably the signs were there all along. Someone has to be watching for them, however.'

Leo pondered. 'The abuse,' he said, not wanting to consider it. 'You don't think . . . I mean, his stepfather. Vincent Blake. You don't think . . .'

'He seems the type, doesn't he? But Daniel was, what? Ten when Blake came on the scene? I don't know. There's no love lost between them, clearly, but . . .' Karen tugged her lips sideways. 'There's something interesting, though. Don't you think? About Vincent's relationship with Stephanie.'

'Hm?' Leo was thinking, churning.

'Vincent and Stephanie. He bullies her and she lets him but . . . I don't know. There's something else at work there too. He's insecure, clearly. Bitter, too, about something.'

'I thought all bullies were insecure,' said Leo idly. 'I thought that's why they ended up being bullies.'

'I suppose.' Karen looked at Leo and smiled. 'You should be sitting where I am.'

Leo did not smile back. 'I'd be glad to,' he said. 'To be honest, I'd take any chair right now that wasn't my own.'

17

'You should have called me.'

'We did call you, Mr Curtice.'

'I mean right away. You should have called me as soon as it happened.'

'It was late. Gone nine. Most solicitors, in my experience, don't like to be bothered by things they think can wait until morning. Most parents, come to that.'

Bobby held open the door and Leo passed through.

'That's up to them. I, on the other hand, would have appreciated being told immediately. You have my home number, don't you? Do you need me to give it to you again?'

'No, that's fine, we have it. I apologise, Mr Curtice. These things happen unfortunately, much as we try to prevent them. They're boys, after all. If there's a way to make trouble, they'll find it. But we'll know for next time to inform you straight away.'

Leo broke step. 'Next time?'

Bobby made a gesture, conceding the poor choice of words.

*

The bruises, it turned out, were not as bad as Leo had feared. A black eye, Bobby had told him; a cut lip. Admirably restrained terminology and yet Leo had envisaged Daniel's eyelids swollen shut, his teeth gapped and veined with blood. In reality it was difficult, but for the discoloration, to distinguish the swelling that had been caused by a knuckle from the puffiness attributable to Daniel's tears. Not that this made the sight of the boy any more bearable. It was not, after all, the degree of physical harm Daniel had suffered that governed how wretched the assault would have left him feeling.

And wretched, from the look of him, was the term. He was a bundle of limbs on the bed, his spine to the wall at the pillow end, his knees drawn to his chin and his arms wrapped protectively around his shins. The curtains in the room were shut but the material was pale and the day bright. Even tucked in the room's dimmest corner, Daniel was exposed.

Leo closed the door behind him. Garrie, the security guard, had not followed him inside but recently he had tended not to. The door, however, would invariably remain open and it occurred to Leo as he entered the room that this was the first time he and Daniel had ever been properly alone: unaccompanied, unguarded, unobserved. It did not alarm him, as once it might have done. Rather, it saddened him; made him feel ashamed somehow, too.

Daniel did not speak. Leo felt the boy tracking him as he crossed from the doorway to the chair. He set down his brief-case, easing it to the floor so that it made no sound. He stood, until standing felt wrong, and then he sat. Daniel looked away, tucking his puffy eyes below the peak of his knees.

'What kind of names?'

Daniel did not reply.

'Pay no attention. Do you hear? It doesn't matter what they say. It doesn't matter what they think.'

Daniel dragged a hand across his cheek. 'S'easy for you to say.'

The boy was on the edge of the bed, legs dangling from the mattress, bare feet protruding from his tracksuit bottoms and just about brushing the linoleum. His head hung and when he spoke he spoke to the floor.

Leo was seated but barely. He had his elbows on his knees and was leaning forwards of the edge of the chair. 'How's the eye?' he said. 'Do you want some ice or something?'

Daniel just frowned.

'For the swelling. It'll make it hurt less.'

'It doesn't hurt that much. My tummy hurts more.'

His tummy. They had hit him there too, Daniel had told Leo. The oldest boy had, while the other two had held him by the arms.

The boy shifted, winced. He wiped again at his eyes.

'Did you speak to your parents?' Leo asked him. 'To your mother? Are they coming to see you?' He checked his watch. If they were coming then surely they would have been here by now.

'Bobby did,' said Daniel. 'He said . . . Mum said she wasn't feeling well. She . . . Sometimes she doesn't.'

'No. Of course. Well. She'll come by soon, I'm sure.'

Daniel raised his head. His features were wrinkled, his cheeks streaked. 'How much longer am I going to have to be in here?'

'Here? What, in your room?' Leo checked the door. 'We can go out, if you like. I'm sure we can. Do you fancy a walk? Or we could go to the games room, see if the PlayStation's free?'

'Not in here. In *here*. This place.'

Leo felt his lips part. He sighed. 'A while, Daniel.'

'Until the rain-thingummy?'

'The arraignment? Yes. At least until then.'

'What about after? Will I have to come back after?'

'That all depends. I'm sorry. It really all depends on what happens.'

'I hate it here.' There was a venom to the boy's tone, a ferocity to his expression, that Leo had almost forgotten he was capable of.

'I know. I'm doing everything I can to get you out. But, Daniel. You need to prepare yourself for the possibility that you will be here, or somewhere like it, for a very long time.'

Daniel stared at the air. Leo, watching him, might have said more. He might have said, here, this place you say you hate: it's not so bad. Compared to the alternatives, it's about as good as you could hope for.

But Leo did not have the heart.

'I didn't mean it, you know.'

Leo raised his head. They had been talking about what Daniel should wear; about his hair – which had been cropped short – and how it might be better, until the arraignment, to let it grow.

'What didn't you mean?' But almost as Leo voiced the question, he realised what Daniel was referring to.

'The girl.' Daniel was staring at his thumbnail, worrying at the flesh around it with the nails on his other hand. 'I didn't mean it.'

Leo swallowed. He folded his own hands together and felt a tension build in his grip. This, the murder itself: it was not something Daniel spoke about. Not willingly. Every detail Leo had so far managed to procure from the boy had been prised from him, and he had so far volunteered no insight beyond those Leo had gleaned long ago from reading the police reports. When Daniel talked about what had happened, it was as though he were describing a scene from a movie. His detachment was such that Leo might have wondered, had he not known better, whether the boy had been there at all.

'What do you mean, Daniel?'

Daniel switched his attention to his other thumb. 'I wanted to talk to her. That's all.' He seemed to ponder this for a while, to the point Leo felt an urge to offer another prompt. But, 'She was scared of me. Even before I'd said anything.'

'Why do you think she was scared of you?' Beyond talking, Leo kept as still as he could.

'I . . . I dunno. Probably cos I'm, like . . . you know. Ugly. Or . . . I dunno.' Still the boy stared at his hands. 'I asked her to kiss me. Just cos I knew she wouldn't.' He glanced but failed to hold Leo's eye. 'I was only joking. I wasn't going to make her. But she – ' again Daniel looked puzzled ' – she made this face. Like . . . Just this face.'

'Go on.'

Daniel dropped his chin. 'She walked away. She was laughing, like she wasn't scared any more, and I . . . I dunno. I liked it better when she was.'

Daniel's hands stopped writhing. He clasped them together, aligning the knuckles of his thumbs.

'She walked away,' Leo said and the boy nodded.

'I followed her. Not on purpose. I just started walking the same way she did and it ended up that I was following her, along the riverbank. It was cold and I . . . I just wanted to be moving.'

'Did she . . . Was she aware . . .'

'She saw me. She pretended she didn't but she did. She started singing. To annoy me. Stupid songs like the Spice Girls and that.'

'Why do you think she was trying to annoy you?'

'I dunno. It was annoying though. She knew it was.'

Leo nodded, once. 'And what happened after that?'

'I was getting closer, just cos she was walking so slow. She did that to annoy me too. I could tell. Walking like she didn't care who was following.'

'Did you speak to her? Did you say anything?'

The boy, almost undetectably, shook his head. 'I got to like . . . I dunno. Like a bus-length away. She was still singing, even louder than before. I . . .' A drop fell from Daniel's eye and burst on the back of his thumb. 'I picked up a stone. I threw it. Not to hit her but . . . I dunno. It landed closer than I thought it would.'

'What kind of stone? You mean like a rock?'

'I don't remember. It was just a stone. I didn't hit her with it.'

'No. Sorry. Go on.'

'She heard it land. The stone, I mean. She turned. She looked, like, angry. Properly angry, like teachers get. She didn't say anything, though. She stuck her tongue out. And then . . .'

Leo waited. 'And then?'

'Then she ran.'

Daniel was crying freely now. The tears drew no sound but they filled the boy's eyes to the point that he was blinking, wiping, just to be able to see.

'Would you like to take a break, Daniel? Can I fetch you some water or something?'

The boy shook his head, more forcefully this time. 'I chased her,' he said. 'Just cos she ran. I wasn't even trying to catch her but she – ' he sniffed ' – she tripped. Slipped on some ice maybe. She fell. It wasn't my fault she fell but when she did I . . . She was just . . .'

'You caught up with her.'

Daniel nodded. He ground his knuckles into his eye sockets. 'She was crying. Shouting, too. Kept going on about her coat. Her stupid coat.'

Her coat. Felicity's crimson overcoat. Leo thought of bulls, of beasts: of the instinct – irresistible; incomprehensible – to charge.

'She said she'd tell. She said she knew who I was and that it was my fault her coat was ruined. Even though it wasn't. Even though I didn't do anything. Even though it was her fault for running, for tripping, for looking at me like . . . like . . .'

Leo could imagine, all too readily, what had come next. An exchange of abuse, perhaps of blows. Felicity's terror dictating her volume; Daniel, the louder Felicity grew, ever more desperate that she should keep quiet. Him seizing her. Her flailing at him. Daniel shoving and Felicity falling and then . . . and then . . .

'I just went mad. Just, like, mad. Her coat – her stupid coat – I ripped at it just to annoy her, to piss her off, to make her as cold as I was. But her blouse, it ripped as well. And I . . . Her skin, she . . . It . . .' Daniel swallowed and his narrow neck bulged. 'I just went mad.'

Mad indeed.

But not mad enough.

'The assault,' Leo said. His voice did not falter. 'Is that when it happened?'

Daniel nodded.

'And Felicity. Was she conscious? Was she awake, I mean?'

Another nod, followed by a shake of the head. 'I hit her. With a stone. She wouldn't be quiet, not even for a minute. So I hit her.' Daniel stared at his open palm. His fingers curled, as though testing the shape of some unseen object, and then balled themselves into a fist. 'I didn't mean to kill her.' He searched for Leo through glistening eyes. 'I didn't. But then, when I saw what I'd done to her, I . . . I looked around me and . . .'

The fairy lights. The gravel. The river. And it was the river, despite what Daniel had believed at the time, that ended her life.

Leo turned away.

He brought squash. He brought biscuits. He set the tray on the floor between them and lowered himself back into the chair.

'I thought you'd be hungry. I know you said you weren't but you should try and eat something.'

Daniel said nothing. He was back at the pillow end of the bed, the sheets covering every part of him now except his neck and his puffed, pale face. Beside him, on the built-in shelf that was the bedside table, was an array of figurines: soldiers, mainly, with rifles abutting their shoulders or grenades poised to be thrown. There was a phalanx facing the window, another angled towards the door. They were on guard, clearly. Against what, Leo could not tell.

He opened the packet of Bourbons. He offered it to Daniel but the boy declined. Leo took out a biscuit for himself. He set it, after a moment, on the arm beside him.

'The arraignment,' he said. 'We still have time – three weeks or so – but at some point we need to decide.'

'I don't want to stay here,' Daniel said. 'Tell them whatever you have to so I don't have to stay here. So I can go . . .'

'Home?'

Daniel glanced. 'Anywhere. Anywhere but here.'

'Is there any reason you wouldn't want to go home, Daniel?'

'I didn't say that. I didn't say I wouldn't go home.'

'No. I know. But Karen – you remember Karen? – she thinks that perhaps there might be some reason why you wouldn't want to go back there. Why, perhaps, you shouldn't.'

Daniel's jaw tensed. 'What does she know?'

Leo brushed at the sugar on the chair from his biscuit. 'She's concerned, that's all. We both are.'

Daniel moved his eyes without turning his head. He knew. From his expression, he clearly knew exactly what Leo was talking about.

'Home would do,' he said.

'Daniel, I . . .'

'I said it would do.' The boy glared, then dropped his eyes. 'It's not like it used to be.'

Leo nodded. There was a silence and he could not think how to fill it.

'This place,' said Daniel after a moment. 'It's not so bad. Is it?'

'What do you mean?'

'I mean, it's bad, I hate it – but there are worser places. Aren't there? They could send me somewhere worse.'

Leo stared. Why he was surprised, he did not know. 'Yes,' he said. 'They could.'

Daniel's face gave a peculiar twitch, as though there was something inside him he was trying to keep from slipping out. 'Tell them what you have to,' he said. He made to say something more but seemed not to trust himself.

'If there's a trial,' said Leo, 'if we plead not guilty . . . It won't be easy. For you. For your mother.' For Ellie, he did not say. For Megan.

Daniel nodded.

'It will be painful. It will be drawn out. You'll have to stay here, at least until the trial is over. And after that . . . After that, there are no guarantees.'

No movement this time. No sound.

'Your barrister: he thinks you should plead guilty, Daniel. He thinks it's your best chance of a shorter sentence.'

Daniel's voice came in a burst. 'What about you?'

Leo took a breath. 'I think . . .' I think it shouldn't be my place. I think someone, somewhere in the system, is forcing me to decide so they won't have to. 'I think what you did was wicked,' Leo said. He expected Daniel to look away but the boy did not. 'But you need help, above all. I think you've been wronged and that someone along the line should have set it right. I think, if you plead guilty, you'd be taking on more than you deserve to.' He paused, then added, 'I think you'd be letting the rest of us off the hook.'

Daniel did not answer right away. 'Do I have a chance? If I do what you say?'

And that, really, was the question.

18

NOT EXACTLY BEACH WEATHER IS IT LEO?

NO LIES NO EXCUSES

<u>*LAST CHANCE. DROP THE CASE*</u>

There were no shards of glass this time. That, by itself, should have been a relief. But the implication that he – whoever he was – had been following, watching, just as he had threatened and despite Leo's vigilance, was somehow more unsettling than if the envelope had arrived barbed with razor blades. And if the intention was to alarm him – to panic him – then whoever wrote the notes could hardly have chosen a more economical turn of phrase. It was, thinking about it, almost as if . . . as if . . .

No. The thought was ridiculous. He was dealing with a lunatic. Someone deranged. There was simply no way that anyone Leo knew . . . That someone from work like . . . like . . . Terry, for instance. Even Terry. He was jealous, certainly, but even Terry would not stoop to this.

Closer to home, then. Who was more eager for him to drop the case than his wife? She had asked, repeatedly, and Leo had refused. They could barely have a conversation, it seemed, without Daniel becoming the theme. Maybe if Megan was even more desperate than she so often seemed? Take the man at the window, for example. Did Leo not half suspect, deep down, that the story had been a fabrication? Or, if not quite that, an exaggeration; a deliberate misrepresentation. And the phrasing. *Not exactly beach weather*. Hadn't Leo, speaking to Megan, used virtually the same expression himself?

Or Ellie. What about Ellie? She had been at the beach too. And Ellie, in her quieter, more solicitous way, seemed more upset even than her mother. Leo had put it down to the incident with the ink, her troubles at school, but perhaps the last note had also been a clue. A confession. How would *your daughter* like it? Was that Ellie's way of saying –

Your daughter. Your wife. For Christ's sake, Leo!

He wrapped the note in his palm. It crumpled easily, along the scars it had suffered after Leo had tossed it, the first time he had read it, into his office bin. He felt an urge to hurl it again but instead slid open his bedside drawer and shoved it beneath his socks and his emergency cash, atop the other two notes tucked away in their envelopes. He stood and the mattress sprung and he turned towards the door.

'Was that it?'

Ellie was at the threshold. She was sockless and damp-haired and wrapped in a dressing gown that sagged from her shoulders. She bore a towel, damp like her hair, and a book and a hairbrush. Her cheeks were flushed: from the heat of the bath water, Leo assumed, though if he had encountered her in any other guise he might have wondered whether his daughter had in fact been crying.

'Ellie. I didn't hear you.' Leo stepped away from the bedside drawer and towards the doorway, resisting the urge to glance back.

'Was that it?' Ellie said again. 'That thing you were reading?'

'Sorry? Was what what?'

'The article. I heard Mum,' Ellie added when Leo frowned. 'Is she going somewhere? Why was she talking about leaving?'

'Leaving? What do you mean? Who's leaving?'

'I don't know. Mum was talking to Grandma. She said something about . . .' Ellie ended the sentence by shaking her head, as though she were not sure, actually, what her mother had said.

'Ellie? Please. Start at the beginning.'

'I heard Mum,' his daughter said. 'On the phone, through the floorboards. She was talking to Bernice. Something about an article.'

The article. The piece in the *Gazette*. Leo had seen a copy just that morning but he had thought, if he ignored it, maybe Megan would never have to know. He had reckoned, clearly, without Terry's wife: briefed by her husband, no doubt, on Leo's hesitancy in agreeing to the interview in the first place, and with nothing else to keep her awake at night but getting to the bottom of why. 'But . . . What's this about someone leaving?'

'Mum called Grandma. Afterwards. She said . . . She definitely said something about going to stay. Or . . . I don't know. Something, anyway. It was quieter so I couldn't hear but . . . Are you breaking up?' Her tone teetered as she voiced the question.

'What?'

'You and Mum. I mean, why else would she be—'

'No! No one's breaking up. Honestly, Ellie, I promise. You misheard, that's all. I'm sure you must have misheard. She was talking about visiting, I expect.'

'She sounded angry. Talking to Grandma. She said . . . What was in the article, Dad? What did it say?'

'The article? Nothing. Nothing at all. I don't know why you think your mother would be angry.' Except, in truth, he did. He could just hear Megan's voice. *One minute you're chasing the press away, the next you're preening for the cameras.* Never mind that Leo had done his best to back out of the interview. Never mind that the article, anyway, made no mention of the Forbes case. Leo, inevitably, would be at fault. But calling her mother. *Leaving.* There was no question: Ellie, surely, had misunderstood.

'You should dry your hair,' Leo said. 'You'll catch a chill.' He made to herd his daughter towards her bedroom but Ellie held her ground.

'Ellie? Please, I really need to . . . ' Leo looked behind him at his bedside drawer. He looked through the doorway towards the stairs.

'It's not fair,' Ellie said.

Leo's attention settled on his daughter. The colour on her

cheeks had intensified and there was an unmistakable sheen now across her eyes. 'What's not fair?'

Ellie swiped at a tear. 'Just . . . Everything. School; Sophie; you and Mum. Everything.'

'Sophie?' Leo said, consciously sidestepping the you-and-Mum part. 'What's happened with Sophie?' More than his daughter's closest friend, Sophie seemed Ellie's only friend. Since they had moved to the estate – since Ellie had switched schools – even her childhood friendships seemed to have withered and she had struggled, in the bigger school, to fill the void. 'Did you argue? Look, darling. It's natural, at your age, to have disagreements.'

'It wasn't just a disagreement! And stop treating me like a little kid! I'm not a fucking five-year-old!'

Leo recoiled. 'Ellie! Mind your manners! I won't have you using language like—'

Ellie did not wait for the rest of the rebuke. She rolled her eyes and turned away.

'Ellie. Wait. Ellie!'

She stopped. She angled her shoulders towards her father but not her face. She dragged a baggy sleeve across each eye.

'Look at me. Ellie. Please. I'm sorry. Okay? You're not a kid. You're grown up enough to decide for yourself what language is appropriate. Okay?'

But when she looked at him, finally, she did not seem grown up. She seemed the child he always imagined her: confused, anxious, unsure of herself and the world.

Until she took a breath and seemed to inflate. 'You're the

one behaving like a child,' she said. 'Hiding things from Mum. Hiding things from me.'

'Hiding things?' Leo thought of the notes. 'I don't know what you're . . .' But: the article; the *Gazette*. 'I wasn't hiding things. I was just . . . I forgot to mention it, that's all. It didn't seem important.'

His daughter looked doubtful.

'You were telling me about Sophie,' Leo said.

Ellie dropped her chin. 'There's nothing to tell. She hates me, just like everyone else.'

'Ellie. Really. Why would she hate you? You're best friends. Aren't you? I thought you two were inseparable.'

'Not any more. Just this week, it's . . . Something's changed. It's like she doesn't want to talk to me, not if anyone else is around.'

'Maybe she's . . . I don't know. Maybe there's some simple reason . . .'

'It's not just her, Dad. It's everyone. Even the teachers treat me like an outcast.'

'The teachers? Come on now, Ellie, don't be ridiculous.'

'I'm not being ridiculous!'

'No. I'm sorry. I didn't mean—'

'You don't know! How could you know? You're not there! You're always at work. With *him*.'

Leo felt his jaw tighten. 'You've been talking to your mother,' he said. 'If you have questions about my work, Ellie, you should really come and speak to me.'

'Why?' she countered. 'What would you say? What could I say that would make things any different? Ever since Grandad died you never seem to notice what any of the rest of us are feeling. You don't seem to care!'

She had. She had been talking to Megan. It was the only explanation as to why they kept accusing him of the same failings.

'I'll go to your school again. I'll talk to the head. If you feel like you're being victimised then it's important that someone—'

'No! Don't! Please, Dad, don't!'

Leo sensed his exasperation showing. 'Look, Ellie. If you feel like the teachers are being unfair somehow, I don't see what other option—'

'Dad! Don't! I mean it! Please!'

'What then?' Leo spread his arms. 'What else do you want me to do? I can't just . . . It's not like I don't have other things to . . .' He shook his head and gripped his forehead.

'I want it to be over.'

Leo looked up. There were no tears now in his daughter's eyes, though the burn on her cheeks endured.

'The case. You and Mum. Sophie ignoring me, people hating me. That man taking pictures of me at the beach. I just want it all to be over.'

'It's not that simple, Ellie.'

'You asked me. You said, what else could you do? I'm telling you.'

'Yes. I know. But . . .' The plea. The trial. Leo had avoided telling his family about Daniel's decision but it was getting to the point where he would have to.

'So? When will it be over?'

'It depends.'

'On whether there's a trial.'

'Right. Exactly. On whether there's a trial.'

'Do you think there will be?'

'That's not up to me. That's up to Dan . . .' Leo, for some reason, stopped himself saying Daniel's name. 'That's up to my client. As a solicitor, I can only do as I'm instructed. It would be unprofessional of me to try to influence his decision either way.' Which seemed an odd thing for him to say – now, here, in the circumstances. But at least it was out there. He would not, he hoped, have to say it again.

'But you must know. You must have an idea.'

'Ellie. Really. It's not my—'

She stopped him with a look.

'Probably,' he said, exhaling. 'At the moment, the way things are looking, it seems likely that there will be a trial.' He flinched at the sight of Ellie's despair. 'But until the plea is entered . . . I mean, technically, at this point in time, at least until the arraignment . . .'

'But . . . How long? How long will a trial take?'

'I . . . It's difficult to say.'

'What does that mean? Days? Weeks, even?'

Leo hesitated. Weeks, certainly. Months – years, probably – counting the appeals. 'It might take a while, yes. But really, Ellie, there's no need for you to worry.'

'That's what you said before. At the start. That's exactly what you told me then!'

Which was not fair. He had warned her. That day in the car. He had said, things might get uncomfortable. He had used those very words. He would not remind her of that now, of course, because heaven knew how she would respond.

'Now you're angry.'

'What?' Leo said. 'No I'm not.'

'You are. I can tell.'

'Ellie. Don't. Don't cry, please.'

'I'm not crying,' she said with a sniff. 'I'm just . . .'

'What? Ellie, tell me.'

'I'm scared, Dad.' The tears ran now and she did not try to stop them.

'It's all right. Ellie, darling. There's nothing to be scared of.' He attempted a reassuring laugh but heard, from somewhere, a voice.

How would you like it? How would your daughter?

Leo held out an arm and Ellie allowed herself to be enfolded. Through the heavy cotton of the dressing gown, her body seemed barely to have substance at all.

19

A knock. Two beats of a knuckle. As though knocking, in this house, were the way things had always been done.

Leo waited for the door to open. It did not, right away, so he ventured a *come in* – just as his wife slid her face into the room.

'This was on the mat with the junk mail,' she said, waving an envelope and then depositing it on the nearest surface. 'And I'm ready when you are.'

Leo rolled his chair back from his desk. 'Oh. Right.' He checked his wrist.

'Whenever you are,' Megan said again. 'There's no great rush. School's not out for another half an hour.' She pressed her lips together – as close to a smile, in the past few days, as she had managed. She turned to leave.

'Meg. Wait.' Leo used his heels to drag himself closer to the door.

Megan stopped, turned. The smile, her expression said, had been a blip.

'How . . . um. How much are you taking? I mean, my golf

clubs. Should I take them out of the boot?' Were they even in the boot?

'There's a case each. And Ellie will have her school things when we pick her up.'

A case. A case was a holiday, a week away.

Megan seemed to sense his optimism. 'Mum has spares if we run out of anything. And I'll be able to borrow her car when I work out what else we need.'

Leo's focus fell to the floor.

'Are you sure?' he said. 'That it's necessary, I mean?'

Megan swallowed. 'There's a casserole in the freezer.' She faced the kitchen and spoke as though Leo was looking where she was. 'I've split it in two. Give it half an hour in the oven once it's defrosted, or blast it for a few minutes in the microwave. If you stick it in the oven, don't forget to put it in an oven-proof dish.'

'Meg.'

'Also, there's a frozen pizza. Ham and pineapple. And there's a pork chop in the fridge. You need to eat it by—'

'Meg. Please.'

Megan raised a hand to her brow. 'We've been over this, Leo.'

'We have.' They had. 'But . . .' But what?

'I need a break. From the house as much as anything. And it's clear you need to focus. If you really feel you need to do this, it would be better, for your sake, if you did it without any more . . . distractions.'

Leo nodded – not conceding the point, just bobbing past it. 'The thing is,' he said, 'I was looking at some recent cases.

At the coverage in the press once things actually got under way. And what happens is, when a trial begins, there's actually less attention in a way because of all the restric . . .'

Leo stopped himself. From the look on Megan's face, the coverage was not the point.

'I'll be in the kitchen,' she said. 'Let me know when you're ready.'

'Meg. Megan!'

He checked the kitchen. She was not in the kitchen. He checked the living room.

'Megan!'

Jesus Christ. Jesus H Christ.

'Megan! Meg! M—'

'Leo.' Megan emerged from the kitchen. 'What's wrong? I was just in the . . .' She hitched a thumb towards her shoulder but Leo crossed the hall and grabbed her arm.

'Leo!'

'Where are the car keys? Have you got the car keys?'

'For heaven's sake, Leo, what's got—'

'The car keys! Where are they!'

'On the hook! The same place they always are!'

Leo dragged his wife towards the rack by the door. Halfway there he checked himself, pulled up short.

'We should ring. Have you got the number?' He released his wife and reached the telephone table in three long strides. He picked up the receiver. 'The number. For the school. What's the number?'

'The school?' Megan's eyes broadened. 'Why? What's hap-pened? Did they call? I didn't hear the—'

'They haven't called! We need to call them! What's the number!'

Again Megan pointed towards the kitchen. 'It's in my address book. In my bag. Shall I—'

'Never mind.' Leo made to replace the receiver but missed the cradle. He let it lie. 'We'll just go. Let's just go.'

'Leo! Will you please tell me what's going on!'

Leo had hold of Megan's wrist again but this time she planted her feet.

'What are you doing! Let's go!' He pulled but Megan sidled.

'Not until you tell me what's going on!'

'I will.' Leo dragged a finger along the key rack and plucked the fob with the Volkswagen logo. 'In the car. I promise. I'll explain when we get into the car.'

'What about my suitcase? And Ellie's? I need shoes at least, Leo!'

'Here!' Leo grabbed a pair from the jumble on the mat. 'Now come on!'

Megan was in the passenger seat beside him, her finger at her heel and her cheek pressed against the dashboard. She was cringing, muttering, struggling to squeeze her feet into her daughter's trainers.

'Well?' she said. 'Are you going to explain?'

But Leo was focused on the traffic. Even on a weekday, in the middle of the afternoon, the dual carriageway was a procession.

'Leo!'

He thrust at the brakes and Megan caught her weight on her outstretched hands.

'Slow down, will you!'

Leo cursed. He flashed his lights. The driver of the bus in front responded with a gesture from his side window and seemed, deliberately, to slow. Once again Leo swore. He craned to see. There was nothing up ahead, no reason for the bus to be plodding at . . . Jesus Christ. Twenty miles an hour, when the speed limit here was, what? Sixty? They passed a sign. Forty, then. Leo made to undertake but there was a camper van mirror to mirror, with a kid driving who must have been drunk or stoned or something because he was beating the steering wheel as though it were a kettledrum.

'Leo! Please! Whatever you're rushing for, this isn't going to get us there any quicker!'

The bus, finally, gathered speed. The needle on Leo's dial nudged forty, forty-five. They were making ground now but less quickly than they needed to. An ambulance passed the opposite way – on a clear carriageway, naturally – and Leo thought of sirens, of the police, of how maybe he should have called the police. But the police would have asked him whether he had spoken to the school, told him to ring the school and then ring back, and by the time he did, by the time he explained – to the police, to the school, to the police again – they could have driven to the school themselves. If it weren't for the traffic, that is.

'Leo. Please. You're scaring me.'

A Range Rover drew alongside and Leo twitched the steering wheel as though to veer into it. The 4x4 fell back. Leo swerved into the gap and accelerated towards the roundabout.

'Where are we meeting her?'

'What? Leo!' Megan clutched at her seat.

'Ellie! Where are we meeting her!'

'At the gates! Just . . . The usual place.'

Leo slowed, slightly, yet took the roundabout in third. There were speed bumps blistering the side street and Leo surged over them, scraping the Passat along the tarmac on each downward lunge. The sound was like the world tearing and Megan, each time, gave another yell. She pressed one palm to the ceiling and clung with the other to the handle on the door. She was crying, Leo realised.

There were cars corked up ahead and children breaking from the school gates. Leo wrenched the handbrake. He opened the door and lunged with a foot but his seat belt was attached and it hauled him back. He fumbled, found the catch, and lurched once more into the street.

'Ellie!'

Leo heard his name in the wake of his daughter's, his wife's voice echoing his. Whatever she said afterwards, though, was muffled by the shrillness of the schoolyard.

'Ellie!' he called again.

There was a hatchback moving off the way Leo had arrived and he caught its bonnet with his open hands just as it slammed to a stop. Someone shouted, swore, but Leo spun away and on, through the gaps between the double-parked cars. He collided with a coat, rebounded into an open door, and somehow found himself on the pavement.

'Ellie!' He paused, raised himself on tiptoes. People were stopping now, turning to look, but when they angled their bodies towards him they only made it harder for him to see. He shoved his way through a chorus of protests and emerged into a vacuum beside the gates.

'Where is she?' He whirled, spotted Megan approaching, but not close enough yet to answer his question. He grabbed the shoulder of someone passing. 'Have you seen Ellie? Ellie Curtice?' The boy made a face and shrugged Leo off.

'Excuse me. Hey.' Leo seized someone else, a girl this time, Ellie's age, but the girl seemed unable, in her fright, to respond at all.

'Leo! What are you doing!'

'Meg. Where is she? You said here, didn't you? You said to meet here?'

'Yes but . . .' Megan checked her watch. She frowned, as though it was later than she had realised. 'Maybe she . . .' She cast about, letting the sentence dwindle. 'Ellie?' she said. 'Ellie!'

The crowd around them was drifting to a halt. It was thinning anyway beneath the reddening sky but the pupils and parents who were yet to leave had ceased chattering and were turning to stare. Leo spotted a teacher inside the gates, watching Leo with a look of alarm. He saw her collar a pupil, then propel the girl towards the main building. Leo searched the faces searching his. He yelled his daughter's name.

'Mr Curtice?'

A girl's voice; one Leo recognised. He checked about him for its source. 'Sophie!' Leo stooped and clasped his daughter's friend by the shoulders. 'Have you seen Ellie? She should be here. Have you seen her?'

Sophie was already shaking her head. 'No, she—'

'Sophie!' Megan, crouching beside him. 'Have you seen Ellie?'

'No. I was just saying. I saw her in lessons this morning but after lunch she was gone.'

No. Please God no.

'Gone?' Megan said. 'Gone where?'

'I dunno. She—' Sophie grimaced. 'Ow. Mr Curtice, you're hurting me.'

'Let go of her, Leo, for pity's sake!' Megan tugged Leo's arm and shoved at his shoulder. He released his hold at the same time and stumbled backwards, colliding with the gate behind him. He slid until he found himself sitting.

'Gone where, Sophie? Where did Ellie go?' Megan was gripping the girl's shoulders herself now, locking Sophie's eyes with her own.

'I dunno. She wasn't at the shop at lunchtime so I figured she'd gone to the park. I mean, just lately we . . . we haven't been . . .' The girl looked towards the ground. 'When I didn't see her this afternoon, I just assumed she must've gone home. That maybe someone had said something or something. To upset her, I mean.'

Leo could only watch. He could only listen. He wanted to lift a hand from the floor but sensed, if he let go, that he would not be able to stop himself falling.

Megan, in front of him, was standing, scanning the street. Coatless, she shivered, but made no move to wrap herself in her arms. She started to speak, to nod, and Leo was aware, vaguely, of a voice drawing closer from across the playground. Ms Bridgwater. The head teacher. Stamping her authority on a situation that was already beyond her control. And Megan again, raising her voice now, hurling gestures towards the school, along the street, back to the school and then —

And then she stopped. She fell silent. She looked at Leo and angled her head. She said something, a question, and Leo looked up at his wife but could not answer. Because he was right. Now that he had let go it seemed like he was tumbling, like the world all of a sudden had given way. In its place there was just a void, an encroaching blackness, and the words on the page he had drawn from his pocket and was somehow holding out towards his wife –

YOU SHOULD HAVE LISTENED

YOU DONT DESERVE A DAUGHTER

– scrawled in blood and underlined with Ellie's hair.

She is early herself but he is already seated. It is not like him, she thinks. But then who is she, these days, to be able to judge?

She slides from her coat but no one offers to take it from her. When no one comes to direct her to the table either, she drapes the coat over her arm and makes her own way across the restaurant floor. It is busy for brunch-time and she has to weave and hoist her coat and apologise, more than once, for knocking other patrons' chairs. Feeling hot, and damp from the rain, and conscious that her hair, probably, is a frizzy mess, she arrives. Leo stands to greet her.

This, ridiculously, given what she has come here to say, is the moment she has been dreading. Not the act of coming face to face after such a long time but the decision, once they are within range, about how she should greet her husband. A kiss, she thought, on the cheek but Leo is caught between the table and the leather bench and Megan, to reach him, would have to lunge. An embrace – a hand on the shoulder, a brief coming together – is her backup but this, in the circumstances, would prove awkward too. A handshake is out of the question so in the end Megan flounders. She says hi, then hi again, then smiles, sort of, and just sits.

He is staring. Megan does her best, with a surreptitious palm, to smooth her hair.

But, 'You look well,' Leo says. 'You really do.'

In spite of her relief, she could take offence – what did he expect? – but his manner is earnest and his expression uncertain and she thinks that today she should endeavour to be kind. Compliments, she knows, are not her husband's vernacular. He utters them, when he utters them, with the same failed fluidity that defines his French.

'You look well yourself,' she says. And this is indeed being kind because Leo looks anything but. He has shaved and is neatly turned out – a shirt collar beneath a V-neck jumper and the colours even vaguely coincide but there is no dressing up a dishevelment that runs deeper. His skin is wan, sunless. He has lost weight. He had some to spare but it has slipped most noticeably from his cheeks. As for his hair: when she last saw him it was already deserting him and he has pre-empted the sedition of the rest by clipping it tight. The result, a stranger might say, was making the best of a bad lot – better than a combover, certainly. But it is not Leo.

She decides. If she was not sure before, she is sure now.

'Would you like a drink?' Leo already has a coffee but is directing a finger at a passing waiter. The waiter – a boy, practically, and east European, Megan predicts – has stopped mid stride. He does not have long, the bustle and his bearing convey. Quickly now, please: what will it be?

'A cappuccino?' says Leo. 'Right?'

The waiter nods and is about to dart on but Megan reaches. 'A Bloody Mary,' she says. 'Lots of spice.' Again the waiter nods. Megan fails to look at Leo as she turns. She needs the drink. She is under no obligation to explain why. And now, she realises, she might un-decide. Such is her see-saw antagonism, her decision might tip on the weight of what Leo says next.

'So,' Leo says.

Megan lifts her head. Her husband is staring at his coffee. 'So.'

'You heard, then. The news.'

'I did.' She has an urge to reach across. 'Leo, I'm . . .' Don't say it. You're not, so don't say it. 'What happened? Do you know?'

Her husband has a gesture. It is not for strangers because it would be construed as rude. But for friends, family, Leo has a gesture – a flick of a finger, a turn of the head, a tightening across the lips – that says, I don't want to talk about it. He will, Megan is convinced, use it now.

Instead he sighs. He picks up his teaspoon. He does not seem to know what to do with it so he puts it down again. 'The short version?' he says. 'Or the long?'

Megan's Bloody Mary arrives. It is a bouquet of celery in a blood-red vase. She would laugh, ordinarily. 'I don't have anywhere I need to be,' she says instead. It is not true but she says it anyway.

Leo regards her, as though uncertain whether she means what she says. But he seems, in the end, to be convinced. He sighs again.

He is grieving, Megan realises. After all these years and after everything that has happened, he is suffering. For this child, this boy – this man, in the end: Leo is aching from the loss.

Megan shivers. She cannot help it and she cannot hide it. Her husband, though, does not notice. He is searching for his voice in his coffee cup.

'It was the guards,' he says. 'Two of them. Allegedly, of course. They haven't admitted anything and from what I hear each one's covering for the other, blaming some mysterious inmate. But the guards. Can you believe it?' Leo smiles and shakes his head.

Megan looks at her hands.

'He was up for parole,' Leo said. 'Or he would have been. Maybe that was why. Huh. I didn't think of that. Maybe just the thought of them letting him out . . .' Leo shakes his head again. 'Such rage,' he says, as much to himself. 'So much rage.'

'Don't tell me you can't understand it, Leo. Not now. Not after everything that . . . that we . . .' Megan's anger, from nowhere, overwhelms itself.

'What? No. Meg, please. I didn't mean . . .'

She turns her cheek. She presses her lips. Leo, she can tell, is searching for the words that might appease her but she could save him the effort because there are none, not in that moment. Her husband, however, seems to have reached the same conclusion because the silence stretches.

When Megan turns back he avoids her eye.

'It was the guards,' Megan says. Her voice is taut but composed. 'You were saying: it was the prison guards.'

Now Leo looks: a child peeking from beneath the covers.

He nods, tentatively. 'That's right.' He clears his throat. 'That's what people seem to think.' He sits straight.

'What did they . . .' Megan, too, adjusts herself in her seat. 'The guards. How did they . . .'

Leo does not answer right away. He is staring again. He wants to ask, she can tell: do you really want to know? Probably she does not but she can hardly confess to that now.

'They stabbed him,' Leo says and that, Megan thinks, is that – at least now they can move on. Leo, though, is not finished. 'They stabbed him,' he says again, 'and punctured his lung. They locked him in the shower block and they watched through the glass as he drowned in his own blood. Allegedly,' Leo adds. His smile, on anyone else, would seem dangerous.

Megan shuts her eyes. She makes a motion with her hand, as though Leo had not already stopped talking.

When she recovers herself, he is watching her. There is something in his look that was not there before.

'He's dead, Megan. Daniel Blake. He's dead.'

She shakes her head. What is that supposed to—

'That's why you're here. Right? That's why you wanted to see me. He's dead, I promise you. They've had their blood.'

And so, his expression seems to say, has she.

'Leo. Really. Is that what you . . . Surely you can't think that I . . .'

He waits.

'. . . that I wanted – ' she lowers her voice ' – *this*.' She is shaking her head and Leo seems suddenly uncertain.

Until: 'The divorce,' he says and his shoulders wilt. 'Right? Closure, finally. That's what this is about?'

214

Still Megan shakes her head. 'No. Leo, no.' She almost laughs. How has she behaved? How has she treated him that he holds her intentions in such base regard?

Leo is searching the tablecloth for direction. He looks at Megan and his eyes draw narrow. Well? he does not say. What, then?

'The house.'

Coward.

'The house? What about the house?'

Nothing. Forget the house. This has nothing to do with the house.

'I'm planning . . . I'm planning to sell it.'

Leo takes a moment to react. 'Okay,' he says. 'That's up to you.'

'I saw an agent. You wouldn't believe how much he said it was worth. I mean, we'd split what was left, obviously. After we pay off the mortgage.'

'Sure. That's fine. It's up to you.'

'You don't mind?'

'Why would I mind? It's your house, Meg. That's what we agreed.'

'I live there. That doesn't make it mine.'

'No, that's true but . . .'

'It's a lot of money, Leo. Aren't you interested in knowing how much?'

So much for the sweetener. So much for softening the blow. But how, really, did she expect him to react, given how much each of their attitudes towards money has changed? After Ellie, it hardly seemed important to either of them. It is the reason

– one of them – why their parting was so effortless. There was nothing, no complications even, to bind them together.

'I earn enough, Meg. I trust you. Sell it for what you can and take what you need.'

Megan nods. She fiddles with the straw in her drink.

'Meg.'

She looks up.

'This isn't about the house,' Leo says. 'Is it?'

And the surprise, this time, must surely show on her face. But again, why should it? She knows him; he knows her. After the greater part of twenty years together, there is no escaping that.

Except, if today proves nothing else, it is that Leo does not know Megan as well as he might think. He does not know, for instance, how furious she is, how it feels sometimes like she is choking on hate. He does not know how atrophied her heart has become, how ruthless that allows her to be, how pitiless. He does not know, after twenty years of being together and a decade now of being apart, what his wife is capable of.

'No,' Megan says. 'It's not.'

And he does not, above all, know what she has done.

20

He was conscious, through it all, of the contradiction. On the one hand he willed an acceleration because everything, it was clear to Leo, was taking far too long. People walked, they did not run. They asked, then asked again, then went away and came back with the same questions. Just to clarify, they would explain, even though Leo – in the first instance; certainly by the third – had been perfectly clear. He knew he had been clear because he knew too the effort it was costing him: to reason when he wanted to rage; to be considered, considerate, when the only consideration he had was finding his missing daughter. Some of those he spoke to suggested he sit. They offered him tea or coffee or water or anything at all and they actually suggested he sit. No one sits! he wanted to scream. No one drinks! No one eats, sleeps, shits until we find my *fucking* daughter!

As though he were entitled to rage. As though he were entitled to direct his anger anywhere but at himself. More haste. More speed. It seemed, on the one hand, the only prophylactic to insanity.

But on the other. On the other, every minute was a minute lost, every second a second wasted. Each tick, each tock, was a slice stolen from his daughter's life, another moment of Ellie suffering. It was time, moreover, they needed to be using. Leo knew enough about these things to know that. He knew, or could guess, what every passing hour was costing them; how for each day they lost, so their chances on the next would diminish. And so he checked the time incessantly, to monitor it, scrutinise it, see that it did not snatch. It was like a gluttonous child, he decided, reaching with flabby fingers as soon as Leo turned his back. And it stole, when it stole, by the fistful.

Speed things up. Slow things down. He would have had it both ways if he could have, though of course he ended up with neither. There was just his grief – a wound that was tearing at the edges – and the suffocating clasp of his guilt.

Leo saw his wife suffering too and in a way it was the hardest thing to bear.

Their marriage, within hours, became a coalition. As Leo watched his wife watching him recount to the police the litany of his stupidity, he became aware of this shift in status, this downgrading. Megan was only at his side, from that point on, because they had a common goal, a common enemy. Finding Ellie was all that mattered. Everything else would wait.

The waiting. They should not give up hope, they were told – there was every chance Eleanor was alive. Writing notes is one thing but taking a life . . . That was something else.

But the waiting, they would find, was the hardest part. The lack of news, the lag in knowing, it's always the thing that hurts most. Which was codswallop, actually. Utter crap. Leo would have taken not knowing over what he did know. He would have taken waiting over the fear, swelling in his gut, that the waiting would turn out to be in vain.

On the first day, anyway, there was no time for it. They were at the school, then inside it, then at the police station Leo already knew so well. There were questions and more questions and statements and tears, followed by a trip in a marked unit to Linden Park. A forensic team, when they got there, was already packing up, having taken what they could from the perimeter of the house. Something, Leo overheard them saying, probably nothing. There was another police officer inside, discreetly established beside the telephone table and offering, as her training seemed to mandate, to stick on the kettle. Her colleagues already had possession of the notes – Leo had told them at the station where they could find them – but the officer who had driven them needed a photograph, if they didn't mind: something recent. He tried insisting he only needed one but Megan sent him off carrying a shoebox.

The waiting, Leo supposed, might have started then. Megan, though, made calls – to friends, relatives, boyfriends, suspected boyfriends, hospitals even though the police were taking care of the hospitals. Leo, at first, listened through the kitchen door. There was no spare phone line – Megan was using a pay-as-you-go the police had given them and the landline, it went without saying, was to be kept free – and there was no one, phone lines aside, Leo could think to call. What could anyone, anyway, have told them? They already knew who did not have Ellie. They knew where their daughter was not. So Leo listened, until Megan's family began to arrive, at which point he unsnagged a scarf from the coat rack and cast himself into the night.

He meant to drive. He had the car keys, somehow, in his palm but no recollection when he reached the garage of what had happened to the car itself. It was at the school, presumably. Double-parked in the middle of the street. It would not have been, of course, but it made sense, sort of, to go back and look. It was close to the place Ellie had last been sighted and so as close to his daughter physically as Leo could imagine how to be.

The cold forced him on. Three hours later, with the car keys still in his hand, it forced him back. He craved news as much as his extremities demanded warmth. But he knew, as he reached the edge of the estate, not even to within sight of their house, that there would be none. He could feel it in his gloveless fingers and see it in the bruise of the dawning sky. There would be nothing to do when he reached home except pick up a coat this time and head out again.

He was joined by Megan's brother. Until the press briefing, it was how Leo spent the second day: in the front seat of Peter's Volvo, discovering how sprawling a city this small town of theirs really was. How many walls there were, how many doorways. How many alleyways and cellars and outbuildings and bushes and vans and car boots and bins.

She could be anywhere. There, here, there, and all they were doing was driving past.

'Stop,' Leo said, and Peter stopped. It was the first word either one of them had said since Peter had started the engine.

'There.'

Peter looked and he did not argue. They got out of the car and they searched, then returned an hour later with mud on their shoes and rips in their jackets and fifty square yards better off.

At the press conference, Leo did the talking. They did not discuss that he would but Megan was in no state to do anything except sit by Leo's side. Before it began Leo felt strangely detached. He listened to the audience tuning up and knew the performance was about to start but was somehow convinced it never would. It was only when they led him on set and the lights and the shutter clicks hailed him did the enormity of his task cause him to falter. Here, now: this was it. His best and perhaps only chance to make up for what he had done to his daughter. To save her, his family too. To plead for help and for mercy and for forgiveness, all while holding back the tears.

So: are you ready, Mr Curtice? Over to you.

He did great. That is what they told him. Even though he did not finish. Even though he made it barely halfway through the statement and stuck, like vinyl, on a single word. Please, he said.

Please.

*

It was Ellie's blood. It was Ellie's hair. Not that there had been any doubt. Not that the absence of doubt made the news, when it came, any easier to bear.

This is what he would do.

He would take a knife, like this knife in his hand, just a kitchen knife but sharp enough, easily, to slice through flesh, and what he would do is, he would stab him here. Like *that*. Just above the belt buckle. And he would grasp the hilt, hold it tight, and it would resist, he imagined, because of the muscle, but he would drag the knife up, like *this*. To the ribcage, maybe; until he hit bone. Then, what he would do is, he would twist. He would adjust his grip on the handle and he would take his time about it and he would make sure he could see his eyes, that *he* could see *his*, and he would twist, like this, and keep twisting and keep twisting, until—

'Mr Curtice? Is everything okay?'

Leo spun.

He nodded.

He released his grip on the knife and laid it on the kitchen counter.

There was a sighting. Dozens, actually, but this one, on day three, seemed something more. Annie, the female officer who had her finger, always, on the kettle switch, told them as soon as she got off the phone. They should not get their hopes up, she said. A sighting was nothing more than that. But the witness seemed reliable and the description accurate and it had been verified, independently, by more than one source.

Even Annie, as she spoke, could not suppress a smile. See, she told Leo and she placed a hand on his forearm. Didn't she say he had done great?

She made tea. They waited for Annie's colleague to arrive and as they burned their mouths on the bitter brew, Annie told them what she knew. The original call had come from an old lady. Old-ish, she amended when she saw Leo's face, and she didn't even wear glasses. She had seen a girl matching Ellie's description at the town end of Bonhay Road. She saw her twice, in fact, which is why the woman noticed her. The first time the girl was with someone, the second time she seemed to be alone. A man, Annie added, before they could ask: the girl was with a man. The witness could not describe him other than that he was tall, broad and definitely older than the girl. The girl, though. Her height, her hair, her shoes, her coat – everything seemed to match. And this was yesterday. Late evening. Which meant . . .

They did not need to be told. It meant, if it was true, that their daughter, twelve hours ago, had been alive.

And, 'She was with someone,' Leo said. 'But then she wasn't.'

Which might have meant something too.

They searched door to door, alley to alley, garden by garden.

Over a hundred officers, they were told, which made it the biggest concentrated police operation the county had seen in . . . Well. Annie glanced at Leo. In a little while, anyway. There were volunteers, too. The type of people who had started writing the Curtices letters. The search had been going on already, of course, but not in such a tightly defined area. Before the sighting the police had been scattered: in the streets around Ellie's school but also in the wasteland along the Exe and among the garages in the corners of the trading estates. Dumping grounds, in other words. Places where something, girl-sized, might easily be disposed of. Now, though, they had a lead. A chance, was the unspoken implication, that they might actually find something.

It went on all day. Into the night, too, with a helicopter borrowed from the Met tracking its spotlights along the line search. Leo and Megan asked what they could do to help but the answer, inevitably, was drink more tea. They obliged, grudgingly, but only because they were invited to do so in the trailer that became the central command post. From their seats in a dimly lit corner they heard everything they needed to and several things, unredacted, they almost certainly were not supposed to. That the girl had been found, for instance. That her name was Caitlyn. That she had been out the night before arguing with a boyfriend her mother did not know she had. That she were the spitting image, Sarge, but that it weren't her. That the only thing left, the sarge supposed, was to drag the river.

It did not get any worse. Surely. Feet yielding to the mud, skin scored by the wind and rain, convinced every diver was about to emerge with your daughter's body. Not that the mud mattered. Not that the weather mattered. And he was forgetting how much worse, in an instant, things might be.

*

They spoke about currents. They said it might look calm but down below, at this time of year, and shook their heads. Someone glanced over at Leo, not having realised he was standing so close. Leo, shivering, turned his gaze towards the sea.

The fingerprints surrounding the letter box belonged to the postman. The footprints around the window were barely footprints at all. There was a thumbprint on one of the notes but a thumbprint, without a thumb, was about as much use as . . . well . . .

The sentence hung.

On day five, in the kitchen, he broke the mugs. Every one of them, starting with the one in his hand that was full of tea. He did not ask for it. He did not want it. So he carried it into the kitchen and looked for somewhere to put it down but he did not want to put it down, he wanted to throw it.

He hurled it at the hearth. He opened the cupboard and reached past the saucers and one by one hurled the other mugs too.

Every.

Last.

One.

The noise was exhilarating. The action of it, too. When the mugs were done he considered the saucers but by that point there were people in the room.

What happened? What's going on? Are you all right, Mr Curtice? The moment passed. The madness. Leo breathed and almost laughed. He said it's fine, everything's fine, and then crunched across the china to fetch the broom.

They decided, in the end, to release the sketch.

Leo watched his wife consider the picture and could tell she did not think it right. But this was, what? The fifth version? It looked like the first, which in turn looked nothing like the man Leo had imagined. Not that it should. It was Megan who had seen the face at their window: the man, they assumed, who had kidnapped their daughter. In spite of Leo's instincts, they had no choice but to trust Megan's.

'The beard is right,' Megan said, exactly as she had said the previous five times. 'But the rest . . .' She closed her eyes, as though to summon the face. She opened them, glowered at the sketch. 'Maybe the first version,' she said. 'Or . . .' She glanced at the policemen, seated side by side at the kitchen table. They in turn shared a look.

'Take your time, Mrs Curtice.'

Again she stared. 'No,' she said at last. She slid the sheet of paper towards them. 'This is the one. I . . . It's as close as I can get.'

The policemen, once more, caught each other's eye. DS Bromley, the more senior, blinked a nod.

'It's two eyes and a beard,' Leo overheard the junior detective whispering later. 'Take away the beard and we'd be looking for an egg.'

Whomever he was talking to laughed. 'Let's just hope he doesn't shave.'

*

Megan's brother had the couch. Her mother took the spare room. Megan slept, if that was the word, in Ellie's room. She would have anyway, Leo told himself.

A week passed.

There were phone calls but none that counted. There were letters but none like before. It was baseless but today, somehow, was the day they had been working towards. It was the day, more accurately, they had been working against.

It felt no different. It felt like yesterday, like tomorrow. It felt like it would always feel like this and Leo wondered, as he rose in the still-dark and fumbled for the bed sheets he had tossed onto the floor in the night, whether that were true. What would change, and when. How long it would be until Annie stopped coming, until Peter returned home, until Megan's mother left and took Megan with her. What he would do when Megan went. Whether he even deserved to care.

He wondered, most of all, about Ellie – about how long he would be able to keep wondering. Because beyond the press of some arbitrary deadline, Leo sensed the imminence of something greater. It was like a beast, stalking him, that he knew would not be kept at bay forever. He could not yet see it but he could smell it and imagine its grip around his throat. It was acceptance. It was certainty. It was knowing, not just suspecting, that his daughter was already dead.

21

The room, when Leo entered, fell silent. He hesitated at the threshold and considered, briefly, turning around. There were people in their seats but none of them – not John, nor Alan, nor Stacie – seemed able to hold Leo's eye. There was a temp, though – Amy, Leo thought her name was – and when Leo noticed her she smiled, just barely, and it was enough to draw Leo in. He nodded and smiled back and ventured, through a snag in his throat, a good morning. He dropped his chin and aimed himself towards his desk.

John twitched a greeting as Leo passed. Alan, likewise, dipped his head and even managed Leo's name. Leo uttered Alan's back. He set down his briefcase beside his desk and fumbled frozen-fingered with the buttons of his overcoat and managed, after a struggle, to free his arms. He shook the coat straight and held it up as he turned, meaning to arrange it on the back of his chair. His chair, though, was gone. In its place was something older, limbless, with a wound deep into the sponge of the seat. The upright segment appeared flimsy and Leo was unsure whether it would withstand the weight of his coat.

'Um.'

Leo turned.

'I think, um,' said Alan, on his feet now and standing close by. 'I think maybe Terry . . . er . . . borrowed your chair.'

Leo looked across the aisle towards Terry's desk. Leo's chair, unoccupied, was alongside it, set low and adorned with matching coccyx cushion and lumbar roll.

'Oh.' Leo considered the chair he had been allotted in exchange. He sat, gingerly, and placed his coat in a bundle on the floor. The chair squawked as he moved.

'I'm sure he was only . . . That he wouldn't mind if . . . I'll wheel it across for you, shall I?'

'Sorry?' Leo looked up from his desk, which had become home in his absence to nothing he recognised. 'No, really. It's fine.' He lifted a ream of copy paper from his mouse pad.

'Here. Let me take that at least. And these.' Alan used the block of paper as a tray, stacking it with junk mail and discarded folders and uncovering, as he cleared the surface, a picture of Ellie.

They both saw it. They both stared. Alan made a noise like something in his throat had slipped sideways.

The external line rang and Alan turned but John was quicker.

'Corker and Copeland,' he chimed, hunching as he spoke as though the atmosphere in the office were a squall. Leo, involuntarily, tensed. He watched for John to turn, to say, Leo, you need to take this, and for a smile to displace his discomfort. But, instead, 'He's in a meeting,' John said, not even looking Leo's way, and he offered, quite cheerfully, to take a message.

Leo swallowed. He faced his monitor. For no other reason than to escape his reflection, he turned the computer on. Something clicked, whirred, and Leo was content while he waited just to sit. He felt his focus begin to smear and that was fine too because it meant the world, temporarily, softened.

The machine chimed. It was waiting for his password. Leo allowed himself to be entranced for a moment by the blinking cursor, then reached one finger to the letter e.

'Excuse me. Alan?'

'Leo. What's up, buddy?'

'I was just . . .' Leo pointed to his workstation. 'I was looking for some files. From the Daniel Blake case. I thought I'd left them on my desk but . . . Would someone have moved them, do you know?'

'The Blake case?' Alan made a face as though Leo had lost his mind. 'Is that why you're . . . I mean . . .' He recovered himself. 'Howard might have them. Or, um, Terry.' He twisted away as he said the name, perhaps hoping that Leo would not quite catch it. He tipped his head towards Howard's office. 'Howard's in with Jenny, running through some paperwork, but Terry – ' he leant to see the clock on the office wall ' – Terry should be back any—'

'Leo?'

'Ah!' said Alan, gesturing. He beamed at Leo and then sank

into his chair, immediately busying himself with something – anything – from his in-tray.

Terry was hauling at his scarf as he drew close. His head was set at an angle, in part because the scarf seemed to be forcing it that way but as though he were wary, too, that Leo might be an apparition. He offered his hand, cautiously, and Leo took it.

'Leo? What are you doing here? We thought you'd be . . . well . . .' Terry's eyes caught on something at Leo's shoulder. Leo's chair? 'How are you though?' Terry said. 'And . . . er . . . Mandy? Your wife. How are you both coping? Have you heard any—'

'We're fine. Thank you, Terry.'

Terry took a moment to consider Leo's response. 'Good,' he said. 'That's . . . er . . .'

'I was just asking Alan,' Leo said. 'About the Blake files. I wondered whether you might know where I could find them.'

Terry was halfway out of his jacket. 'The Blake files?' He glanced at Alan but Alan's eyes leapt for safety. 'They're on my desk, Leo.' Terry smoothed his jacket over his arm. 'Most of them, anyway. The rest are with Howard.' His tone was kind but overly so.

'I see,' Leo said. 'May I have them back?'

It was a joke, Terry seemed to think, with a punchline that had gone over his head. 'Have them back?' He turned to Alan, half laughed. 'Why would you want them back?'

Leo did not return Terry's smile. 'They're my files. It's my case.'

'But you're . . . You've been . . .'

'I've been gone a fortnight. Not even that. And the arraignment's not until Friday.'

'Yes. But. Leo, I—'

'There's no reason for me to relinquish my responsibilities. I know the case; I'm up to speed. Unless there have been any developments I should be aware of?'

'Well,' said Terry, 'actually . . .' and then he shook his head as though to clear it. 'Why are you here, Leo? I thought . . . I mean, this thing with your daughter . . . Shouldn't you be . . .'

'What?' said Leo. 'Shouldn't I be . . . What?'

Again Terry shook his head. 'I don't know.' He gestured towards the door to the street, turned back with an upraised palm.

'You think I should be out there?' Leo said. 'You think I should be checking the dustbins maybe? The gutters? You think perhaps I've been sitting on my arse for two weeks, catching up on daytime television?'

'No. Of course not. I didn't mean—'

'I haven't forgotten about my daughter, Terry. I'm not here because I woke up this morning and thought, wow, actually, it'll probably all turn out fine. I might as well just head into the office.'

'Leo. Look, I—'

'I don't need to be reminded. That's all. Not every second. Not in every conversation I have.'

'Please. Leo. If you'll just—'

'I'd like the files please, Terry. *My* files. Daniel is my client, my responsibility. I'm not just going to forget about him. Not now. Especially now. I mean, Ellie, she . . .' Leo's voice faltered. Whatever he had intended to say, he could not bring himself to say it.

The telephone rang. No one answered it.

Someone coughed and Leo focused.

'Terry. May I have the files. Please.'

Terry ran his tongue beneath his upper lip. 'I'm sorry, Leo. I can't give them to you.' He folded his arms – slowly, as though to temper the hostility of the gesture.

Everyone in the office, Leo knew, was watching to see how he would respond. He tapped his fingertips against his thigh. 'They're on your desk. Is that what you said?' He began to turn. 'In that case, maybe I'll just—'

Terry seized Leo's arm. His hands were in proportion to the rest of him but his stubby fingers had a strangler's grip.

'Leo. Stop. Talk to Howard. Okay? Let's both of us go and talk this through with Howard.'

Leo looked at Terry's hand on his arm. He gave a jerk and recovered his shirtsleeve.

He led the way.

'Listen, Howard. Before Leo says anything, I think I should tell you—'

Their boss was seated at his desk. Jenny was standing at his shoulder, studying the same sheet of paper he was. Terry had blundered in without knocking but Howard's surprise, on seeing Leo, cut him short.

'Leonard,' said Howard, raising his head.

'Howard, listen I—'

Howard held off Terry with a finger. 'What are you doing here? What about your . . . Shouldn't you be . . .'

'Have they found her, Leo?' said Jenny. 'Did they catch him?'

Leo, from the doorway, looked at Jenny and his eyes, unexpectedly, stuck. He had never before noticed the resemblance. She was fair, like his daughter, and just as freckled. She was taller, slightly, and older, obviously, but she might have been an image of Ellie as, say, an undergraduate. The Ellie he would never get to see.

He reached for something to hold on to.

'Leonard? Are you okay?' Howard rounded his desk.

'Howard, listen. It's ridiculous. He can't possibly expect to walk in here and just demand—'

'Terence! Please! Can't you see the man is unwell?'

Howard drew closer. Jenny, as though startled by Leo's reaction, wilted into the corner.

'I'm fine,' Leo said. He steadied himself. 'I'm just . . . just tired, that's all. I'm fine, really.' He held off Howard's outstretched hand. He stood straighter.

'Would you like some water, Leonard? Or a hot drink? Some coffee maybe, or some—'

'No! Thank you. Really, Howard. I promise you I'm fine. I'd like to . . . I wanted . . . I'm here to talk about Daniel.' He felt an urge to look again at Jenny but resisted. 'Just Daniel,' he said.

'Daniel? Daniel Blake?'

Leo nodded.

'It's being taken care of, Leonard.' Howard smiled. 'Really, there's no need for you to worry. You obviously have more important—'

'It's my case.'

Howard looked to Terry. Terry looked knowingly back.

'Of course it is,' Howard said. 'And you've done a fine job. But with everything that's happened, no one's expecting you to—'

'Daniel is. Daniel needs me.'

Howard's smile began to fray. 'Leonard. Really. Terence here has your notes, he's familiar with the case.'

'He has my notes. He doesn't have my relationship with the boy.'

Terry grunted. 'A good thing too,' he muttered.

Howard, caught between his two employees, seemed suddenly unsure of his bearings. He glanced about. 'Let's sit. Shall we?'

No one moved.

'I just need the files, Howard. I'll catch myself up and then go and see Daniel this afternoon.'

From her spot in the corner, Jenny took a step towards the door. 'If it's okay with you, I should probably . . .' She pointed out her escape route but hesitated and lost her opportunity.

'For pity's sake, Howard,' said Terry. 'Just tell him. Can't you?'

Leo glared. He turned to Howard. 'Or if it's a question of time. If you think we should try for a deferment . . .'

'Deferment? Christ, Leo, what the hell do we need a deferment for!'

'The Crown would agree,' said Leo, ignoring Terry and facing his boss. 'Surely. Given the circumstances.'

'That's not the point!' Terry, too, appealed to Howard. They might have been advocates in a courtroom, their boss the sitting judge. 'Howard. Really. Don't you think—'

'Enough!' Howard raised his hands, lifting his palms close to his ears. 'Gentlemen, please. That's quite enough.' He glared at Terry and only reluctantly, it seemed, addressed Leo. 'Leonard. Listen. Things have moved on. Surely you can understand that. Your priority now should be your family. Don't worry about Daniel Blake.' He attempted another smile. 'It's being taken care of. Terence here—'

'Terry doesn't give a damn about Daniel! If it were up to him, the boy would have been strung up by now in his cell!'

Terry brandished a finger. 'Now wait just a minute—'

'Terence is a professional, Leonard.' Howard's expression set stern. 'As, may I remind you, are you. There is no need for acrimony, particularly given that Terry has acted entirely properly since assuming your responsibilities. The boy's parents are happy, the barrister's happy, even your psychologist—'

'Karen? You spoke to Karen? And Dale. You spoke to Dale?' Leo swung his ire from Howard to Terry and back again.

'Someone had to,' Terry mumbled and Howard stung him with a look.

'Naturally we did,' Howard said to Leo. 'The arraignment, as you know, is on . . . Let's see . . .'

'Friday.' Leo and Terry spoke as one. They exchanged scowls.

'Friday. Exactly. So obviously we didn't have time to—'

'What about Daniel?' Leo interrupted. 'You said his parents were happy, that Dale was happy. What about the client?'

Howard was content, this time, to let Terry answer.

'The client,' Terry said, emphasising the word just as Leo had done, 'is happy enough too. I saw him this morning. That's what I wanted to say to you,' he told Howard. 'He's given me my instructions. He couldn't have been clearer. He's happy, finally, that someone has spelled out to him exactly what's at stake.'

Leo faced him. 'What's that supposed to mean?'

Terry splayed his hands. 'Just what I said. I'm not going to start criticising, Leo. Not given what's happened to your kid.'

'Don't let it stop you, Terry! Criticise away, if you feel the urge!'

'Gentlemen! Please! Let's try and keep this amicable, shall we?'

Leo glared and Howard recoiled. Leo might have said something too but Terry's words finally resonated. 'What instructions? What did you do, Terry? What did you say to him?'

His parents are happy. The barrister's happy. Even Karen . . .

'Terry? Answer me. What did you tell Daniel he should do?'

Terry, though, did not reply. His expression said enough.

22

He had not planned to be here. He had been awake from three and in his car by five and here, from seven, only by an accident of his subconscious. For some time he had sat, in the cinch of his seat belt and with the engine mumbling, until he had overcome his reluctance to test the silence. At first it had been consuming – overwhelming, almost – but it fissured after a moment and the world outside became audible through the cracks: the sleepy groan of the sign on the roadside wall of the pub; gulls or gannets, not yet in full voice but clearing their throats once in a while as they sketched shapes against the pallid blue sky; the river, beyond the bank bordering the car park, bloated from the rain and spilling itself either side. And the cold. Leo could hear it, somehow. Scratching its icy fingers against the windscreen and beckoning him from the waning warmth of the car's interior.

He released his seat belt, let it slide across his chest. He tugged his woollen hat below his ears and searched the car seat next to him for his gloves. Beneath the maps and the flyers and the half-eaten sandwiches wrapped in foil, he found only the left. The right was not on the floor either, nor tucked down the side of the seat, so Leo settled for wearing one.

The air, unexpectedly, was still. The sign continued to creak and the treetops continued to lurch but where Leo had stopped the car he was sheltered from the wind by the walls of the pub. It was as cold as he had feared, however, and he drew the zip of his anorak tight to his chin. He checked about, as though uncertain in which direction to walk, though he had known what route he would take, really, the moment it had registered where he had arrived. He drove his hands deep into his pockets and crunched across the gravelled car park in the direction of the river.

He suspected he was being watched. Not because he felt it, in the hairs on his neck or otherwise, but because it was inconceivable his presence was not being tracked. He had seen her every day, the landlord had said. Every school day, at least. From his morning spot by the window in the kitchen, he noticed everything that passed his pub between just gone seven until just about nine. Which was not a lot, as it happened. And if he had noticed Felicity on the day she was killed – if he knew, as he did now, that he had been the last person, but one, to see her alive – how could he fail to be watching on every day that followed?

Leo wondered what the landlord – Lodge? Loach? – would be thinking of him if he were watching. Whether he would assume Leo was a journalist, slower or more persistent than all the others, or some morbid breed of tourist, of which he had no doubt also seen plenty. Leo glanced towards the building, to the windows most likely to belong to the kitchen, but he saw only blackness cast back; the glint, on the upper floor, of the freshly dawned sun.

He turned his back to the pub and crossed the footbridge, his heavy winter boots unleashing what felt like a localised earthquake. On the far side he turned south, just as Felicity had, but hesitated when he reached the stile. Beyond, the path tapered and curved out of sight. It was the same mix of mud and grit as the ground on which he stood but somehow the space beyond seemed a different country. It was as though the stile were a border; a crossing into somewhere wild. Although if Leo had learnt anything in the past few weeks it was that such clear delineations, in this world, did not exist.

With his ungloved hand, he grasped the post, in the same place Felicity would have had to grasp. He stepped and hoisted his leg and dropped down onto the other side. He tugged at his coat where it had ridden up and, wincing against the head-wind, trudged on.

He was looking for his daughter. It was what he told him-self. Because it was logical, in a way, that of all places he should be looking here. He was being punished – Ellie was – for what Daniel had done to Felicity. Was it not reasonable, then, that he should look for parallels, for clues in Felicity's fate as to Ellie's? Felicity was found along this stretch of river, not far from where Daniel had caught up with her. She was killed at this time of day and her body discovered almost two weeks after she went missing, just as two weeks had passed since Ellie's disappearance. There had been a search, for both girls, that at first had yielded nothing. The parents had been through denial, anger, desperation, grief. So it was time. Wasn't it? According to the rules by which Ellie's abductor was playing, the game was up and Leo had lost. Ellie had. Leo knew that already and yet he did not – which was why he was here, now, tracking Felicity's path in search of his daughter.

Not logical, then. Not remotely. But even with such a brittle thread he was able to bind what Daniel had inflicted on Felicity with what was being done to his daughter. And was that not, after all, the real reason he was here? To assuage his guilt. To displace it with anger. To cast Daniel in the same light as the man who had taken Ellie and excuse his failure to face up to the boy he had once considered his ward. Because if Leo had been wrong to feel sorry for the boy – if he accepted that he had been wrong – how much easier would it be to accept that the fate awaiting Daniel was right?

He was looking for his daughter. It was what he told himself. It was true because it would always be true and if there was a chance he would find her then that was all the logic, brittle or otherwise, he needed.

He saw nothing. The riverside, unsurprisingly, was deserted. But it was not quite so cut off as Leo had expected, even this far from the city centre. There was road noise, for instance, faint but incessant. And on the hills to the north, buildings were visible: student dorms, mainly, with only the majority of the windows shrouded. There were dog tracks in the mud; horse prints, too. People used this path, though perhaps less these days than before.

At a bench, Leo paused. He did not sit but read: that Tom had 'fucked Natasha', that 'exstacy' ruled, that Exeter was a 'shitwhole', that Plymouth FC played like 'flids'. The bench was a noticeboard, though most of what was written, to Leo's eye, was undecipherable. He imagined Daniel seated sideways, scratching some remark on the plasticised wood. Although, given the boy's state of mind, a comment seemed somehow too constructive. There were gouges – chiselled scores that seemed estimable only by their depth – and these were more likely to have been Daniel's work. Perhaps that was what he had been doing, here, until Felicity passed, the day that had cost them their lives.

He was a killer. His life be damned. Would Leo wish to spare the man who had taken Ellie should the choice ever – please, God – be his to make? Would Leo urge mercy, understanding, compassion when the victim was his daughter and not a stranger's? Would he care about *why* then?

Maybe not.

Certainly not.

But it was different. Wasn't it?

It was different because Daniel was a child. Not old enough, in the eyes of a government he was too young to choose, to buy cigarettes, have sex, get a tattoo: to make any mistake but the most heinous. And, more than a child, he was a victim. He had been failed and failed again. That he had killed had been not just his crime but his parents', his schoolteachers', his social workers', his peers'. To greater and lesser degrees, of course, but was condemnation, in this context, anything other than self-exoneration? Why should Daniel pay the price, exclusively, without understanding, when he had pulled the trigger on a gun someone else had placed in his hand?

And yet.

And yet, this man who had Ellie: what was he but a child grown up? A victim himself, probably, but one who had managed to survive in the world a little longer. Not sane, clearly, but not in care, not cared for. Someone else who has fallen through the gaps but further, harder. Should it therefore have been *his* parents who were held to account? Or his parents' parents? At some point, surely, there was a line to be drawn.

Maybe the victims should decide. Felicity's parents, in the girl's case; Leo, Megan in Ellie's. That seemed right. It seemed just. Except Leo knew what he would choose were he ever to be placed in that position. He knew what he would have done to the man, would do to him himself were he afforded the opportunity. Everything society wished on Daniel – what the crowds outside the courtroom were clamouring for; what the newspapers in their columnising sought to incite – he would visit tenfold on this man, whoever he was, whatever his story, however he might seek to explain *why*. And such would be Leo's right. It would be *right*. Given how good it would surely feel, how could it be anything but?

From the bench, Leo edged closer to the bank. The water, below him, was as grey and impenetrable as stone. It did not seem to be moving but Leo knew enough by now not to be fooled. He knew what the river might swallow, how reluctant it was to discharge what it caught.

He continued his walk, careful of his footing on the uneven ground but not as careful, perhaps, as he might have been. He did not want to fall. It would not matter, particularly, if he did.

There was the sound of something flapping, cracking, in

the wind. Leo turned, spooked, but there was nothing behind him but where he had come from. The sound came again and this time he caught its bearing. There: the tree. An ash, ashen and cankered, its only foliage a strip of blue and white barrier tape left behind by the police. It leapt, then wilted, then leapt again.

He had arrived.

The place – the scene – was as empty of life as any other he had passed that morning. Of life, or otherwise. Everything except the remnant of tape had been swept aside by the wind, washed down by the rain. It was clearer here than it perhaps should have been. No litter or junk as further up the river; nothing that had not already been bagged and consigned to an evidence room.

Leo wiped at his eyes. It was this wind, he told himself. He turned against it and wiped his eyes once more.

Back then. Or head on? It was hard to decide when there were no pros, no cons, nothing on which to balance reason. And anyway his reason felt used up. Worse, it felt useless. Left, right, this way, that. He was floundering, whichever way he turned. He had been floundering, in truth, since his father had died. Looking back when he should have been looking forwards. Looking in when he should have been looking out. Doubting what he had accomplished and ensuring, in doing so, that the one thing he had achieved would crumble, soon enough, into nothing.

What was he doing here – *really*? What, in his search, did he actually expect to find?

A way out.

Escape.

The freedom to cast Daniel aside.

There was the hope, of course, that the boy's life would be the price of his daughter's. That it would be enough for him – whoever *he* was, this faceless stranger with a beard. That Daniel pleading guilty would be the key to his daughter's chains.

But he did not believe it. If he did, he would have made the exchange in an instant. Take him. Take my limbs too if that's the price, just give me back my heart.

Not hope, then. It was, he realised, fear that was driving his search – his flight, rather, from a truth he had carried with him all along.

Ellie was lost. Daniel was too. In failing one, Leo had sacrificed them both.

23

'WICKED AND DEPRAVED ...
AN ACT OF BARBARITY AND EVIL'

By Tim Cummins

Daniel Blake, aged 12, pleaded guilty yesterday to the sexual assault and murder of Felicity Forbes.

Daniel, pictured, was sent to prison for "many, many years" by Mr Justice Murdoch, who described the boy's crime as "an act of barbarity and evil", adding: "It was wicked and depraved."

The boy showed no signs of remorse as he entered his plea. Only as the youngest convicted murderer of the new millennium was led away did he deign to shed a tear, as much perhaps in sorrow at his own fate as that of his victim.

Eleven-years-young Felicity was brutally assaulted and murdered on a cold, bright day in January this year, and her body dumped and discovered only two weeks later.

Continued on Page 2

246

KILLER'S TEARS . . . BUT ONLY FOR HIMSELF

Victim's father expresses relief but maintains the nightmare will never end

Continued from Page 1

Daniel Blake, named in public now for the first time, was arrested and charged at the beginning of February.

"By your actions you have torn a family asunder," said the judge. "You have broken hearts and lives and deserve to be imprisoned for many, many years – until the Home Secretary is satisfied you have repented and are fully rehabilitated."

As the judge concluded his remarks there were isolated cheers in the public gallery. Felicity's mother was not present but her father, seated with other family members, maintained a dignified silence throughout proceedings.

Explaining his decision to overturn the order banning identification of the defendant, the judge stated that the "tragic and unique circumstances of the killing puts this case in a class of its own".

Public interest

He accepted the argument, set forth by this newspaper among others, that it was "in the interest of fair and balanced reporting" that Daniel Blake should be named.

Such a callous murderer "should not be allowed to hide from his crimes", the judge said, particularly "in light of the complete lack of mercy he demonstrated towards his victim".

He spoke of a "moral imbalance" in consigning the victim's family to a life in the public eye but offering the killer "a shield of anonymity".

Blake's mother, Stephanie, and his stepfather, Vincent, showed no reaction when the boy they raised admitted in open court to having brutally murdered an innocent and popular young girl.

The boy's mother reached for her husband's hand but neither made eye contact with Daniel until the boy was led by his social worker from the dock.

Supt. George Morrison, who led the investigation, expressed his satisfaction that justice had been done. "There is not a doubt in my mind that this boy is wicked beyond belief," he said.

"There is nothing to provide any excuse for him."

The only mitigation offered by Dale Baldwin-Tovey, QC, acting for Blake, was a suggestion that his client had demonstrated "sincere remorse" at every stage since admitting the crime and had pleaded guilty at the first available opportunity.

Blake, while in custody, was understood to have undergone psychiatric evaluation by Dr Karen Mitchell, who was also present during proceedings. No reference was made by the defence team to her findings.

Daniel's solicitor Terence Saunders, who took over the case from Leonard Curtice after the abduction of Curtice's daughter ("A family's grief", *page 19*), described himself as "disappointed at the tone of the judge's pronouncement". He reiterated his client's repentance and expressed a hope that the Home Secretary would take this into account when deciding upon the boy's sentence.

The Forbes family's solicitor Colin Share, meanwhile, said: "No sentence the court might pass could adequately punish this boy for his horrific crime."

"Felicity's father and mother are of course relieved that this stage of proceedings are over but unfortunately for Roger and Anna, their ordeal will never end."

Comfort

After a session in court that lasted barely an hour, it was back to his hotel-quality accommodation for Felicity's killer, perhaps to listen to a few CDs in his private room or play video games on his taxpayer-funded Sony PlayStation.

As Blake was driven from the court building in an unmarked van, a crowd of 400 including mothers with toddlers in their arms screamed abuse. In an echo of events at the boy's first remand hearing in February, the protesters surged forwards and had to be held back by a straining cordon of police officers.

Cries of "Scum!" and "Murderer!" drowned out appeals from the police for calm. Objects were thrown at the van, including eggs and at least one brick. No arrests were reported to have been made.

The Home Secretary refused to be drawn on his likely intervention in the sentencing of Daniel Blake, commenting only that he was horrified by the killing and by the age of both victim and perpetrator.

248

24

The morning, on any other day, would have seemed a blessing. The sun sat bold in a cloudless sky, softening the breeze and warming the colours of the breaking season. A new beginning, was how a churchman had put it in his thought for the day: 'The morning after the nightmare before.' And it was indeed as though the city, the country, sensed it had been purged; rinsed clean of something distasteful.

The effect, mercifully, did not seep beyond the doors of the detention centre. The mood within seemed more closely to match Leo's own, though partly this may have been down to the pall Leo knew he carried with him. He saw it – had seen it since Ellie had been taken – cast back at him by everyone he encountered. He only had to enter a room and the light within would immediately seem to dim.

He waited beside the security desk, the two guards on the other side of the counter conspicuously evading a collision of eyes. They were intimidated, Leo realised. By his presence. By the absence his presence brought home.

He coughed and one of the security guards squirmed.

'Mr Curtice.'

Leo raised his head. Bobby had appeared through a doorway. He edged closer, looking the way Leo felt whenever he was forced into conversation with one of his daughter's classmates.

Had felt.

'I wasn't expecting you. Did you call? Nobody mentioned ...' Bobby exchanged glances with the men on the desk, who said, without speaking, don't look at me.

'No,' Leo said. 'Sorry. I should have. I wasn't sure I was coming, to be honest. Not until I got here.' Which did nothing to set anyone at ease.

'Daniel is . . . I mean, I assume that's why you're . . .'

'Will he see me?'

'I think . . . I think he was expecting you sooner.'

'I know. I'm sorry. But will he see me now?'

Bobby winced. 'Look, Mr Curtice. Leo. I don't know whether that's such a good idea.'

'Please,' Leo said. 'I'd like to talk to him.'

Bobby started to shake his head but Leo spoke before the gesture could gather momentum.

'Please. Just ask him. Can't you? I only want to explain. That's all. Please.'

Once again Bobby looked towards his colleagues. Expressionless, curious, they peered back; and Bobby, eventually, sighed.

'Wait here.'

*

It was a mistake. That much was clear from the outset.

Daniel had agreed to see him but not in his room. There was significance, clearly, in the stipulation, no doubt less obscure to a twelve-year-old mind than to Leo's. When Leo entered the visitation room, however, all ambiguity fell away. He was not welcome. Whatever he had come here to say, Daniel was not interested in hearing it.

'Leave me alone.'

'Daniel. Listen. I know I'm probably the last person you—'

'Leave me alone! Do you hear? That's all I've got to say. That's the only reason I told them to let you in.' He was on his feet, his hands feeble-looking bundles at his side. He turned to Garrie, who was guarding the whitewashed wall at the back of the room. 'You can kick him out now. We're done.'

Garrie moved but only fractionally.

'Wait.' Leo held up a hand. 'Please. I'm only asking for a minute. That's all. Just one more minute.'

'You lied. I hate you. Your mate too. You're all liars!'

Daniel's words made Leo flinch. Not the part about him being a liar: he had expected that. It was, rather, the boy's expression of hate that struck him. Ellie had once told Leo the same thing – months ago, now; a lifetime, it felt like – and it cut, this time, just as precisely.

'You're right,' Leo said. 'I let you down.' Daniel was standing beside the table and Leo edged to within touching distance of the adjacent chair. It was the only thing between them in a room that was for the most part empty space. 'But I didn't lie, Daniel. Even Terry: he didn't lie. We were wrong, that's all. We were both wrong.'

'What's the difference?' Daniel backed slightly away. 'You said you'd help me!'

'I wanted to! We both did. I thought I could but . . .' But what? But no one could have? How to convey to a twelve-year-old that hate, often, trumps humanity? That justice, sometimes, is blind, deaf, dumb. 'I was wrong,' Leo said. He reached a hand and Daniel permitted it to settle on his shoulder. 'I'm sorry, Daniel. I'm really desperately sorry.'

The boy jerked away, lashing out at Leo's arm. There were tears budding in Daniel's eyes.

'Why did you go? If you're so sorry, why did you leave me in the first place?'

Leo, for a moment, floundered. He didn't know. He had assumed that Daniel would know.

'Did Terry not tell you?'

Daniel shook his head, more than was necessary to convey an answer. His mind, in that instant, seemed as ragged as his appearance implied. His clothes were dishevelled, his eyes raw and his hair a pillow-chafed mess. All, probably, much like Leo's.

'He said you were on leave or something. On holiday!'

'What? No!' Again Leo reached, to stop Daniel edging back, but the boy shrugged him off. 'It was my daughter. She was . . . She needed me. She needed my help.'

'So did I!'

'I know but Ellie, she . . .' You killed her, Daniel. Me and you together. 'I would have been here. I promise. I tried but . . .' But it would have made no difference. It would have been longer, harder, the disappointment all the greater. But the outcome would have been the same.

Leo let his head drop. He tucked his fingers into his hair.

'Did you see?' said Daniel, after a moment. 'The papers. I'm in all of them! That's what they told me. Every one of them.'

Slowly, Leo nodded. He slid a hand across his mouth. 'I know,' he said. He recovered himself; tried to. 'But listen to me. Daniel? Are you listening?'

The boy made a noise: why should I listen to you? But he fell silent.

'It will pass. I promise you. The coverage, the outcry, everything you're feeling now: things will settle down. I prom—'

'Stop! I don't wanna hear your promising! All you ever do is promise and it always turns out to be a lie!'

Which was unfair. He had never promised, not once. He said he would try, that was all.

He had never said the words. That was the only difference. The promise had been inferred.

'Have they . . . You know they'll protect you, don't you? And later . . . after . . . You'll have a new start. A new identity. They'll keep who you really are a secret.'

'Like now, you mean? Like you said they would this time?' The boy had moved against the wall. Leo remained two paces away but Daniel acted as though cornered, driven back by a press of hostility.

'This is different, I prom—' Leo stopped himself. 'It's different. No one can overturn it this time.' You're lying, said a voice: half Daniel's, half his own. You're doing exactly what you did before. Just because you hope something is true, doesn't make it any less of a lie.

Daniel, anyway, did not believe him. He was shaking his head, dislodging his tears in the process.

'You didn't hear him. The judge, what he said. If you'd been there, you would've heard him. They hate me. Everyone does.'

Again Leo reached out. He could not stop himself. Daniel recoiled and Leo's hand swung to his side.

'Not everyone hates you.' Again the voice but he ignored it. Better to lie, surely. Better to give the boy something approximating hope. 'They don't understand, that's all. They're angry and they're upset and they're looking for . . .' Blood, was the word that came to mind. '. . . for someone to blame. What you did was an awful thing, Daniel. You do understand that, don't you?'

The boy, a mess of snot and tears, nodded. He sniffed, wiped his nose on his sleeve.

'And when someone does something awful, other people, they . . . they get angry. They get so angry, sometimes, they forget about the other things that matter. Like understanding. Like compassion. Like forgiveness.'

'I said I was sorry! They didn't believe me! But I am! I really really am!'

'I know. I know you are. And they'll listen. In time. The hurt will fade and . . . and . . .' The hurt will fade. To whom was he lying this time? 'The important thing, Daniel, is for you to get help. Karen. You remember Karen? She wants to help you. She's determined to. And there are other people like her. Kind people, not . . .' Not what?

The boy was shaking.

'You need to let them help. That's important too. You need to trust these people, Daniel. Karen especially.'

'She was there! I saw her! She didn't say anything! I thought you said she was gonna say something!'

'I know but it's . . . it's complicated. She—'

'And you! I trusted *you*!'

Leo looked down, away. He caught Garrie, the security guard, watching. Leo had forgotten he was in the room. Neither man held the other's eye. There was just the sound, in that moment, of Daniel crying and trying not to.

'What'll happen now?' the boy managed to say. 'Where will they send me?'

Leo pressed his lips, shook his head. 'I don't know.'

'Stash, one of the older boys: they sent him to prison. Last week.. Proper prison. With murderers and that.'

'He was eighteen. Grown up. Didn't you tell me that? You're twelve, Daniel. They'll send you somewhere like here. Not a prison but a . . .' Leo shook his head again. The semantics, once again, failed him.

'But I'll *be* eighteen! In, like, four or five years or whatever. They'll send me to prison then. Won't they?' The boy stared hard, watching for the lie.

Leo hesitated, then nodded, as fractionally as he could manage. Even such a minor affirmation, though, was enough. The boy seemed to wither. He let out something between a moan and a wail.

This time when Leo reached, Daniel allowed himself to be

enfolded. The boy pressed his face to Leo's chest and gripped with an intensity that belied his narrow frame. Leo, in turn, wrapped his arms around the boy's shoulders, encircling them easily. Daniel was Ellie-sized, Leo realised: just as meagre, just as fragile. 'Shh,' he said, 'hush now,' and, thinking of the last time he had held his daughter, he had to stop himself from clinging too tight.

Bobby was waiting for him in the corridor. That he had been watching, listening, seemed unlikely but the expression he wore – apprehension, tenderness; mainly sorrow – would no doubt have been the same if he had.

'He'll be grateful,' Bobby said. 'When he gets a chance to think about it, he'll realise he was glad you came.'

Leo said nothing. He wiped an eye.

'I'll walk with you,' Bobby said. 'Shall I?'

This time Leo nodded. They fell into step.

Leo cleared his throat. 'Have his parents been? His mother?'

Bobby inhaled, nodded on the out breath. 'They came. They weren't here long. She . . . Mrs Blake . . . She seemed to take it hard. The stepfather too, in his way.'

They reached a set of doors, negotiated them awkwardly. For several paces afterwards they walked in silence.

'What about Daniel?' Leo asked. 'How long will he stay here?'

Bobby drew his lips sideways. 'As long as they let him. Not long, probably. Not once the Home Secretary makes up his mind and they draw up a sentence plan. But it was only ever a stopgap, as you know. We're not really set up for boys as young as Daniel.'

Leo sniffed. 'Is anywhere?'

Bobby turned slightly, as though deliberating whether to take offence on his peers' behalf. 'There are some good institutions around, Mr Curtice. All things considered.'

'All things considered?'

Bobby shrugged. 'Facilities like ours don't tend to be a priority. In terms of funding, I mean. We're up there in government minds with asylum seekers and single mothers. Down there, rather.'

'That doesn't surprise me.'

'No. I don't suppose it does. But we do okay. We do, others do. It helps when you get the right people. You'll find, actually, that boys of Daniel's age receive the best care of all. It's only as they get older, turn into adults, that sometimes they . . . I mean, it's inevitable really that at some point they're . . .'

'Set adrift.'

Bobby glanced.

They walked on.

'He's scared, you know,' said Leo. 'Terrified, actually.'

Bobby nodded. Both men watched the floor as it passed beneath their feet.

'Is he right to be, do you think?' Leo regretted the question almost as he finished asking it. He shook it off. 'Don't answer that. It was a stupid thing to ask.'

They passed through another set of doors and found themselves in the main lobby. They slowed, then stopped alongside the security desk.

Bobby exhaled audibly. He seemed actually to be considering Leo's question. 'You never know,' he said, finally settling on his answer. 'He's due a little luck, wouldn't you say?'

He was, that much was certain. And, possibly, he would encounter some. But that Bobby could think of nothing more encouraging to say did nothing to give Leo hope.

Bobby held out his hand. Leo took it.

'Listen. Mr Curtice. About your daughter. I just wanted to say . . .'

But Bobby got no further. He seemed to realise that Leo was no longer paying attention. Leo was looking, instead, across Bobby's shoulder, at the two guards chuckling now behind the desk. The younger man, lank-haired and wispy-chinned, and with a complexion that suggested he worked too many night shifts, had said something that had made his older, fatter colleague laugh. And Leo had heard every word.

'You.' He let his hand slip from Bobby's and moved beyond him, towards the desk. 'What did you say?'

The guards looked up. They were seated, chairs drawn together, but they rolled apart slightly as Leo edged closer. The younger man swallowed.

'Say it again,' Leo said. 'What you just said.' He reached the counter and peered across it. On the surface, spread between the two guards and two empty coffee mugs, was a copy of the morning's *Post*. Daniel's Photoshopped features projected outwards from the newspaper's front page.

'Mr Curtice? Is something wrong?' Bobby was at Leo's shoulder. Leo raised his finger and pointed.

'You. Say it again. What you just said.'

The younger guard shied from Leo's glare. 'I . . . I'm sorry, Bobby. I was just . . . It was a joke. That's all.' He looked to his colleague, who looked conspicuously away.

'What did you say? Mervyn? What did Mr Curtice hear you say?'

Leo stared at the newspaper. At the picture in the newspaper.

'I just said . . . All I said was . . .' Another look towards his friend. 'That some people would . . . um . . . do anything. To, um. To get their picture in the paper.' He said this last part in a rush. 'It was a joke, Bobby. That's all. I didn't mean for anyone to hear.' He glanced through his eyebrows at Leo.

Leo was shaking his head. 'You said kill. You said, some people will kill to get their picture in the paper.' He did not look at the guard as he spoke. He just stared at the *Post*'s front page.

25

It was shabbier than he had expected. Or as shabby, perhaps, as he should have expected, given the outfit that was operating inside. It was a four-floor box of bricks, devoid of architectural flourish and dating, probably, to some time between the wars. The windows on the bottom two levels were papered off, as though the rooms beyond were being used for storage. Indeed, the building as a whole had the look of one of those places people rented by the square foot to dump their junk. Only the sign – the *Exeter Post*'s red-on-white masthead, underscored with the name of its listed counterpart – confirmed to Leo that he had found the right place. The sign, and the clutch of hacks smoking in the doorway.

He was not among them. Leo got a good look at each of their faces because, after he had raggedly parked his car on the double yellow lines in front of the building, every one of them turned to study his. But the face for which he was looking was not there. Assuming Leo would recognise it. He would, though, surely. He had to.

He shoved his way through the group and towards the

entrance, knocking someone's arm and catching his on an outcrop of ash. He said sorry, did not turn, and pushed, pulled, until he found the right combination to open up a gap in the double glass doors.

Another security desk awaited him; another guard. This one seemed to have noticed the minor scuffle Leo had generated outside and rose, as Leo lurched across the lobby towards him, onto his size twelves.

'Can I help you?' He voiced the question as a challenge.

Leo was already looking over the guard's sizeable polished head at the floor directory on the wall; and, beyond that, to the staircase and a treacherous-looking lift. There was no listing for the art department, if such a thing existed, but editorial was on the third floor. He aimed himself at the stairs.

'Hey!' The guard stepped and grabbed. Leo tried to dodge but found himself rooted.

'Let go of me!' Leo tugged at the man's grip.

'Do you have an appointment? *Sir?* You can't just walk in here, you know.'

'I'm not, I'm . . . I'm a solicitor! I'm here to see . . . to see . . .'

'To see who?' The guard released his hold on Leo's lapels but built himself into a wall across his path.

'One of your journalists. Covering the Forbes story.' It was the only thing he could think of to say. He barely had a face to go on, after all, let alone a name.

'Oh yeah? Which one?' The gorilla folded its arms.

And then it came to him. Not the name he needed but a name nonetheless. 'Cummins,' he said. 'Tim Cummins.' The name on the byline. A man he had encountered, once in a while, amid the press gang that haunted the local courts.

The guard frowned. His lips gave a twitch and his arms, reluctantly, loosened.

'Is he here? Please tell him Leo Curtice is here to see him.' Leo straightened his jacket, settled his shoulders and fixed the man looming over him with his best supercilious stare.

Tim Cummins emerged from the lift with a finger in his teeth. He was precisely as unshaven as he was the last time Leo had seen him – on the steps outside the police station the day following Daniel's arrest – which made him think the man's sloth might be affected; a provincial attempt at Fleet Street flair. But then he withdrew his finger, nibbled at whatever piece of breakfast he had dislodged and extended the same hand for Leo to shake.

'Mr Curtice. Leo! What brings you to these parts?'

'Tim. Thanks for seeing me.' Leo swallowed his distaste. He glanced towards the security guard, who was loitering with malcontent.

Cummins seemed to notice too. 'Relax, Tiny. Stand down. Mr Curtice here is a personal friend.'

From the snarl that bubbled on the guard's lips, he appeared not to appreciate the nickname.

The journalist herded Leo away from the guard and towards the lift. 'Hey,' he said, 'listen, buddy. I am *so* sorry about this business with your daughter.' He shook his head at the floor, worked a fingernail once more between his teeth. 'But if there's any way I can help. I mean, you'd be surprised how much traction an interview will get you. Have you thought about that? A one-to-one. Just me and you. We'd keep things tasteful, I promise. Tug a few heartstrings but all for a good cause.' He raised an eyebrow.

'Actually,' said Leo, 'there is something you can do to help.'

'Really? Great. Just say the word, buddy.'

'I'm looking for a colleague of yours. A photographer.'

Cummins let his disappointment show.

'He said he was freelance. He was young, ish, and wore a cap. It had a logo on it. A picture of a shark or something. It looked American. From a baseball team maybe.'

'Football. The Miami Dolphins. But . . . er . . . I'm not sure who you mean. We have so many snappers, Leo – particularly the jobbing kind. It's a big paper, buddy.'

It was not. It was a local rag with tabloid airs. And Cummins was lying.

'Listen, Tim. This is important. It's to do with my daughter. I'm asking for help. Please. I need your help.'

They reached the lift. Cummins jabbed a button, summoning his means of escape. 'Sorry, Leo.' He spoke to the lights above the doors. 'Can't help you. I'd love to, you know I would, but Tiny over there: he probably knows more of the faces that come and go here than I do. Why don't you ask him?'

The guard was on the phone now, seated and angled towards the wall.

'This photographer,' said Leo to Cummins. 'He followed us. Me and my family. To Dawlish. All we were doing was buying ice cream.'

Cummins glanced.

'He said he was working for the *Post*,' Leo said.

Cummins hit the call button again. He sniffed, gave his head a single shake. 'I can only apologise, Leo. Darryl Blunt, our lifestyle editor: he thinks he's running *OK!* I'll have a word with Daz on your behalf. Tell him to keep a leash on his paparazzi.' He studied the lights, tapped his foot.

'It was you,' Leo said. 'Wasn't it? You sent him. You've been sniffing for an angle on the Forbes story from day one.' How does it feel: isn't that what Cummins had asked him, that day outside the police station? How does your family feel about your involvement in this case?

The lift arrived. Cummins beamed.

'Well,' he said, 'this is me. Good to see you, Leo. Thanks for stopping by.' He seemed to consider holding out a hand but did not. 'Best of luck with . . . er . . . everything.' He darted into the empty compartment and started jabbing at one of the numbers.

'Tim. Please! I just need his name. His address. Anything!'

Cummins gave a lazy salute. 'Take care, buddy.' The doors of the lift began to close.

Leo glanced over his shoulder, at the guard still whispering into his phone. He looked at Cummins, at his fleshy grin about to vanish behind a sheen of metal. And then he sprung: between the doors and into the lift, in pursuit of his very last hope.

He had lied. The address was a fake. The name too, probably. Leo had half a mind to go back there. Not half a mind:

he would. Right now. He would call the police if it came to it, or threaten to, or—

He stopped mid-step, squinted at Cummins's scrawl on the scrap of paper. Unless . . . this was it. Was it? The address, after twenty minutes searching, seemed to match. Flat 2, 2b Plymouth New Road, which did not sound like a real address at all – but here, on a door that looked like a fire exit, was a 2 and a drunken b. There were no names on the buzzers so Leo pressed the middle one of the three. He held it, until the buzzing gave way to static.

'Yeah? Who's there?'

'Mr, er . . .' Leo checked the name again, then changed his mind and slipped the note into his pocket. 'Er . . . Archie? Is that you?'

'Yeah. S'right. Who's that?'

'This is, um, Tim Cummins. From the *Post*.' Leo put on his deepest, fattest voice. 'I need to talk to you.'

'Tim? What's up? Can it wait? I'm not exactly up yet.'

Leo looked incredulously at his watch. 'No! It can't! I mean . . .' Deeper. Fatter. 'Just let me in. Er, buddy. It's important.'

There was a groan, followed by a rasping sound: an intercom receiver, perhaps, being dragged across sandpaper skin. And then a pause, which extended – until a siren-loud buzzing beckoned Leo in.

The hallway was windowless and unlit. Leo stood blind amid a stench like bins until a cleft of light broke the darkness on the landing.

'Hit the lights,' came a voice. 'The switch right beside you.'

Leo reached for the wall, then pulled back. He headed instead for the hulking shadow of the staircase.

'On the wall. Right beside you. Oh for God's sake. Here.' Movement: the silhouette of a shuffling dressing gown. And then the bulb in the hallway came on, casting a light as thick as the lingering odour. Leo was only halfway up the stairs.

'Tim? Is that . . . You! What the hell are *you* doing here?'

Leo accelerated. He started bounding up the stairs two by two.

Archie, the photographer, took fright. He did not wait for Leo to explain but dived from the light switch on the landing back towards his apartment door. He tripped, on the cord of his dressing gown, and fell through the doorway. He landed with a yelp just as Leo scrambled to the threshold.

'What do you want? What are you doing here?' Archie rolled onto his heels and hands. He scrabbled backwards as Leo advanced.

'The photographs. The ones you took of my family. I need to see them.'

'But how did you . . .' Archie collided crown-first with a wall. His hand slipped beneath him and he crumpled once again onto the grubby carpet. He reached for his head and screwed up his eyes. 'Ow. Fucking *ow*.'

Leo hesitated. The man in front of him was a mess. Beneath his robe, which was hanging from one shoulder and gaping across his girlish frame, he had on boxers and a vest: the type Leo wore, and that made even Leo feel old. His eyes were slits and his skin pale. Symptoms of spending too much time in a darkroom, Leo would have said, had he not seen the man looking perfectly healthy the last time they had met.

'What's wrong with you? Are you okay?'

'No. I'm fucking not.' The man shuffled until he was sitting, shifting his weight onto his backside and hooking his arms over his knees. He hung his head. 'I'm fucking dying. What the hell do you want?'

'I told you, I . . . Look. Really. Can I get you something?'

Archie laughed, as though tickled by his impending wit. The laugh turned into a cough. 'Some morphine, maybe. A replacement head. Even a Bloody Mary might do the trick.'

A Bloody Mary? Leo took another step. He leant and he sniffed. 'You're hungover?'

'Actually, scratch that.' Archie pressed the heel of his hand to his forehead. 'Just the thought of vodka makes me wanna . . .'

Leo dropped beside him, grabbed his dressing gown and shook the man straight. 'The photographs! Where are they!'

'Ow! For fuck's sa—'

'I don't have time for this! I need the photographs *now.*'

'Seriously! The decibels! I told you, I'm fucking dy—'

'I DON'T CARE.' Each word seemed to strike like a blow. Leo tried standing, meaning to drag the photographer upright. 'STAND UP. STAND UP!' He hauled but the man was like a ton of sleeping cat. 'I'M NOT GOING TO ASK YOU AGAIN! STAND UP! I SAID, STAND—'

'Okay!' Archie reached a hand to the wall. He started to claw himself vertical. 'Just stop shouting, will you?' He found his feet and dragged a hand across his pallid face. He blinked.

'The photo—'

'The photographs. I heard you. Just give me a minute. Okay? Five fucking seconds.'

He looked left, right, then stumbled deeper into the apartment. Leo followed. At the doorway to the living room, he stopped short, marvelling at the scene beyond. It was carnage. A battlefield, with the casualties yet to be removed. There was a girl curled between ashtrays on a flammable-looking sofa, and a man strewn across an armchair. Beneath Jimi Hendrix posters sagging from the smoke-stained walls, record sleeves vied with beer bottles for floor space. There were patches, too, of visible carpet: person-shaped, suggesting not all of Archie's guests had failed to make it home.

'I told you I'd delete them. Didn't I?'

Leo turned. Archie seemed to be searching for somewhere to slump. He settled for a spot furthest from the daylight that was seeping through the blinds, in the shade of a gargantuan rubber plant.

Archie was right. Leo had forgotten. Not forgotten: he had not believed what the photographer had told him in the first place. 'Did you?'

Archie shrugged, shook his head. 'Nope.' He extended a foot, prodded a laptop beside the coffee table with a toe. 'They're on there. Help yourself. But hey! Mind the carpet!'

Leo, in his rush, had toppled a highball. The liquid inside merely merged into a pre-existing stain.

'It's not working.' Leo was kneeling now, pressing, holding, prodding the computer's on button. He looked at Archie, who had his eyes closed.

'The battery's buggered,' the photographer said. 'You need to plug it in. But seriously!' At the sound of clinking beer bottles, Archie opened his eyes and raised his drooping head. 'You're making a mess!'

Leo knocked over another bottle as he lunged for a power socket. He ignored Archie's remonstrations and beat the plug into the wall.

'What's the password?' Leo said, when the screen on the laptop prompted him. 'Archie! What's the—'

'Jimi!' Archie snapped back. 'That's i, m, i, all lower case.'

Leo typed two-fingered. 'And the folder. Which folder? Jesus, Archie, there's hundreds of—'

'The date! They're sorted by date. You're really not helping my headache, you know. I should call the fuzz or something.'

Archie grumbled on but Leo stopped listening. He was searching the photographer's hard drive, which was mercifully better organised than the man's living space. Kneeling over the screen and working his fingertip clumsily on the touchpad, Leo located a directory that was arranged by month. He found February, and then the week, and then the day of their trip to Dawlish. He clicked again, twice in succession, and the screen was filled with thumbnails of his daughter. On the village green carrying her ice cream. In the parlour choosing the flavour. Outside, on the pavement. Emerging, further up the street, from the clothes shop with Meg. In her seat, on the train, marvelling at the sea.

Leo dragged the computer to the top of his thighs and leant his head in close. His daughter. Image after image of his daughter and in not one of them, it struck Leo, was Ellie smiling. He reached a fingertip to touch his daughter's cheek. He felt instead the coldness of the laptop's screen.

'You were on the train,' Leo said. 'You were taking pictures of us even before we got there?'

Archie was a ball on the floor, his eyes shut once again and his nostrils pressed into the carpet. 'I was following you,' he mumbled. 'You went by train. *Er*-fucking-*go*.'

Leo scrolled again through the thumbnails, focusing on the images of his family crossing the green.

'How do I enlarge these?'

Archie did not answer but Leo had worked it out for himself. He double clicked an image, scanned it, closed it again. He checked another, and then another, and then another. There was nothing, no one. He zoomed in, then reset the image. He opened another, zoomed, panned out again. A beard. Anyone with a beard. Anyone who looked even remotely like the man Megan had seen at the—

A face. Masked, almost, by an upturned collar, a beanie pulled low over the eyes. Leo zoomed. He stared. And he heard the voice.

Not exactly beach weather is it, Leo?

26

This was harder. At least before it had felt like they had been through the worst of it. Their oxygen had been cut off and, after the initial panic, they had submitted to asphyxiating slowly – not without pain but numb to it. Now, waiting, it was like they had been instructed to take a deep breath while someone worked on fixing the supply. They had no idea how long it would take or whether it could even be done. All they knew for certain was that this was their very last gasp.

Leo, for the first time in a while, was attempting sitting. He beat the table, drumming out his fretfulness through his fingertips.

'Leo.'

Megan was standing beside the sink, her arms around her middle and her back to the room. In front of her was a plastic milk bottle and a mug of half-made tea. Either she had forgotten what she had been doing or she was drawing out the ritual for as long as possible.

'Leo,' she repeated. 'Please.'

Leo, with a glance, settled his fingers. He stared at his flattened hands.

What if he'd fled? He must have known, surely, that they would catch up with him. Somehow, at some point – in this day and age. So if he fled. If he panicked. If he suspected he was running out of time . . . He would let her go. Wouldn't he? Surely he would. It was the only rational course of action. He was caught anyway. Why make things worse? Not just worse: intensely, immeasurably so.

'Leo.'

Even to someone as addled as this . . . this *lunatic*.

'Leo, you're . . .'

And he was that. A lunatic. Someone deranged. Quite what had happened to make him so, Leo could not begin to imagine. It wasn't rage, this, after all. Or if a mist had descended, it had settled. Low enough to obscure any guiding light but not so dense that the man was unable to plan, to scheme, to act as though—

'Leo!'

Megan was facing him now across the breakfast bar. Something in her seemed to have shattered. 'Stop!' she said. 'Please! Stop drumming your blasted fingers!'

Leo swallowed. He slid his hands into his lap. Sorry, he tried to say but his throat, his mouth, was gummed dry.

Megan, eyes closed, said it instead. She started to say something more but turned back in silence towards the worktop. She stood facing the sink. She flicked on the kettle. It must have been the third or fourth time she had set it to boil.

Leo studied her. She had on her pyjamas, as well as the

jumper that had emerged from her closet on day two: a polo neck, the one she described as her hot-water bottle and only ever wore when she was ill. It was fraying at the joins and two sizes too big, so that the sleeves hung to her knuckles and the shoulders overlapped her arms. Her hair was gathered in a shabby bunch and her skin was sallow and free of make-up – and not just because it was the middle of the night.

Leo swallowed again. He slid back his chair. It scraped on the ceramic-tiled floor and he saw the sound rattle Megan's spine. She twitched her chin in his direction, then gripped the handle of the kettle, as though impatient for it to steam. Leo touched the chair, the table, the dresser. He moved from one piece of furniture to the next. He closed on Megan's back and reached his hands towards her shoulders.

'Don't.' Megan stepped away and turned. She pressed herself against the roll of the worktop and wrapped herself tight.

'Meg.' Leo took another step and his wife seemed almost to flinch.

'Don't,' she said again. 'Please.'

It was the please that hurt most.

'Meg. We need to talk. Don't you think?'

She did not answer – and her silence, suddenly, was more than Leo could bear. After weeks of this. The skulking, on his part; the passive loathing on hers. Nothing said, everything implied, even through the cold formality of the words they did exchange. No physical contact of any sort, though Leo longed to hold his wife, to be held in turn by her. They had collided, once or twice, in doorways, around corners, and he had caught the scent of her – the warmth of her – only for Megan to bear it briskly away. She had not even unpacked. The case she had filled the day Ellie had been taken lay distended on their daughter's floor. Her family had returned to their homes – to their beds, anyway, though Megan's mother was invariably back with them by nine – but Megan herself behaved like a guest: sleeping apart, eating apart, confining herself to narrow corridors of space. Not a guest, then. A prisoner. Someone trapped. And even though Leo had tried everything he dared to free the both of them, she refused to look beyond what in her mind had the inviolability of scripture: that everything that had come to pass – all of it – was Leo's fault.

'I didn't mean for this to happen, you know.'

Plaintive, he was dimly aware, would have been a better tack: healthier, more nourishing, less like gobbling grease to sate a hunger. Yet he could sense his fury gathering, barging its way towards the surface. 'Is that what you think?' he heard himself saying. 'That I meant for this to happen? That this was somehow my plan all along?'

Megan remained silent. Everything about her seemed to tighten.

'I'm sorry, Meg! I don't know how many times you want me to say it!'

She watched him. Just stared at him.

'She's my daughter too. I want her back too!'

No movement. Nothing. Not a twitch – until he stepped.

Megan slid away, towards the open part of the room. 'Don't,' she said once more.

Don't. Don't, don't, don't. Leo held up his hands. 'Fine.' He backed as far from his wife as the kitchen units would allow. 'Don't talk to me. Don't touch me. Just carry on acting like I don't exist. Like you're the only one who's feeling any pain.'

Megan made a sound. It was difficult to read. Disdain, most likely. Or pity?

'We need to get past this, Meg. We need to talk about it. Because when they find him. When they find El—'

'Don't! Don't say it!'

Not pity then. Leo felt his chin fall. 'What? Why not? They'll find her, Meg! How can they not? One way or . . .' He shook his head. He had not meant to start that sentence. 'The picture,' he said, 'It's all they needed. With the picture they—'

'Stop it! For God's sake, Leo! Don't you think you've taunted fate enough!'

'Fate?' Leo felt his lip curl. 'Fate has nothing to do with this!'

'No. Of course not. I forgot: this is about you. Right from the start, this has only ever been about you!'

He shook his head. 'That isn't fair. You know it isn't.'

Megan angled her chin as though studying him. 'You think this absolves you. Don't you? You think finding some blasted picture makes everything else all right. Well it doesn't, Leo! It only goes to prove how much you're actually to blame!'

Leo spread his arms. 'I just said! Didn't I? I said I was sorry!'

'And what? I'm supposed to forgive you?' She touched her forehead, let her hand rebound. 'Of course. I forgot. In

Leo-land, that's how it works. As long as you're *sorry*, you can get away with anything.'

Leo smiled. He looked at his watch. 'Congratulations, Meg. You made it, what, a whole thirty seconds this time before bringing up the case?'

'I didn't say anything about the *fucking* case!' She wiped her chin with a sleeve. 'And anyway so what if I did? I can't mention it? We can talk about your daughter being abducted but Daniel Blake being convicted of murder – sorry, that cuts too close to the bone.' Megan pressed a palm to her brow. She opened her mouth to say something more but seemed suddenly overwhelmed by the futility of it, the effort of it. She made, instead, to walk away. Just walk away.

'It doesn't absolve me,' Leo said. And a voice, after, added: stop. Leave it there. Let Megan go and be grateful that you did. But this was something. Shouting, fighting: it was better than doing nothing. He wanted to keep Megan there because he could not face going back to where they had been. He would do anything to avoid that.

'It doesn't absolve me. I never said it did. But at least I've done something. At least I've been doing *something*.' He paused, peered over the edge. 'What have you done, Megan? Between blaming me? Between pining, making tea? What have you actually *done*?'

'Excuse me?' The warning sign on Megan's face was plain to read. Leo hurtled past it.

'I've been out there. Every day. Driving, walking, searching. And I found something. Something important. All you've been doing is—'

'How dare you!' Megan moved with a speed that caught Leo by surprise. She flung a hand and Leo, reacting, caught it. She flung the other and hit Leo on the upper arm. She swung again and this time Leo caught her other hand too. She was thrashing in his grip, yanking at her wrists to try to free them.

He pushed and she stumbled away. She made to come again but Leo held out his hands to ward her off.

'Megan! What the hell are you doing! Calm down!'

'You *wanker*. You *bastard*!' Her hair had come loose. Her jumper had twisted and she writhed to try and straighten it. She started to cry. More than that, she began to heave, gulping and sobbing all at once. She gave up on the jumper and tried to drag her hair from her mouth, as though to make space for air – but it was stuck there by her spit and her snot and her tears. Leo had never seen her look so wretched; so wounded and terrified both.

'Meg.' He took a step. Megan sniffed, sobbed again but marginally recovered her breathing.

'Meg, I'm sorry. I'm so, so sorry. I didn't mean . . .'

She recoiled.

'I need you, Meg. More than ever. You need me too, I know you do.'

Which made her look. Into his eyes and beyond them. It was just a look but as clear an answer as Leo could have asked for.

'Meg.' Leo could feel his own tears now, massing though yet to break. 'Meg, please. Don't. Just think for a minute before you—'

A ringing. The sound they had been waiting for.

Leo was closer. He looked at the phone and back at his wife. She was motionless all of a sudden, her hand halfway to her cheek, her lips pressed tight. A tear fell and she let it.

The ringing. Once again Leo turned. His feet pointed one way, his shoulders the other.

'Answer it.'

Leo looked at Megan.

'Answer it!'

Leo scrambled. He lunged and snatched up the receiver. 'Hello?'

There was quiet for a moment at the other end. A rustling, voices in the background, then finally a cough. 'Hello?' said a voice back. 'Mr Curtice?'

'Inspector?'

'You're there. Thank God.'

'What's happened? What's going on?'

'Are you . . . Can you get down here?'

Megan, Leo was aware, was beside him. He turned and held the receiver so that she might hear.

'Of course. But what's happening? Have you got him?'

'We've got him but . . . Look, you need to come down here.'

'Why? Inspector? Have you found my daughter? She's not . . . Please don't tell me she's . . .'

'Don't drive, Mr Curtice. Just stay put. A car's already on its way.'

27

'He says he won't talk to anyone but you.'

They marched along the corridor, Detective Inspector Mathers supposedly leading but Leo setting the pace. He was surprised, given the hour, how busy the station was. It was kicking-out time at the city's nightclubs, which explained the bustle in the lobby, but here, amid the back rooms, they had barely passed a room without a light on.

'He's refused a solicitor, too,' said the DI. 'Doesn't want a duty. Says you're the only lawyer he trusts. Seemed to think that was amusing until I reminded him what it was he was doing here.'

Leo broke step. He was laughing? He was sitting, waiting . . . laughing?

They stopped outside a windowless door. Mathers reached for the handle and held it. 'Listen,' the DI said. 'I realise this is going to be hard for you but it's important that we keep our cool. We still don't have your daughter, Mr Curtice. Whatever he says, whatever he does, you need to keep that in mind.'

*

Vincent Blake was pacing the edge of the room, tapping his cigarette packet against his thigh. From the door side of the table, a constable roughly double Blake's size tracked his progress. Other than a chair either end of what looked like a 1980s school desk, there was nothing and no one else in the cell.

Keep your cool. The words, briefly, tethered him. But when Blake turned; when he spotted Leo and smiled – *smiled*, as though genuinely pleased to see him – Leo felt his fury snap its leash.

He surged. He felt a touch on his shoulder – a flailing grip – but he was free of it and past the table and through a chair and falling against his cowering prey. He seized Blake's throat. He pressed him to the wall. He smelt sweat and soured smoke and the scent was like a taste of blood.

'Where's my daughter!' He squeezed and Blake's eyes bulged. 'Where is she! If you've hurt her I swear to God I'll . . .'

A hand on each arm: rough, strong, prising at his grip and wrenching it away. Another set around his middle, yanking until Leo tumbled. He searched for Blake's face but saw only the constable's, the inspector's, and felt himself hurled against something solid. He cracked his head. He barely noticed. He tried to push himself forwards but there was a weight across his chest that pinned him: a forearm, the size of Leo's lower leg.

'Mr Curtice!' DI Mathers appeared around his colleague's shoulder. Their faces were in Leo's, blocking his view of the coward in the corner. 'Look at me. Look at me!' Leo, reluc-

tantly, allowed his focus to settle. He saw Mathers growling.
'I said cool, didn't I? I said we needed to keep our cool!'

Leo jerked. The constable held him still.

'Okay!' Leo struggled again but less forcefully. The policemen were a wall in front of him and he would have said
anything to get a glimpse of the man beyond. 'Okay,' he
repeated and this time Leo held the inspector's eye. Gradually the pressure across his chest began to ease. The constable
drew back. The inspector, though, held his ground.

'Cool!' He showed Leo a finger. 'Got it?'

Leo nodded. He shifted and there he was: Daniel's stepfather, his cigarette packet crumpled at his feet and his
nicotine-stained fingers massaging his throat. The man
coughed. He hacked and he spat. He glared at Leo and Leo
glared back.

'Sit,' said the DI. 'Both of you.' He dragged Leo towards a
chair. The constable, less tenderly, assisted Blake.

'Hey!' Blake resisted but the policeman shoved him down,
then slid the chair so Blake's stomach impacted against the
table. He took up position at Blake's shoulder. Leo sensed
the DI looming over his.

'I could do you, you know,' said Blake, spluttering. 'Him
and you both.' He jabbed a thumb at Leo but spoke across
his shoulder to the PC. 'That's assault. So much as touch me
again and I'll have you for ABH.'

The policeman said nothing. He stared at the opposite wall.

'Settle down, Mr Blake,' said Mathers. 'I don't think you
really want to broach the subject of formal charges just yet,
do you?'

Blake faced them. He glowered.

'Now. The matter in hand. We're listening. Mr Curtice here: he's listening.'

Blake, tentatively, moved his gaze to meet Leo's. He licked his lips. He made a motion to lean forward but, catching something in Leo's expression, changed his mind. He propped his elbows on the surface and spread his fingers.

'Curtice,' Blake said. 'Leo.' He wetted his lips again. 'I sent the notes. Okay? I admit it. But this business with your daughter . . . I swear to you I had nothing to do with it.'

Leo made no movement.

'Please,' said Blake and this time he did lean forward. 'You need to tell them. You need to convince them I'm telling the truth. Because they won't listen. They just won't. I mean, you know what they're like, right? You have to deal with them all the time. Right?'

Leo twitched and Blake flinched. Mathers, at Leo's shoulder, edged closer.

'Where is she?' Leo's voice, in his head, sounded distant. It seemed steady, under control, when Leo felt anything but. 'Blake,' he said. 'I helped you. I helped Daniel, your family. Please. Just tell me where my daughter is.'

Blake was shaking his head as Leo spoke. 'Listen to me. Please. You're not—'

Leo held up a hand. 'Even if she's . . .' Leo registered the horror spreading on Vincent Blake's face. 'You just need to tell us. Now.' He had intended to sound intimidating. On the final word, however, Leo's voice cracked.

There was silence. Leo, the men around him, watched Blake.

Blake looked at each of them in turn, as though willing for someone in the room to admit the joke. He focused on Leo.

'Curtice. This is me!' He pressed his fingers to the faded logo on his sweater. 'You know me,' Blake was saying. 'You know my family. You said it yourself. You were trying to help us! Why would you help us if you didn't trust us?'

'Not you,' Leo hissed. 'Never you!'

Blake shook his head. 'I admitted it. Didn't I? I wrote the notes. But that's all. Honest! That's all I did!' He checked around again in desperation. 'Okay,' he said, and splayed his hands again. 'Maybe I sent a mate of mine round to your house and all. But he didn't do anything, did he? Gave your wife a bit of a scare but there was no harm done. Was there?'

Leo sat motionless. The man with the beard. The man Megan saw. Leo had forgotten all about him.

'I told him you owed me money,' Blake was saying. 'I said to him, throw a brick into your living room or something. But he couldn't even manage that, could he?' Blake reclined slightly and muttered, as though revisiting some lingering grievance. 'Twenty-mill units, he tells me. Your double glazing. Says he took a proper look but a brick would have bounced right off. But if he'd done it right, if he'd chucked it at one of the corners . . .' He raised his eyes, seemed to realise he owed the room an explanation. 'Glazing's my trade,' he said. 'Pat's, too: my useless mate. It's how I got this.' He fingered his crooked nose, the scar across it. 'Cash-in-hand job. Almost lost a bloody eye. At least I get my disability now but I should probably be claiming for the undercover work too.' He tested the room with a smile. It faltered. 'The beach,' he explained to Leo. 'The day I followed you. I mean, I was wrapped up pretty tightly so I'm assuming my ugly mug's how you . . .'

Leo made to cut him off and Blake held up his hands.

'Whatever,' he said. 'It doesn't matter. The point is, you've got me all wrong. The notes, the brick: I had my reasons. But that was it, Leo. Honest. That, for me, is where it stops.'

'Why?'

'Why what?'

'You said you had your reasons. What were they?'

'What does it matter? I told you what I did. I told you what I didn't do. It's not helping your kid, keeping me here like this.'

'You're lying. You can't explain, which means you're lying!'

'No!'

'Where is she? Tell me where she is!' Leo half rose from his chair. He felt a hand settle lightly on each of his shoulders.

'Mr Blake,' said DI Mathers. 'You said you wanted to talk to Mr Curtice. So far you haven't told him anything you haven't already said to us.'

Blake fiddled with something unseen. 'No. Well. I said Curtice, didn't I? I didn't say you and Hulk Hogan over there too.'

'Meaning what, Mr Blake?'

'Meaning it's none of your business!'

'Mr Blake—'

'Actually. You know what? I'm leaving. You've got no evidence. You haven't charged me. You haven't even arrested me!' Blake stood and appeared surprised when the constable let him. He seemed to take heart – until the detective inspector cleared his throat.

'Vincent Blake,' he said. 'I am arresting you on suspicion of murder.'

Blake's eyes stretched wide. 'Wait a minute,' he said. 'There's no need for—'

'You do not have to say anything unless you wish to do so—'

'Wait! Just wait a minute!'

'— but it may harm your defence if you do not mention, when questioned—'

'OKAY!'

The room went quiet.

'Okay,' Blake said again, more softly this time, as though wary of severing the silence. 'Here,' he said. 'Look.' He sat down. 'I'm cooperating. Okay?'

The inspector, at Leo's side now, folded his arms.

'But I'm not gonna say anything till we're alone. Till you guarantee me nothing's being recorded.' Blake pointed at Leo. 'And Curtice here,' he said to Mathers, 'is a solicitor. Which means I'm covered. Right? Leo? I'm covered, right?'

Leo had no idea what logic was playing in the man's head. 'Right,' he said.

Mathers looked across the room towards his colleague. He considered Blake, then Leo, seated at the table. Then, with a grimace, he gestured for his junior to follow him out.

'Hey,' said Blake and the inspector, in the doorway, paused. Blake glanced warily at Leo. 'Don't go too far,' he said.

'Blake.'

Daniel's stepfather had slid from his chair the moment the

policemen had left the room. He bent, gathered his cigarette packet, and bore the remains back to the table.

'Blake!'

Blake twitched.

'Talk,' Leo said. 'Quickly. Your so-called reasons.'

Blake set aside his plunder. He glanced over at the door and scanned the ceiling, as though to check they were not being monitored. 'It wasn't personal,' Blake said. 'Okay?' He smiled. 'I like you, Leo. Always did. So just remember that this had nothing to do with—'

'I don't care! All I care about is my daughter!'

'Okay, okay.' Blake shuffled. He edged his chair a little further from the table. 'I'm just saying, that's all. But you wanna know why, right? And that's the problem, Leo. You were always banging on about *why*.'

Leo felt his face crease.

'*Why* this, *why* that. Wouldn't shut up about the bloody *trial*.' Blake sniffed another smile. 'The why's the why. Get it?' He drew a cigarette from his pack.

'The trial? You wrote the notes to put me off a trial?' Leo watched Blake watching him through the flame of his lighter. 'That doesn't make sense. What difference would it have made to you if we'd gone to trial?'

'What difference?' Blake winced at the stupidity of the question.

'A trial would have been about Daniel!'

'Bollocks,' said Blake, sputtering smoke. 'It would've been about us. Me and Steph. Steph most of all. *Why*, right? You wanted everyone to find out why.'

'For Daniel! For your stepson's sake!'

'Yeah, yeah. So you say.'

'It's true!'

'So what if it is! Daniel wasn't the only one with something at stake. Ask your shrink friend if you don't believe me.' Blake put on a voice. 'Tell me about his past. Tell me about *your* past.' He sneered, shook his head. 'Dragging shit up is all she was doing. Looking for someone else to blame.' Blake dragged, exhaled, dragged again. He threw the filter to the floor.

Leo watched him. 'We were right,' he said. 'Weren't we?'

Blake turned.

'About the abuse. About what Daniel went through.' Leo tightened his eyes. 'You. You abused him.'

'No!'

'Is that why you married her? Because she had a child? Someone you could get at whenever you—'

'No!' Blake stood. 'I said, no! Okay?'

Leo hesitated. 'Who then? His father? His real father, I mean.'

Blake, slowly, settled himself. He shrugged. 'No. Maybe. I don't know.'

Leo waited.

Blake looked and looked away. 'There was a bloke,' he told the floor. 'One in particular. One of Steph's friends.' He spoke the word with disdain. 'This was after Frank left her. She kind of . . . fell apart. Started drinking. Started seeing blokes. Started, you know. *Being* with them. It was how she "got by",' he added, as though mimicking – ridiculing – a phrase that, in private, had become a euphemism. *I coped.* Isn't that how Stephanie had put it talking to Karen?

'So this bloke. He was a regular, shall we say. Before my time. He'd show up, have his fun, then bugger off. In a week, a month, he'd be back again. For her, Steph thought. She always told herself he was coming back for her.' Blake met Leo's eye. Something passed between them. Even Blake, it seemed, could comprehend the horror of what Daniel would have suffered.

'But that's . . .' Leo forced himself to focus on Ellie. 'I mean, if it wasn't you . . .'

Blake made a face, like Leo was struggling to keep up. 'It was Steph. Wasn't it? She knew what was going on. She drank but she still knew. He turned up, she opened the door. You ask *why* and the answer points to her.'

Leo made no sound. He swallowed. 'No,' he said at last. 'Not necessarily. I mean, one could argue . . .' He was not sure where the sentence was headed but Blake, anyway, cut it off.

'It wasn't just that.' He leant in, studied his hands. 'There was other stuff. When Daniel was a baby. Bad stuff, like . . .' He glanced at Leo. 'Bad stuff,' he said.

The hospital visits. The trips to A & E. The times Daniel almost died.

Leo stared.

'You read about it all the time,' Blake said. 'Someone gets done for something they did like a million years ago. Like the Nazis, the fucking Yids hunting them down. Not letting bygones be bygones.'

Still Leo could say nothing.

'She was wrong. She knows she was. I'm not trying to make out it was accidental or anything but . . . She was ill. Sick. She

288

saw doctors, shrinks like your mate, but all they ever did was give her pills. When she got better it was on her own. With me.' His voice, momentarily, conveyed pride. 'But a trial. That would have been, what? Another year?' He gave his head a sharp shake. 'She couldn't have handled it. She's barely handling things as they are.'

'Stephanie,' said Leo. 'Did she . . .'

Blake's head snapped up. 'She doesn't know. She didn't. The notes, all that: it's down to me. Okay?' He looked around the room, as though speaking to whomever might be listening. 'I wanna make that clear right now.'

Leo, watching him, found himself struck. 'You love her.'

Blake seemed puzzled by his tone. 'I married her,' he said, as though that, surely, were evidence enough. 'I'm not the hugs-and-flowers type but that doesn't mean I wouldn't do anything for her.' His frown deepened. 'You're married, right? You know what it's like. What kind of man lets something happen that he knows is gonna hurt his wife?'

Leo, to that, could offer no answer.

Blake took his silence as an accusation. 'I know what you're thinking,' he said. 'You're thinking about the boy, that I screwed him over. I would have.' Blake straightened his shoulders. 'I'm not denying it. He's the guilty one, right? And Steph's better off without the little sod if you ask me. But it would have made no difference anyway. Would it?' Blake paused but not long enough for Leo to reply. 'Like I said, right at the start. If he'd pleaded not guilty it would've been a show trial. A publicity stunt. Guilty, not guilty: whichever way you played it, Daniel was always gonna end up on a plate.'

The abuse. Maybe if they'd been able to prove Daniel was abused . . .

But even that, Leo knew, would not have been enough. Nothing, short of madness, would have been enough.

'I was right, wasn't I?' Blake said. 'At least my way Steph was spared.' He took another cigarette from his pack. 'I mean, I'm sorry,' he mumbled. 'About the notes and that. Maybe, I dunno. Maybe I could have played it some other way.' He did not, listening to himself, sound convinced.

'You could have just said. About the trial. You could have insisted . . .'

'I did insist!' Blake glared at his failing lighter. 'Fucking tried to anyway.' He shook it and the lighter sparked.

'But Daniel: Stephanie's his mother, you're his stepfather. You could have just told him . . .'

Blake scoffed. 'Tried that too. But there ain't no telling Daniel. Me and him, in case you hadn't noticed, don't exactly get along. He resents me, is what it is. Can't handle the fact I'm cuddling his mummy.' The cigarette was refusing to light. Blake plucked it from his lips and grimaced as he flicked it aside. 'And as for her,' he said. 'She lets him do whatever he wants. That's part of the problem, if you ask me: spoiling him like it'd make up for what happened in the past. And Danny boy: he said he liked you. Said he trusted you. Said he'd do what you told him to, which in the end meant that was that.'

It was down to him. Once again it was all down to him.

'I'm no expert,' Blake was saying, 'but something about it ain't right. The boy's twelve. Not even old enough to know what shaving foam's for. But stick him in front of a jury and suddenly he's the man in charge. That ain't right. Surely? You're the lawyer, you tell me. Is that right?'

Leo could only shake his head. Once he started, though, he found he could not stop. 'I don't believe it,' he said. 'I don't believe *you*. You sent the notes. You said you did.'

'S'right. And I said I was sorry. They were only meant to rattle you, mate. Give you a nudge, that's all.'

'And my daughter's hair? Her *blood*. What was that supposed to do?'

'What? What are you talking about?'

'I don't deserve a daughter. Isn't that how you put it? Explain the hair, Blake. Explain the blood!' Leo was standing now, leaning towards Blake over the table.

Blake tried to slide away his chair but its rear legs caught and the chair tilted. 'Hey. Calm down. I honestly have no idea what you're—'

Leo was around the table and upon him. He gripped Blake's collar and bore his weight as the chair beneath him fell away. 'The note! The final note! It was written in Ellie's blood! They tested it! They confirmed it! What's your story for explaining that!'

Blake stuttered. He shook his head. 'Honestly! Leo! I haven't got the foggiest—'

'If you wrote one, you wrote them all! And you couldn't have written that one unless . . . unless . . .'

Leo's eyes locked. He saw the notes in their envelopes in his bedside drawer. He saw his balled-up socks and his stash of emergency twenties. He saw Ellie's blood. He saw her hair. He saw the words on that final note and he saw that the words, all along, had held the truth: who had written them, and why.

She does not need to look to be able to see it. She tries, though, to view it through her husband's eyes, to reconcile the image with what they both, probably, would have expected.

The woman is thin. That much is programmed into her DNA. Not a worrying, wiry thin, however. Just the wrong side, in Megan's mind, of a size ten. A pound or two extra would not hurt, particularly on those narrow hips, but overall she appears fit, healthy.

Her hair has been dyed dark. It has been cropped, too, into a boyish cut that Megan does not care for but hair grows, styles change. She recalls some of the hairstyles she wore when she was young. The perms, for instance. My God, the perms.

The pallor has gone. There is a depth of colour to her freckles that worried Megan at first. In this country, she reasoned, only people who spend most of their time outdoors develop such tone to their skin. Gardeners, for instance. Street sweepers. Street sleepers. But she convinced herself, in the end, that the colour was a good thing. A lack of it, after all, would have worried her more. And anyway the shot, from the fullness of the trees, appears to have been taken in the summer. Last summer. Which made it recent, when Megan first saw it.

Would Leo have recognised her, if he passed her on the street? Would Megan have? The answer scares her, every time. Place the woman side by side with the sketches they had drawn up, for instance, and you would not assume you were looking at the same person. Ellie might have seen her face on a lamp post and not realised she was looking in a mirror.

Megan shifts to disguise the shiver.

'Who's this?'

She glances at the tip of Leo's finger, at the chin nestled on her daughter's shoulder. She turns back to face the road.

'Her friend. Samantha. Maybe more than a friend – I haven't worked it out.'

'Have you met her?' Leo's eyes do not move from the photograph.

'No. But she keeps saying.'

Leo shakes his head slightly, ousts air through his nostrils. It is a mannerism, in the course of the drive, she has become used to.

'Look,' he says. 'Look at her grinning.' Ellie, he means. Their daughter. 'You remember what she used to be like in photos? How she used to scowl? You had to sneak up on her just to get a shot. Remember?'

She does. She smiles.

Leo shakes his head again. He turns to the window and seems to register for the first time where they are, where they are headed. He peers along the motorway and frowns. 'Are we nearly there yet?'

Megan just laughs.

'What?'

'Nothing,' she says. Then, 'An hour, I'd say. Maybe less. Are you hungry? There're some services coming up.'

'No. Keep driving. Unless you'd like me to?'

Mcgan's hands slide to greet each other on the steering wheel. 'I'm okay.' She glances and Leo catches her.

'What?' he says again. 'What's wrong?'

This time she allows her exasperation to show. 'You,' she says. 'Being nice. Offering to drive.' She glares at the tarmac.

'What? What's wrong with that? You're tired, I expect. I should have offered earlier.'

'You know what I mean.' She glances again and sees that he does.

'Look. Meg. She wrote to you. She didn't write to me.'

Megan says nothing.

'You only did what she asked you to. I can hardly blame you for that.'

She shakes her head, expels a breath. Leo turns away, as though happy to leave it at that.

Megan, though, is not. 'I had no right.'

'Meg—'

'I didn't! If it were you . . . If you'd been me . . .'

'Please. Don't start that. She asked you not to tell me. She *told* you not to.'

'But it was up to me. Wasn't it? Whether or not to agree.'

'I'm not sure it was, actually. Knowing our daughter, I'm not sure you had very much choice in the matter.'

'I could have argued, though. How do you know I even argued?'

'Because I know you.'

'But . . .' Megan sighed. 'So many times. So many times I nearly called you. And I was always going to, you know. It was only ever a question of when.'

'You've told me now, Meg. I know now. Let's leave it at that.'

'I was terrified, Leo. You understand that, don't you? I couldn't have faced losing her again. I kept saying to myself: after the next time I see her. Or the next letter she sends. I'll tell him then.' Megan turns from the road, watching for Leo's response. 'Can't you be angry at least?'

'Because that will help, do you think?'

'Yes!'

Leo shakes his head. 'I can't. Not with her. Not with you.'

Megan glowers but her husband just watches the road. 'It was my fault too, you realise. She ran from the both of us, not just you.'

'I know.'

Megan is thrown momentarily by his answer. Which part of what she said, exactly, is he agreeing to?

Leo notices her expression and shrugs a smile. 'We made mistakes, Meg. Both of us, just like all parents do. But mine were bigger.'

He does not give her time to consider an answer.

'Can I see them again?' he says. 'The letters?'

'What? Yes. Of course.' As though he should not even have to ask. As though at any point in the past six months, all he ever had to do was ask.

He dips into the footwell towards her handbag.

'Oh,' she says. 'I almost forgot. My purse. It should be in there.'

Bent double, he shows it to her. 'What do you need?'

'At the back. Behind all the receipts. There should be two twenties.'

He rummages, finds them. They unfold by themselves and he holds them out.

'They're yours,' she says and smiles at his frown. 'She gave me a cheque, made me promise to cash it. Said if ever I got a chance, I should slip the money into your wallet.'

Two twenties. The same number as were missing, when Leo finally got round to counting, from his bedside drawer. The place Ellie found them. The place, looking for the maga zine article that had so angered Megan, she had discovered Vincent Blake's notes.

Leo folds up the money. 'Petrol kitty,' he says and takes his time tucking them back in the place he found them. He takes out the letters instead and leans back with them piled on his lap. He casts his focus through the windscreen, at the spots of lazy rain and the cars beginning to bunch at the approaching junction.

'It's the thing she regrets most, you know,' Megan tells him as the car slows. She checks for some reaction. 'The note,' she continues. 'She doesn't say so in the letters but it's what she told me. Last time. I know she meant it.'

Leo looks at the letters in his lap. He picks up the topmost envelope. He puts it back and flips the pile the other way up.

'She was angry, Leo. Scared above all. Especially when she saw what that man wrote.'

'I don't blame her,' Leo says. 'I told you.' He takes a letter – the first one, this time – from its envelope. He lifts it closer to his face as though he were short-sighted. For everything else that has deteriorated about him . . .

No. Not deteriorated.

For everything else that has altered about him, Megan knows there is nothing wrong with her husband's eyes.

He is smelling it.

She turns to conceal her smile. He seems to notice and coughs his embarrassment. He angles his head to show he is reading.

If he asked her to, she could read the letter to him. *Mum*, it starts. *I don't really know where to begin.* She has committed to memory all twenty-seven lines, as well as all fifty-six from the second letter, each and every one of the third, fourth, fifth. And sixth. There are six letters in total. The first arrived with the photograph last autumn, for no reason that her daughter has been willing so far to reveal. Because she is happy, is Megan's guess. Because her happiness has given her strength. The other letters came one at a time every four or five weeks. Not enough. Not nearly enough. Especially as they say so little: gossip, mainly, about Ellie's friends. But that she has friends is in itself wondrous. Her friends and also her smile. Plus, now, they have met. Three times; roughly once in each of the past few months. At Ellie's suggestion. Only ever at Ellie's suggestion. Which is fine, not fine, all Megan can ask for. It is building. Re-building. It is killing her but it is making her whole.

Mum. I don't really know where to begin.

She looks at Leo. She watches him read. She turns back to face the road and recites the lines in her mind along with him.

'Here. Or a bit further in. This is the nice part. The expensive part. Acton's cheaper. Closer to Ellie, too. Although I'm not even sure I can afford Acton.'

Leo, she can tell, is exaggerating his interest. He is impatient. He would rather not have taken the detour.

'I'm sorry,' she says. 'I'll turn around. Head back to the ring road.'

'No. Honestly. It's fine. I'd like to see.'

She narrows her eyes at him. 'Now you're stalling.'

'I'm not. What kind of place are you looking for?'

'You are. Just a flat. Three bedrooms, if I can.'

'I'm nervous. That's all. Three bedrooms sounds okay.'

She smiles. She is not beyond feeling nervous herself. 'Two,' she says. 'It will probably be two. I'd like a garden for Rupert but it seems like a frivolous expense.'

'Rupert?' Leo turns. 'Rupert's still alive? But she must be . . .'

'. . . on her last legs. That's what I mean. I have my doubts, actually, that she'll make it to moving day. That's why I've never mentioned her to Ellie.'

'You should,' Leo says. 'She'd be pleased.' He shakes his head again at the never-ending wonderment.

'Either way,' says Megan, thinking once more about the flat. 'There'll be a spare bedroom. In case you ever . . . I mean, if anyone ever . . .'

She flushes. She turns away. She does not even pause to see whether Leo has reddened too.

Her husband, after a moment, clears his throat. 'I'm up here a lot, as it happens. You know. For work.'

Work. It is how he has been referring to it since she asked about it. He is, in Megan's opinion, belittling himself with the term.

'How's that going?' she asks.

'Oh,' he says, 'you know.' He does not think she genuinely wants to hear.

'Tell me. Please.' They reach a roundabout and Megan swings the car the way they have come.

'Slowly,' Leo says. 'The campaigning part, I mean. But we've made a nuisance of ourselves, got some backbench support. Lib Dems, mainly.' He shrugs. 'But still.'

But still indeed. She thinks of Leo's father. She wonders if Leo realises how proud Matthew would be.

'And Karen? She's working with you?'

Leo nods. 'Karen's involved. She's a big part of it, actually, especially after her experiences with . . . I mean . . . Given her experience.'

'With Daniel.' Megan says the name and, for the first time she can remember, she does not shudder.

Leo looks at her. 'That's right. Also,' he adds, 'a barrister I used to work with. He was involved with Daniel's case too. And there are others. Other lawyers, other therapists, a judge.

It helps that it's people who work with the law who are arguing that the law is an ass.'

'And the *pro bono* stuff?'

Leo's face shines. 'It's good. I mean, Howard's been great.
He's retired now but he was the one who helped me get it all
set up.'

'You work with kids, you said? Just kids?'

'Exclusively. Which means I travel a fair bit. Around the
south-west mainly. Also, here.' He gestures at the North
Circular. 'Believe me, there's plenty of work. Hardly anyone
specialises in it, you see. No one's qualified to. Which is frus-
trating enough in itself.' He finishes with a shrug.

'You do look tired, Leo. Are you eating properly?'

Leo purses his lips, as though to snip off a smile. 'When I
can,' he says. He seems to consider for a moment. His expres-
sion hardens. 'It sounds heartless, probably,' he says. 'But
Daniel: what happened to him. It will help. In the long run.
I won't let it not.' There is a hint of a challenge in his tone.
Megan does not rise to it.

'Not heartless, Leo.' She indicates, turns, glances. 'Never
that.'

They have been parked, by Megan's estimation, for thirteen
minutes. If they leave it any longer, they will be late.

'Leo. We should go.'

Her husband stares at the shopfront, as though the coffee-
shop signage were something outlandish.

'Leo. It will be fine. I promise.' Will it? Does she?

Leo turns to her. 'I shouldn't be here.'

'What?'

'I shouldn't have come. It's not fair. She should have warning.'

The thought has occurred to Megan too. More than that: it has nagged at her, like a child growing fitful in the back seat. What if I ruin it? she keeps thinking, the very thought that stopped her telling Leo from the start.

'Don't be silly,' she says. She opens the car door before she can stop herself.

'Megan. Wait.'

She shuts it again.

'What should I say to her?'

'What?'

'When I see her. What should I say to her?'

She would dismiss it as a foolish question. But she knows, having been there, that it is not.

'She's studying, you know: catching up,' Megan says. 'She wants to be a lawyer.' She slightly overplays her disdain. 'So you could tell her, for starters, to get a proper job.'

Leo, clearly, does not get the joke. He is staring again; working himself, she can tell, into a state.

Megan checks the clock again. She sighs. She says, 'Leo,' and taps her watch and then gestures through the windscreen towards . . .

Her daughter. *Their* daughter. Standing in the coffee-shop doorway. And it is clear, now, why Leo is staring so. She has been here, too. On the brink. Toes to the edge. Dazzled by the thing before them and praying – not quite believing – it is really real.

Their daughter. *His* daughter. Searching now, stepping now – and finally spotting them.

Both.

'Go.'

He does not move.

'Go. Leo!'

She leans. She opens his door. 'Go,' she says again. 'Go ahead.'

Because she was right that this was right. She can see, with her own eyes: her daughter with her hand across her mouth; her husband, standing, trying to, hauling himself up by the door frame of the car. He takes a step. She does. And Megan watches as her family comes together.

Acknowledgements

Love and thanks, as ever, to my unfailingly supportive family and friends. For their help and insight during the research and writing of this book, I owe a debt in particular to Sandra Higgison, Darryl Hobden, Andy Hood, Hanne Stevens and Amanda Thornton. Without their collective generosity, in terms of time and expertise, I would still be staring at a blinking cursor. Thank you, equally, to all at Macmillan, Penguin, the Zoe Pagnamenta Agency, Andrew Nurnberg Associates and Felicity Bryan Associates. Emma Bravo, Kathryn Court, Sophie Orme, Zoe Pagnamenta, Maria Rejt, Tara Singh and Caroline Wood all deserve an extra special mention.

I would like, as well, to detail here the books that have most informed and guided my research for *The Child Who*: Blake Morrison's heartbreaking, exceptional *As If*; Gitta Sereny's *The Case of Mary Bell*, as well as her astonishing series of articles about the James Bulger case published in the wake of the resultant trial in the *Independent on Sunday Review* (and available now as appendix to the aforementioned book); Alex McBride's fascinating and entertaining *Defending the Guilty*; and, finally, *Infant Losses, Adult Searches* by Glyn Hudson Allez, a devastatingly insightful analysis.

Last, and above all, I would like to say thank you to Sarah, my wife, and to my two sons, Barnaby and Joseph: for being there, and for being who they are.

Writing *The Child Who*

BY SIMON LELIC

In November 1993, Jon Venables and Robert Thompson were convicted of the murder of James Bulger. They were ten years old when they committed the crime; eleven by the time of the trial. Seventeen years later, after both boys (now men) had served their sentences, Jon Venables was returned to prison on charges you can't have failed to read about in the national press.

It was during this more recent furore that I decided to write *The Child Who*. Specifically, it was as I listened to a man named Laurence Lee being interviewed on Radio 4's *PM* programme. Lee was Venables's solicitor during the Bulger trial. He had no professional involvement in the 2010 case against Venables. At the time of the interview, I'm not sure the details of the charges were even publically known. But what was clear from Lee's tone – which struck me as considered, weary and, above all, upset – was how emotionally engaged with Venables's fate he remained.

Lee knew Venables. When Venables was ten, it had been Lee's job to gain the boy's trust; to spend hours, as I later discovered, playing computer games and darts matches with him in an effort to get him to open up. I've never spoken to Lee, I feel I must stress. I deliberately decided, as I wrote the book, not to try and contact him. But what became obvious to me as I listened to Lee being interviewed was that his life, from the moment he first encountered Venables, was irrevocably changed. And for all the countless column inches that his former client's crimes have inspired, few have had the opportunity Lee has had to examine and understand what really went wrong.

There are no definitive answers to this, of course. But what infuriated me as I started my research into the Bulger case, the Mary Bell trial and other similar cases, was how reluctant so many people seemed to be, in more general terms, even to ask this question. I began to get a sense of why Lee, on the radio, had sounded so weary. It was after five; maybe he'd simply had a long day. But maybe, too, he was tired of the sensationalism, the puddle-deep journalism that seeks to answer, in rapid-fire bullet points, 'WHY KIDS KILL!'.

And worse: since the Bulger trial, we (at least in England) seem to have gone backwards. At the time Venables and Thompson were put on trial, the courts were still obliged to consider whether a child aged fourteen or under was able to tell right from wrong (yes, was the answer in the cases of Venables and Thompson). Today in England, this is a done deal. If you're ten (in Scotland it's twelve, up recently from eight), you're legally responsible. You're not old enough to smoke, to have sex, to get a tattoo: the assumption is that the decision would be emotionally beyond you. But if you break the law, you know exactly what you're doing.

This is the main reason *The Child Who* is set when it is. There is a back story, of course (Daniel's story; the bulk of the book), as well as a contemporary strand, but for all my research about the Bulger case in particular, I wanted events in the novel to take place at a time existing legislation applied. The book is about Leo Curtice and his family – about the effects of Leo's involvement in such a high-profile and emotionally engaging case – but it is also about his perspective of the law. He is forced to consider, virtually for the first time in his career, how things could be done differently. How, for all our sakes, they could be made better.

Questions for discussion

1. After Leo's first meeting with Daniel Blake, he describes his client to his colleagues as looking '[just] like a scared little boy'. Why do you think this provokes such a scathing reaction, even before Daniel has been convicted of a crime?

2. Leo is warned by his boss that the Daniel Blake case will be 'like nothing you have experienced before'. Why is Leo so quick to dismiss Howard's concerns? Is he being naive? Reckless? Or realistic that the public will realise he is not necessarily 'on Daniel Blake's side'?

3. With increasing intensity, Megan asks Leo to give up the case. Is she entitled to ask? Is Leo entitled to refuse?

4. What is your reaction to Daniel's experiences at school, as recounted to Leo by Daniel's former head teacher? Where do you think the responsibility for Daniel's failure to integrate at school lies?

5. In his dealings with Daniel, does Leo overstep his professional responsibilities? Does he neglect his personal ones? How much sympathy do you have for him in his attempt to balance the two?

6. Leo tells Daniel, 'I think, if you plead guilty, you'd be taking on more than you deserve to. I think you'd be letting the rest of us off the hook.' What does he mean by this? Is he right?

7. Does Leo miss any signs that Ellie's troubles are more serious than he has assumed? How would you, in his position, have reacted to the evidence of her distress differently?

8. In spite of his actions, is Vincent Blake a good man? Would you say he is motivated by selfish or selfless concerns?

9. Who, ultimately, is to blame for Daniel's crime? Do you feel, as Leo seems to, that Daniel Blake should be considered a victim too? Who else in the book, other than Felicity, might also be considered a victim?

10. Restorative/reparative justice is an approach to justice that focuses on the needs of the victims, the offender and the wider community, typically involving dialogue between the parties involved. Around the time of the James Bulger case in England, for example, there was a similar case in Norway. The young offenders, rather than being prosecuted, remained in their community and were treated with compassion and counselling. Would such an approach work in the UK? Should it be tried?

If you enjoyed **The Child Who** you'll love

RUPTURE

Simon Lelic's debut novel

Will you remember his name?
In a year. In a month. In a week.
Will you remember his name?

In the depths of a sweltering summer, teacher Samuel Szaj-kowski walks into his school assembly and opens fire. He kills three pupils and a colleague before turning the gun on himself.

Lucia May, the young policewoman who is assigned the case, is expected to wrap up things quickly and without fuss. The incident is a tragedy that could not have been predicted and Szajkowski, it seems clear, was a psychopath beyond help. Soon, however, Lucia becomes preoccupied with the question no one else seems to want to ask: what drove a mild-mannered, diffident school teacher to commit such a despicable crime?

Piecing together the testimonies of the teachers and chil-dren at the school, Lucia discovers an uglier, more complex picture of the months leading up to the shooting. She realises too that she has more in common with Szajkowski than she could have imagined. As the pressure to bury the case builds, she becomes determined to tell the truth about what hap-pened, whatever the consequences . . .

The first chapter follows here.

I wasn't there. I didn't see it. Me and Banks were down by the ponds, pissing about with this Sainsbury's trolley we found on the common. We were late already so we decided to ditch. Get in, Banks says. You get in, I say. In the end, I get in. I'm always the one getting in. He pushes me for a bit over the field but the wheels keep seizing up, even though the grass is short and it hasn't rained in a month. Sainsbury's trolleys are shit. There's a Waitrose just opened up where the Safeway used to be and their trolleys are built like Volkswagens. Sainsbury's get theirs from France or Italy or Korea or something. They're like Daewoos. Although Ming says Daewoo means fuck yourself in Chinese, which is the only reason I'd ever buy one.

How many was it in the end? I heard thirty. Willis said sixty but you can't trust Willis. He reckons his uncle played for Spurs, years ago, in the eighties or something, and that he can get tickets whenever he likes. He never can though. I've asked him like four times but he always comes up with some excuse. Not cup games, he says. He can't get tickets for cup games. Or I asked too late. Says I have to tell him weeks in advance.

Months. Not the day before, even though it wasn't the day before, it was a Monday or a Tuesday or something and the game wasn't till Saturday.

So how many was it?

Oh. Really? Oh.

Just five?

Oh.

Well, anyway. That's where we were when we heard: down by the ponds. There's this track that runs round the edge. It's made of planks. There are gaps where the wheels can get wedged and it feels like you're off-roading in a Skoda but you can get up some speed. You have to watch the flowerpots. They stick out into the path and you can't move em cos the council have nailed em to the floor. I dunno why they bothered. They're full of Coke cans now, not flowers.

When I say we heard, I don't mean we heard it happen. School was half a mile away, back across the railway tracks. But these year eights turn up just as Banks decides to have a go in the trolley. He gets his foot caught and sort of falls, not arse over gob but enough to make me laugh. I shouldn't of. He gets pissed and starts having a go. And then the year eights turn up and even though they haven't seen him trip, Banks decides to have a go at them.

It was weird though. They're crying, the year eights. Two of em are, any rate. The other one just kind of stares. Not at anything in particular. Like he's watching TV on the inside of his glasses.

So anyway, Banks starts having a go but the year eights just kind of let him. They don't run or mouth off or try to fight or anything. I recognise one of em. Ambrose, his name is. My sister, she's in year eight too, she knows him and says he's okay so I ask him what's going on. He can't speak. His words come out all squashed and stuck together. Banks turns on him but I tell him to leave it. In the end one of the others tells us. I don't remember his name. Spotty kid. Normally I'd say shut the fuck up but he's the only one making any sense.

Banks wants to take the trolley with us but I tell him there'll be police and that there so he shoves it in a bush and says to the year eights if they take it he'll shit in their mouths. They don't look much interested in the trolley, to be fair. The spotty kid nods just the same, all wide-eyed like, but the other two don't look like they've even noticed the trolley.

I've never run to school in my life. Neither's Banks, I guess. I remember we were laughing, not cos it was funny, just cos it was something, you know?

I say to Banks, who do you think did it?

Jones, Banks says. It was Jones, I know it.

How do you know it?

I just do. He was pissed all last week after Bickle made him sing on his own in assembly.

Bickle, that's Mr Travis, the headmaster. That's what we call him cos basically he's mental.

You won't tell him I said that, will you?

Anyway, I don't say anything for a moment. Then I say, I bet it was one of them Goths. One of them kids with the hair and the jeans and the boots they wear in the summer.

Banks sort of scrunches his nose, like he doesn't want to admit it but he thinks I'm probably right.

Have you seen *Taxi Driver*, by the way?

You should.

We hear the sirens before we see the school. We've heard em already I expect but we haven't noticed em. And when we get there I count ten police cars at least. Shitty ones, Fiestas and that, but they're everywhere, all with their lights going. But I guess you know that. You were there, right?

But you got there later?

Thought so. Cos it's your case, right? You're in charge.

Sort of? What does that mean?

Well, anyway, there are ambulances there too and a fire engine for some reason. Some are still moving, just arriving I guess. The rest are all across the street and halfway up the pavement like someone's asked my mum to park em.

I'm sweating and I stop and I hear Banks panting beside me. We aren't laughing any more.

Everyone's going the opposite way. They're leaving the building, any rate. At the pavement everyone's sort of gathered, hanging together in groups. There are some year sevens near the teachers, just outside the gates. The sixth-formers are furthest away, across the road on the edge of the common and just along from me and Banks. I can't see any of our lot but people keep blocking my view. It's like three-thirty or parents' night or a fire drill or something, or all of them things at once.

Check it out, says Banks and he's pointing at Miss Hobbs. She's carrying some kid in her arms, crossing the playground towards the gates. There's blood on em but I can't tell whose.

Are you sure it was only five?

Well, whatever. So Miss Hobbs is crossing the playground, wobbling and swaying and looking like she's about to drop this kid but no one helps her, not till she reaches the gates. All around her kids are buzzing about and the police, they're going the other way, into the school. Then Miss Hobbs yells, she's got quite a yell I can tell you, like the time she yelled at Banks for flicking his sandwich crusts at Stacie Crump, and one of the ambulance men spots her and legs it over with a stretcher. They disappear after that, behind the ambulance, and that's when I see Jenkins with the others by the lights.

I tug at Banks and I point and we weave in and out the cars and over to the crossing.

Where you been? says Jenkins.

What's happening? I ask him.

Someone went loony tunes. In assembly. Shot the whole place up.

What, with a gun? I say and right away wish I hadn't of.

Jenkins looks at me. Either a gun, he says, or a fifty-litre bottle of ketchup.

Who? says Banks. Who did it?

Dunno. Couldn't see. People were up and running and that before we knew what was happening. Someone said it was Bumfluff but it couldn't of been, could it?

Then Banks says, where's Jones?

Didn't I say? says Terry, who's standing right beside Jenkins. Didn't I tell you it was Jones?

Jenkins gives Terry a punch on the arm. Banks doesn't know it was Jones, does he? He was just asking where he was.

Well, where is he? Terry says but Banks is already moving away.

Where you going? I say but he ignores me. I run to catch up and hear Jenkins behind me. You won't get in, he says but Banks doesn't even look back.

We try the main gates first but there's these policemen there dressed in yellow, they look like stewards at White Hart Lane. They turn us back. Banks tries again and has to scarper when one of the policemen shouts at him and tries to grab him. We go round the back instead, to the side gate by the kitchens, and there's a policeman there as well but he's talking to a woman with a pushchair, pointing at something across the street. He doesn't see us.

I've never been in the kitchens before. I've seen em from the other side, from the counter, but only the main bit and even then you can barely see past the dinner ladies, they're like sumo wrestlers in a scrum. Not that you'd want to. It's fucking disgusting. The main bit, where they serve the food, it's not too bad but in the back, with the cookers and the bins, it's rank. I see what I had for lunch the day before, a pile of pork all glistening with fat like it's been run over by a herd of slugs, just left on a tray in the sink. And there's stuff all over the floor, lettuce gone soggy and brown, and peas with their guts splattered and smeared all over the tiles. I almost throw up. I have to swallow it back down. But I'd rather eat vomit than eat in the canteen again, I swear. Banks, though, he doesn't hardly notice. He lives in a council. I live in a council too but a better one.

We're trapped in there for a bit. We can't find a way out cept for the way we've just come in. In the end we jump up over the counter. I kick at a tray of glasses with my foot, not on purpose, but some of the glasses fall and they break. Banks starts having a go, tells me to be quiet, but no one hears. No one would of cared.

From the canteen we go out into the passageway and along into the entrance hall and that brings us right up to the main doors and there's a crowd there and who should we run into but Michael Jones himself. And we know just by looking at him that it can't of been Jones.

He spots us but doesn't say anything and he's as pale as a custard cream. He's trying to get out by the looks of him but he's stuck behind a wall of sixth-formers. The sixth-formers, they're standing there, waving their arms about and bossing people where to go but it seems to me like they're only making things worse. Bickle's there too, Mr Travis, he's standing by the doors, telling the kids to keep moving to settle down to maintain order to move along. That's one of his phrases that: maintain order. As in, I'm sitting in on this class today to help *maintain order*. Or he'll be marching the corridors, whacking kids on the head, yelling, order children, *maintain order*. He calls us children even though we're like thirteen. The sixth-formers are eighteen some of em. Anyway, it should be our school motto – *maintain order* – not that thing we have in Latin. Something about helping yourself or helping others or doing one but not the other. Something like that.

Bickle spots us too and he looks like he's about to collar us but he's distracted, there's kids pushing past him, banging against him, on purpose some of em I bet, and Banks and me slip past and into the main corridor, the one that leads to the stairs and the classrooms and at the bottom, at the end, the hall, the assembly hall. That's where it all happened, right? The assembly hall.

We almost make it. We almost see it. The whadyacallit. The aftermath. I'm glad we didn't. Banks wanted to but I think I'm glad we didn't. Do you know what I mean?

It's a woman that nabs us in the end, a policewoman and they're the worst. All bossy and up themselves.

Oh.

No offence.

But anyway, we're halfway down the corridor and we can see the doors into the hall and we can see there are people inside, police and that mainly, and we don't see her reach for us. She was in one of the classrooms, I guess. She saw us pass and must of figured what we were doing, where we were going, and she doesn't shout or anything, she just comes up behind us and she nails us. Banks yells at her to geroff but in the end we can't really do anything, I mean what can we do? And she marches us up the corridor, back into the hallway, through the doors past Bickle, who just kind of glares, and all the way to the gates. And then she gives us a shove.

Banks tried to get back in after that but I'm pretty sure he didn't make it. By the time we get outside there's tape and more police and TV cameras and everything's being organised. The teachers, they're calling register and forming lines and that sort of thing. I stand on my own, to one side. I sit on the kerb. Then, I dunno. I just watch, like everyone else.

So that's it, I guess. I told you, I don't know anything really. I wasn't even there when it happened.